random Acts of Vandalism

random Acts of Vandalism

a novel

Patrick Blennerhassett

$[N_1[O_2[N_1$

CANADA

*Publisher's note: This book is a work of fiction. Names, characters, places and
incidents are either the product of the author's imagination or are used
fictitiously, and any resemblance to actual persons living or dead
is entirely coincidental.*

Library and Archives Canada Cataloguing in Publication

Blennerhassett, Patrick, 1982–
Random acts of vandalism : a novel / Patrick Blennerhassett.

ISBN 978–1–926942–01–8

I. Title.

PS8603.L46R35 2011   C813'.6   C2011–905916–9

Printed and bound in Canada on 100% recycled paper.

Now Or Never Publishing
#1101, 1003 Pacific Street
Vancouver, British Columbia
Canada V6E 4P2

nonpublishing.com
Fighting Words.

for all my sins . . .
that they may one day be forgiven

"When you break a man down,
you see how he was built up, backwards."
Anonymous

"Coincidence is just an illusion of chaos."
Eli Anderson

When seen from the suburbs, the city of Vancouver appears almost parallel with the clouds tethered to the surrounding mountains. Full of white, like crack smoke straight from the pipe, they're pearly, creamy, with a hint of grey along the edges, a sign of pending precipitation. Carrying temporarily, ready to burst, they eventually self-crack like egg whites and disgorge themselves over the hills, down the streets, into the gutters and finally the Pacific Ocean's deep blue abyss.

The rain doesn't always come quietly here, but today it has, though it has fallen far enough to pick up speed and collect in thick, splashing drops. It runs down familiar viaducts, a child returning home from school, taking a well-worn path through backyards and corner lots. The rain falls so much here it has its own route. It knows where to go, does not stray from its well-defined trail to the sea. The rain here is simply part of the atmosphere, having tattooed its way onto a shadowed topography.

A young boy leaves his parent's home—two floors, three bedrooms, glossy white-framed photos in the hallways of soccer fields and campsites. He's left the dark corners of his room cluttered with appropriate push-pin posters, pushing out the back door and through the backyard. Dressed in his favourite dark hoodie—Alkaline Trio—white iPod headphones dangle out and back into his sweater. Cheeks just starting to experience acne, still fresh-faced but with red bites, dark eyes—this kid looks worn.

With dyed-black hair pushed across his forehead, he hops a brown fence and its runny, solvent, year-old stain, and lopes past a HomeSense bird feeder hung high in a thick, full-bearded evergreen. When he pokes out from the alley, he cuts left with the rain down towards the ocean, following gravity and the slight slouch this city sits in. He watches the rain trickle and scamper along the sidewalk crevasses, periodically emptying into gutters, only to collect and run out again. Wash sprays up from the odd car, always a new model, always silver, always a four-door, it seems.

Each house has its own complexion, although they all look like relatives of the same species. New paint, big glass window exposing a living room with a fireplace or long flat-screen television. Hedges, bushes that have been trimmed each weekend, and putting green lawns just starting to grow a shag. Everything up here isn't brand new, but seems instead to be constantly entering a period of upgrade. The middle class morphs, mutates and renovates efficiently against its own will into the affluent, revealing a notable hybrid of haves and have-nots.

This boy walks slowly enough that he doesn't seem to have a destination in mind, but with determination enough that he must be going somewhere. The rain streams down his face from forehead to chin as the sun sets somewhere beyond the pall of western cloud, gone for another night, asleep in the ocean bed. It's dusk, everything has a sunglass tint, the smoky smear of grey and blue, though the streetlights have yet to come on.

When the boy reaches a crosswalk, he neglects to push the button, waiting instead for a break in the traffic to jaywalk, checking each side carefully before he proceeds.

Once across the residential road, he sees it loom up before him, lit by neon yellow scales across its backside. The Lions' Gate Bridge rises out of the lush, damp green trees like a massive, steel-constructed dinosaur, reaching across to take a bite out of Stanley Park. Cars crawl across her spine three lanes wide, packed tightly together.

By the time the bridge was built, back in 1937, eleven men had perished during her construction, which had spanned almost seven years. However, back in the '30s, this was considered a low death toll for the height and danger of the project. The city dubbed it a lucky bridge. Since then, ten suicides have been reported, one less than the steel- and ironworkers who perished during its architectural conception.

When the boy sees the bridge, it's as if he's looking at it for the first time in his life. When in all actuality, he's seen it many times. He's driven across it, biked across it and walked its green-railed pedestrian crosswalk. He knows this bridge well—where the best spot to stop and spit is, how close to hug the rail so as not to get splashed by trucks and campers barreling across, how to throw a Styrofoam airplane off it and watch it soar as far as the rail yard some five kilometres away. A lifeless bird following the currents, dipping and diving and pulling back up into the blinding oblivion.

He also knows it's well over 500 feet from the pedestrian crosswalk to the cold, grey water below. When the bridge starts to arch up slightly like a cat's back in a stretch, one can do a 360 degree spin and see the Coastal Mountains, the Pacific Ocean, Washington State and Vancouver Island all in one dizzying turn.

When the boy approaches the bridge he starts to slow, to walk as if he's been dragged by a weight stuck, rammed into the corner of his stomach. It's as if he's carrying something heavy inside him, something that makes his steps start to labour and drag his Chuck Taylors just a little.

In his dark hoodie and tight black jeans he melts into the scenery. His presence is rarely noticed by any of the cars' inhabitants, what with the rain and the darkness and his camouflaged appearance.

With each step he starts to slow now, his hand gliding lightly atop the railing, music pulsing in his ears, his playlist put together specifically for this occasion. He gazes up at the lights stretching out over the span of the bridge. They have turned more white than orange, obscured and diluted by the water collecting in his eyelashes.

A bicycler passes the boy on the sidewalk but does not make eye contact—it's not worth it tonight. Besides, there's not much to see other than the glowing lights, the falling rain, the passing cars and the rising shroud of the blackened horizon.

At the crown of the bridge the boy stops and looks out over the railing, out over Burrard Inlet. Lighthouse Park is barely visible in the distance to his right. It's serene, even quiet as he allows the constant drone of cars to fall into the background. On the boy's iPod, Aphex Twin's "Stone in Focus" begins to play. It pours through his ears, soothes his eardrums, massaging his brain like a quiet lullaby.

After what has been close to twelve minutes, the boy stands up straight, hands still on the railing, and starts to straddle the three-foot high steel divider. He's up and over, hanging from the other side, hands clenched tightly on the slippery wetness of the painted steel. He's broken through a barrier and he knows it. Everything starts to feel a little alien as he steps outside the comfort of his life. The point of no return has come and gone. The boy crouches down to conceal his presence, and now, even from a few feet away, looks like nothing more than a part of the bridge to anyone passing by—perhaps a gargoyle placed there by workers long ago. He could stay here for hours without anyone noticing. But he doesn't. He lets go.

Inside his mind a freedom unleashes him, sucking up all the uncertainty of his short life. He has started his descent into another world, instantly invigorating his heart into near cardiac arrest.

His body starts to tumble, his sweater comes up, his white iPod cords flutter as he falls and then whip from him in an instant. He falls like a rag doll, trying to right himself to see the ground, but he's not powerful enough. The wind currents just above the water, being funneled by the inlet and now the lower mouth of the bridge, take complete control of his limbs.

The boy falls for nearly six seconds, though he doesn't know it. He has blacked out, rendered unconscious by the very act itself. They say fully half of suicide jumpers die from heart attack before they even hit their destination. But this boy is young and his arteries still too free of North American opulence to be clogged enough to turn his motor off. He simply swallows too much air on the way down, the wind literally knocked into him.

An underground mine appears to explode from the dark sea, a plush, backwards-pulsating explosion of white water. A crackle of sound, almost like a cannon, accompanies the eruption of water that reaches up seven feet in the air, sixteen feet wide in diameter. The displaced water comes down and seems to swallow itself, and as quickly as it happened, disappears back into the small greasy waves washing into the bay, as if nothing has happened.

The Novelist

The entire high-rise office building of CBC is colour-coordinated. Blood red, black lined with silver and grey. Even the stalls in the bathroom match that flowery-looking symbol outside the doors here in downtown Toronto. Right now I'm looking at the back of one of these stalls, graffiti-free, staring at it as if I'm trying to see right through it.

My black suit is custom, open shirt one button down—a thin white pinstripe Pierre Cardin. A form-fitting black v-neck cardigan and dress pants. Black dress socks and black dress shoes. None of these clothes have been worn for more than a few hours. I sit in this stall, pants, belt and underwear down around my ankles, waiting for a shit I know will never come. I sit in this stall waiting for this shit that won't come thinking of how I got to this very exact moment in my life. How I am less than half an hour away from an "exclusive" interview with George Stroumboulopoulos, not on *The Hour*, but on *The National*. Peter Mansbridge is on vacation or something, and the producers at CBC felt I would feel more comfortable talking to someone closer to my age. George is the edgy, youthful demographic of CBC apparently. Sure. It's not as if one cares how they are executed. Whether death comes by sling blade, rawhide noose or gasoline fire. Death only leads to one thing in the end. If the pain is swift, it's really all the same. Soften the blow with this national boy-toy for all I care. Paint me up in Technicolor just to tear me down more vibrantly.

How I got to this point in my life. Just over two years ago I started writing a book after quitting my job amidst unusual circumstances which afforded me some time away from the burden of regular employment. The book recounted a lonely boy growing up amidst a chaotic home life. His parents were divorcing, he was dealing with depression and ADHD, and nothing really seemed as if it was going to break for him. I waxed poetic for 295 pages of Generation Y angst—Facebook, sexting, global child and whatnot. *The Globe & Mail* called it "teen poetry angst for the iPod generation."

I literally shat the thing out in a few months, I just holed up in my dad's basement and plowed through it. I dropped 30 pounds and developed a nice cocktail of Vitamin D deficiency, hypersomnia, nicotine addiction and a bad case of the masturbations—as I like to call them. Bottom line was I needed an immediate distraction from life, and drugs, woman and violence weren't as readily available as they had been in previous chapters of my existence.

The novel was published through a relatively small house in Vancouver. Made the critical rounds, stirred up some sales, and got championed by George himself on his show. He loved it, gave it a short plug, and sales went national. I peeked onto the *Maclean's* Bestseller's List for a brief stint. Apparently I had shades of a young Douglas Coupland, one raised in the "shadow of 9/11, the promise of Barack Obama, and the reality of life after the economic downturn."

Six months in though it was just another book on the shelf and I was living off dwindling royalties, a small advance, severance, employment insurance and a small Canadian Council Arts Grant trying to write my follow-up.

I had shit.

Then, on September 23rd, sometime around seven thirty in the evening, 16-year-old North Vancouver resident Michael Vanbiesbrouck jumped off the Lions' Gate Bridge in what would be a very successful suicide attempt. It would be another seventeen days before his body would be recovered deep underwater alongside Stanley Park.

Michael was presumed missing in what turned into a massive man-hunt, spearheaded by the RCMP and the Vancouver Police Department. He was believed abducted, or lost, or dead somewhere in the woods in the surrounding area. The story of the missing boy got local and provincial attention. He was a model student, top of his class. He was an accomplished piano player, having landed a scholarship to the Julliard School in New York.

For Michael to go missing was completely out of character, though his parents were aware he had a darker side. A kid troubled by their secretive ways and his cocktail of anti-depressant medications. A cracked marriage held together only by their promising son. A house long since devoid of feasible love, or viable compassion, or respectable comfort.

Finally, after over two weeks of abrading every lead, endless reports on the evening news, and a personal charity set up to help pay for private investigators, Michael's mother walked into her son's room for the last time.

On the dresser, which she had looked at numerous times, combed through with police and private investigators, was a copy of *Bending Light*, my novel. Inside the jacket cover was a six paragraph suicide note scrawled in black ink.

Stay together for the kids, they always say. Place a child between two opposing entities and see how long before that elasticity snaps. I knew full well what kind of internal terror Michael was drudging through. I'd grown up around it my entire life. Broken homes make broken kids.

At the end of the book, the young character in *Bending Light* jumps off a large commuter bridge outside his own neighbourhood, just outside a large city. My publisher chose the defining image of this bridge at night for the cover, which in itself won a national award. The fact it turned out to be an artistic photo of the Lions' Gate Bridge at night was just dumb fucking luck. It was more allegory than literal; I'd kept the actual name of the bridge vague for obvious reasons relating to my own troubled past.

Once the note was given to the authorities, the police swept Burrard Inlet and found Michael's decaying, half-eaten body stuck against a sunken grate twelve feet under the surface. The press got a sniff of it and, during a slow news week, couldn't find much else to bite into. So they sunk their teeth into the story. Copycat suicide. Endless references to Kurt Cobain, Johann Wolfgang von Goethe and *The Sorrows of Young Werther*, "Gloomy Sunday," and Japanese musicians Hide and Yukiko Okada. I was their brand spanking new info-tainment porn for the cycle. Endless high-end rotation reports in a 24-hour news world. Beat the story to death, then move onto the next. A binge and gorge process I'd watched from the other side until now. Until the weather forecast told me something incredibly, remarkably and uncontrollably different.

I was instantly forced into hiding at my father's house just outside the city. He had a place just past Boundary Road, far enough away that the messy chaos of Van was still background music. It was good because my dad and I never talked. I had his unassuming good looks, symmetrical face with dark, Anglo-Canadian sculpted features—six feet, brown hair, brown eyes, you know the drill. I also had his tendency to go days without uttering much more than monosyllabic grunts. There was also this thick silence he seemed to carry around, at least around me, from as far back as I can remember, even before he left my mom. It was like he was carrying something inside him that prevented him from getting close to me. I never asked what it was. I can't remember him smiling once. It made for a quiet house, which worked, given the current circumstances.

We had to disconnect my phone, e-mail, and set up a private number. I couldn't go outside unless escorted by a bodyguard for the first few days. I couldn't do much other than sit in my father's den and watch the endless smutty television news clips, pictures of myself, the book, the boy, the bridge.

Bending Light also firmly planted itself on top of the *Maclean's* Bestseller's List, perched high above the others not looking to come down anytime soon. It made its way halfway up *The New York Times* Bestseller's List, however never hit number one thanks to Dan Brown and some vampires. I was only clipped by full-blooded Americana exposure. Thank God.

I saw a grief counsellor and psychiatrist once a day, and even took a call from James Frey. However, it did little to quell the swirling emotions and endless rumination controlling every waking moment of my life.

The first few days were a shock. An actual shock where you find yourself dramatically shaking your head when alone, still unable to comprehend the sheer monstrosity perched overhead licking its lips and sharpening its knives.

After the shock subsided, it was replaced by what I would call endless thought. Your brain trying to formulate the best way to respond to this because you know everyone wants to know how you're going to respond to this. You wrestle with the fact that now you are and will be an established writer for the rest of your career, having commuted atop some dead kid's corpse to financial bliss, unwillingly, unknowingly, and without consent. This was not your choice, or your decision. You were not a willing participant.

I lean over in the stall on the 24th floor of CBC in Toronto, rest my head against the toilet paper dispenser, rub my eyes with the pads of my thumbs.

I take a pull from the flask of vodka tucked neatly into my jacket pocket. I'm light-headed, sufficiently tired, half-assed jet lagged and my conscience is still throwing mounds of coal onto the thought fire. I look and feel like shit, but for some reason can't seem to defecate.

Once I emerge from the bathroom, I'm followed closely by my literary agent, my publisher, a publicist and an assistant, my father and a bodyguard. My entourage, a swarm of Gollum-like peddlers hanging onto my flesh like remora. They're all here for many reasons, the majority of which are not really about me at all. Rather their reflection of me within themselves, their place amongst this fifteen minutes of fame. Their places, their thoughts, their goals, their ambitions, anything and everything they want to get out of this. It makes me sick, but I keep a straight face.

Infamy will tax any soul, squeeze any goodness until it's black and hard. Distort any well-wishing into ulterior motives. It leads to infomercials and tell-all books and Levi Johnston and turns idiots into pundits and fucks into fuckers. It's a slime bucket of vile that people can only stomach because it has an endearing spotlight elixir. Entertaining bloodlust, the entertainment in and of others' suffering, and the disease inside all of us that wants to watch that car accident, over and over and over again.

Through the back rooms and hallways of CBC are posters of famous Canadians—Pierre Trudeau, Wayne Gretzky, David Suzuki. Signed photos, big Native artwork. Dark studios with photography lights. Endless black electrical cords snaking across a scuffed floor with ground-in resin and rubber sole shoe marks. Trail marks from moving cameras, gum pressed into the wood, markers, coloured electrical tape in X's that look like they're marking buried treasure.

I've shaken fifteen different pairs of hands today. Women in power suits, men with creamy Italian-styled ties. They've all blended into one person, one producer—I can't seem to tell any of them apart. That vibration bellow of Blackberries in pockets, clipped against belts. Over and over and over.

I met George earlier. He seemed amicable. He sized me up, poked a bit into what he thought some of my responses might be. Tried to distance himself from any Frey-Oprah comparison with a "This really isn't like this at all, the country just really wants to hear what you have to say."

Wrong. The country wants to judge me according to what I have to say. Scrutinize me, hold me up to the light, place me under the microscope. Talk about me as if I'm simply another round of gossip for the chattering class, which I am.

I've become Twitter talk and casual dinner conversation.

The only reason I'm doing this is because I have something to say on air that I need to say. The interview is supposed to last twenty-two minutes give or take, but all I need is one sentence, one breath, to get my message across.

I take a deep breath amidst the talking and lights and confusion and sound checks. My armpits are sweaty, my legs stiff at ninety-degree angles, and I still can't calm the incessant stream of thoughts running through my head. I pray to God the medication kicks in soon.

It's a dark black table, grey background with red trim. On that table sit two brand new black coffee mugs, filled with water. George has a black dress shirt on. With all the lights pointed straight at me, everything else is muted. It's dark out there but blinding in here, and with all the attention focused solely on me, I squirm like a fish out of water, flopping around in the back of a boat, gasping for air.

The introduction is expected, as George rambles off my bio and the story to Camera 1, like when people talk about you like you're not there even though they know you're sitting right there beside them. There's a section of angst growing within me, and now it's starting to spill static across my senses. I can't hear much else but static and a faint voice now. I feel so prodded.

George turns to me. A red light flicks on the camera behind him, pointing directly at me like a floodlight. "How have the past few weeks been for you, I mean in terms of how you're personally handling this?" George, asks, making concerned eye contact. I can see why the ladies ooze over him. He appears sincere.

I hesitate a small second, my mind goes blank and my mouth starts moving. I'm beside myself now, an out of body experience, watching, listening to myself spilling syllables away like a seasoned practitioner.

"I've been okay. It's been tough, you know. It's the type of thing where I'm just trying to take it one day at a time."

"Have you spoken to Michael's parents? Have they been in contact with you?"

I wasn't expecting this question. Looks as though I'm to expect the unexpected this interview then. Fair enough. I'd be an idiot if I thought it would go down any other way.

"No I haven't spoken to them. I'm guessing they're still going through a grieving process right now. I'm probably not very high on their priority list, I'm guessing."

"But you've got to feel as though they would want to talk to you at some point about all of this," he says with that concerned look again. His hands have a tendency to move when he accents his points, much like myself.

"Yeah," I reply, shrugging a bit. "I'm sure they might have some questions for me, and I might have some questions for them. But this isn't something I want to rush into, or even push them into. They can get a hold of me if and when they want to."

"What would you say to them if they approached you today?"

I look over at George. He's prodding and he knows it.

"I don't know. I haven't gotten that far. I'm guessing they would have something to say to me first, some questions they would like answers for. And I would respond to those first before I said anything."

George looks at his notes. He knows he needs to change gears.

"During the writing of *Bending Light*, did a copycat suicide ever cross your mind? Did you ever think like something like this would happen?"

"No, not at all. If you think of how many times suicide has been portrayed in art, it's not something you really fathom. I mean plagiarism and stuff like that is much more on my radar. But someone acting out my book, no, I was not expecting that at all."

I take a sip of water. It's luke warm. I really want a good stiff drink to sip on right now.

"What was your initial reaction though. What was the first thought that crossed your mind when you found out. Take me through that day."

"I . . ." I hesitate. "I mean the first though that crosses your mind is one of sheer unexpectedness. You're blindsided. It feels like a bad prank. Then there's this immediate wave of shock that overwhelms you pretty quickly."

"You saw it online, that's correct?"

"Yeah I was just surfing a news page—Google, I think—and I stumbled over it. It's the type of thing where for the first few minutes you're really just trying to gather as much information as possible. Then my agent and publisher phoned me, and they came over and got me filled in pretty quickly."

George looks at his notes again. I think he wants more out of me, maybe longer answers. But it's not my job to play ball with him today, so I'll just give him what I feel like giving.

"I want to talk about the debate this has stirred," he says. "A few weeks ago, a young boy from Winnipeg was found dead after a similar massive manhunt was undertaken by Winnipeg police. He was playing *Call of Duty 4*, playing it a lot, to the point that his parents actually took the game away from him. This obsession seems somewhat similar to that of Michael and your book."

I shake my head. "No, this is different. Night and day actually. He wrote a suicide note in the jacket cover of my book. The cover played a big part in it too. But this wasn't something where he was obsessed with the book like, say, Mark Chapman."

"Do you feel any responsibility for his death?"

I shake my head again. "I mean, I do and I don't. I want to take responsibility, but I'm not sure it's just to do so. Did I murder him? No. Did I push him off that bridge physically? Did I intend to goad him into suicide like some Heaven's Gate fiasco? Suicide is everywhere, look at *Thelma and Louise*. *The Happening*. *The Virgin Suicides. . . .*"

I draw a blank after that. I'd written down fifteen movies and books and even a few paintings with suicide in them. But it was in my jacket pocket, and pulling it out wouldn't really work right now.

"Are you at all worried about more? About more attempts?"

"I dunno. . . . I mean you can't really think about that."

"What was your train of thought when writing the book? Why have such a promising young character—someone who's obviously struggling in certain aspects of his life—why have him give up like that?"

I take a deep breath of air in, but only a fraction seems to make it all the way into my lungs. "I just didn't want to write a book that had a storybook ending. It wasn't about that, it was about documenting the types of things kids go through these days. I was reading this article in *Vanity Fair* about the cluster suicides in Wales. . . . Something about it spoke to me, but the media couldn't put a finger on it. There were all these kids killing themselves, none of them were extremely poor, they all had internet access and went to decent schools. It's just today, being young, staring out at the abyss that is adulthood and responsibility, it can seem even more daunting in such a globalized world. We can seem so small and insignificant when you hear all these amazing stories about amazing people all day everyday, and here you are, in your one-storey flat with your parents who barely break even and college is for the rich and the gifted, and everything just seems way too big to take on."

I can tell he enjoyed that answer. He lets it sink in for a few seconds.

"Talk to me about the allegations of exploitation within the book. I know that when I read it I definitely didn't feel that way at all, but it does give suicide a very appealing factor."

"It's not an exploitation at all. I'm not romanticizing suicide either. *Romeo and Juliet* romanticizes suicide. I was never suicidal to the point of actually feeling as if I could actually carry it out and do it. All I wanted to do in the book was paint a direct picture of what kids can be hit with these days. It's a bombardment. Maybe that's what Michael agreed with."

He got me to get back to Michael, and I'm moving my hands when I talk, my personal sign of nervousness. Now he's going to use it as his bridge to the next question. The lights are still blinding, and I can't see anyone but George. I'm sure they wanted it this way.

"What do you think you'd say to Michael given the chance?"

I look at him, confused. "Like now, after he's dead?"

"If you got the chance to speak to him before he died. If he contacted you after reading your book."

"I dunno, I'm not big on that question. I'm not his parents. From what it looks like he had a very promising musical career ahead of him. Julliard. The kid was going to be okay. But I can't really answer that. It's not something I want to answer unless it actually happened, and it isn't going to happen."

Someone signals for a commercial break. A bell sounds. Red lights go off. Someone comes up and dabs my forehead with a napkin.

I lean forward, unbutton my jacket, then lean back, exhaling all the air that didn't seem to do me any good earlier. All I can do right now is breathe. George says a few words to me. We're going to be talking about how suicide is portrayed in the media apparently. I nod. My agent struts over brandishing his Blackberry like a weapon, protective. I can smell his designer aftershave.

"You okay, you want anything?" he says, paternal hand on my shoulder. I look up at him, and then I pull out my flask and take a good long pull. He winces, shifting slightly to his right, as though trying to conceal my crutch.

"I'm fine," I say. "Let's just get this over with."

He nods and disappears. Introduction music again. That red light. George speaking, looking directly at Camera 1. I just stare at him. There's not much else to do.

"It's a well-known policy within most media outlets that suicides are very taboo subjects," he says. "Copycat suicides are a very serious threat, especially if a suicide is widely reported. However, if this person is famous, someone of note, it's impossible to ignore. It leaves us in a difficult situation, one between bringing forth information that the public needs, and paying respect to the danger that very information can bring. The nationwide manhunt and media exposure for Michael Vanbiesbrouck ended in tragedy. One of a boy who many believed had simply run away from home, or was abducted. When his suicide became public, and the final words from that young promising boy were etched in a book about teen suicide, it brought forth many questions."

Then George introduces me again, as the "notorious" author of *Bending Light*. The vodka inside me warms my stomach, slightly calms and slows the traffic of blood racing through my veins.

"We talked before the break about other instances of suicide in art. *Thelma and Louise,* you mentioned. *Romeo and Juliet.* This idea of life imitating art, we see it all the time. People quote their favourite actors, dress-up as superheroes on Halloween. We do it all the time. But when tragedy is involved, it really brings this issue to the forefront."

George looks at me, then continues. "Do artists have a responsibility to their fans, to the people who purchase their work? Did you ever feel that with *Bending Light* you were speaking to a particular audience, and by that I mean a very impressionable one?"

I don't answer immediately, choosing to take one good breath instead. "I mean, of course you know you're speaking to someone—it's art, it's public, people are going to read from it, and be influenced by it if they like it. But art is very open to interpretation. I've heard so many different things from so many different people about the book. They all come up to me and say different things, talk to me about different passages and characters. Different themes resonate with different people. So to think that you're ever going to be delivering a direct message to a certain audience, it's preposterous, and very egocentric to presume, I think."

"You've actually talked about some interpretations in the book. For instance, that the ending is possibly a dream, and with the allegory of the piano playing, that this is simply the protagonist shedding his demons and moving onto a better stage in his life. That the suicide in the book is simply a dream sequence, and a somewhat cathartic one."

I nod. "Yeah, definitely. When I wrote it, I wanted a sense of ambiguity. The literal people who read that book will think it's literal, and the ones more inclined to imagery and imagination may think otherwise. I definitely think it's open to interpretation."

"But Michael ended up taking it very literally."

I pause to scratch my nose, clear my throat slightly, buying time to answer. "Once again, I wasn't inside his head. I don't know what was going on in his life. How much of an effect the book had on him, I don't think anyone will ever really know. For all I know he may have read it, hated it, and that day just happened to see it sitting there and chose on a whim to write a note in it, and carry out the act portrayed in the book and on the cover. It may have been completely on a whim."

George starts to ask another question, but I interrupt him. "Look, any artist who believes they're changing the world with their work is an idiot. Art doesn't influence life, life influences art. Without life there would be no art. Art is simply the mirror we hold up to ourselves, to our culture. You can't have the egg before the chicken."

I stop, think about what I said, realize it may have come off as pretentious. George glances across at a producer, who might be signaling something to him.

"Was there any discussion at any time after it was found out about Michael, concerning pulling the book off the shelf?"

I hesitate. "Yeah, we discussed it a few times. I initiated all of the discussions. We had some lengthy conversations about it, my agent, my publisher and I."

"And why did you stick with the decision to keep the book in print?"

"I don't know, partially maybe simply out of our own sense of ego. I mean, the part of me that's ripping me to shreds right now is realizing this is making me really rich. We're working on United States distribution, a translation to French, international rights. Movie deals are starting to surface. I'm not going to lie to you, or anyone, this situation, as horrible as it is, benefits me immensely."

"And how are you dealing with that?"

"I'm not."

"You're not?"

"No, I'm neglecting it, pushing it away. What would you expect me to do? I've learned to cope through tragedy by employing a cloak, just a shield around myself. I watched some-one, someone I loved dearly, die slowly in front of me, but this, I don't know how anyone would ever handle something like this."

"You're taking counseling right now, correct?"

"Of course, yeah, it's been helping me through this. I dunno, I think this is one that's going to stick, going to scar. This will be my cross to bear."

Someone signals for a commercial break again. A bell sounds. Red lights go off. Someone comes up and dabs my forehead with a napkin.

I take a pull from my flask, this time in plain view of every-one. George catches me, smiling ever so slightly, an understanding smile. "Let the motherfucking kid drink," he's probably thinking. Let the pariah have some water.

~

I've cut my hair short, about an inch and a half long, died it bleach blonde, and have started keeping a short beard. I've also been tanning, and have taken to wearing aviator sunglasses fre-quently, all in an effort to change my appearance. To hopefully be able to bypass a few awkward conversations and random encoun-ters with the many zealots that line the streets. I imagine I resem-ble a younger Leonard in *Memento*, and I'm certainly not far removed from his level of lunacy. There's not much I can decipher beyond the shitstorm that's presently engulfing me. Everything is tainted by its putrid residue.

My days are now spent moping around my father's house, sleeping in incessantly, trying to write, failing to write, and drinking copious amounts of alcohol. I feel like Capote trying to write *Unanswered Prayers*, another work of fiction forever hovering over his head. At least Truman had other works in his repertoire. Me, I was quickly moving towards becoming another one-hit wonder, forever known and tied to his first offering. Forever trying to leave the long suffocating shadow it's created. J.D. Salinger. Harper Lee. At least they'd written something memorable. I'd written smut that turned into a snuff book. I could already see my Jeopardy clue: "He was the writer of *Bending Light*, a marginal novel made infamous by a copycat suicide, and perished soon after in a hail of booze, drugs and insanity."

"Who is me, Alex."

Infamy. My bedfellow. She'd moved in, set up shop, ready to stay the night and possibly well into the morning of my life. She was now my Cheshire Cat, forever able to hang above my conscience and appear and disappear at will. She had become my incurable disease—ground teeth, pulsing headaches, wavering consciousness, anxiety clutching at my throat. A choke chain yanked upwards at the most inopportune times.

My mornings usually start around noon or later. A seething cold shower followed by some Oxycotin and Diazepam to sooth my latest hangover. Maybe some black coffee mixed with Bailey's. Anything to set forth on a productive day.

I screen my calls, check my email, turning down about two interviews a day from publications across the globe. But I've noticed lately they've started to become more infrequent, leading me to believe I'm moving beyond my fifteen minutes.

I start with a good stiff drink around one-ish. A double vodka, maybe some tequila straight up. Something to wash the medication out of my stomach and into my bloodstream. Then I sit my ass in front of the television in the downstairs den and flick for hours. I've paid for satellite TV to be installed, and now have over five hundred channels to browse through. I am addicted to television, unable to cope with the thoughts in my head, and am channeling them deeper into the dark vortex this box allows you to be.

The den is dark, dank, poorly lit, and I can hide for days in its corners. Large plush couch, one small window I've covered with a pillow sheet. Boxes and crap lying all over the place. A dining room table and brand new barbecue packed neatly into the corner.

It isn't all bad though. There are bright spots. For instance, my bank account keeps climbing. I will be a millionaire by year's end, not that that's any feat in itself these days, but it's noteworthy for someone like myself. I've started buying random things I've always wanted but never needed: a plasma screen TV, a brand new laptop to replace the old one I've had for years that my parents bought me for Christmas one year, a jet black Porsche, new custom suits and expensive shoes, a blender and, inexplicably, a trampoline I've never gotten around to setting up.

I've stopped listening to myself, and started listening to the television. She has much to tell me, all the time, filling my head with a state of faked informativeness. She speaks a lot, sometimes contradicting herself, but ultimately comforting me with her flashing vociferous colours. The lone boy who's wandered into his closet at night only to find solace in the monster stalking him after the lights go off.

I also have a list. When you watch as much television as I do, you start to play games with yourself to stay occupied during droughts of reasonable programming. First I start tabulating a running list of notable figures I see on any channel. Morgan Freeman and his wise-talking freckles jump out to an early lead, but he is soon overtaken by Paris Hilton, who is then overcome by President Obama. Finally there's a *Lethal Weapon* marathon on one weekend, which coincides with *Braveheart* playing on the History Channel and *What Women Want* on the Life Network, and Gibson runs away with it and I give up.

Now I am tabulating the periodically numbing rotation of abdominal exercise machines. I am at eleven and it has only been two and a half weeks: Ab Slide Torso Track II, Ab Scissor Ultra Abdominal Machine, Ab Lounger, Yukon Back and Ab Machine BAM-160, Ab Rocket, Easy Shaper Ab Exercise Machine, Ab Killer, Super Abdominal Machine, Ab Coaster, Ab Crunch Machine, Ab Roller.

It's not even 2pm on a rainy Tuesday, and I have a good buzz going when my agent comes over. His cream-coloured shirts, and his Blackberry whatever that makes a weird mooing noise whenever it vibrates across the coffee table, make me smile. It's fun to be friends with such smut. I like his sleaze. At least he's always straightforward with me about things people normally aren't straightforward about, which is something.

"Look," he says, sitting across from me in the den, sipping a beer. Whenever I offer one, he accepts after remarking about his shitty wife and stressful job. It's incredibly endearing, this false display of proletarianism. "You ride this out, you're the next James Frey. You keep putting books out and sooner or later people will forget about it. I mean *Bright Shiny Morning* sucked. It wasn't *A Million Little Pieces*. But he's moving on, he's a rich writer, something everyone dreams of. You made a deal with the devil, my friend. So deal with it and move the fuck on."

I nod. It's probably the best advice I've received in months.

Then he tells me to stop writing, in order to clear my head. Go kayaking, wakeboarding, skydiving, he says. Travel to Tibet. Or Australia. Take up knitting, adopt a kid with Down Syndrome, do something, anything to dislodge my mind from its present inertia. Get a girlfriend. Or boyfriend. Buy a dog. Start running drugs. Anything, he says. Anything but nothing.

Later that evening I'm out driving around drunk in my Porsche. It's a quiet night, the city is dead. I'm dressed in a grey suit, white dress shirt. I've started wearing all the suits I have, pretty much all the time. I figure why not, break them in. Falling with style, I like to call it.

I drive around, put back a six-pack of lime-less Coronas, then head to the liquor store for more. Denied. I smell like booze. I head to the next liquor store where the brown clerk more than happily serves me a large quantity of beer.

I head up to the hills, but on my way I spill a beer in my lap. Dismayed, I pull into the first parking lot, behind a shopping mall. It's a covered lot, dark, sparse, and behind it there's a set of train tracks and large bushes before a tract of residential housing commences. Beside the parking lot, down an embankment, sits a quiet car dealership. Shiny BMWs tucked neatly into the turnoff to the highway.

I look over the parking lot, down the embankment, to the lights of the cars parked neatly in compartmentalized lines. I smoke a cigarette and pound a beer gazing down at the cars, lit in the night by overhead lighting. The highway off to the right, vehicles streaming by with their coloured tails in the daze of dark. The stars peaking through the tall trees to the left, guarding this quiet little automotive sanctuary.

I head down the embankment, my dress shoes slipping a little in the mud. I hop the chain-link fence with ease, though I almost stumble upon recovering from the jump down.

No alarms, no dogs. I walk down the little aisles of cars. Beer and smoke, dress shirt halfway open, hair crusted from day-old gel. Behind the service shop I find a tire iron lying beside the door, ostensibly used to prop said door open during the day. I pick up the tire iron, finish my beer and whip it off the hood of a yellow BMW 3-Series. It smashes beautifully, everywhere, all over the hood and windshield.

I glance around. Nothing. Cars slip past on the highway. A dog barks off in the distance. Smiling, I put my smoke in my mouth and bash the driver's side window. The sound of glass shattering is music to my ears. Millions of fragments, like a diamond rain splashing over the car and concrete.

I glance around again. Still nothing. The cars must not be alarmed. Guess they install them after you pay for it. One of those hidden little costs. Another driver's side window is smashed. And then another. And another. I stop. Listen.

Nothing.

I get up on the hood of a black BMW and go to work on the front windshield like an ancient axeman. My smoke falls to the ground as I pound and slash with the tire iron, sending shards of glass flying into my face. I kick with my dress shoes, knocking the window in. Then I hop down, break a few headlights, and another windshield. I stop. Nothing.

I'm breathing heavily, smilingly, as I create my own little economic recession here, car industry be damned.

I smash in another front windshield with a series of violent home run swings and overhead tomahawks. A deep sense of peace washes over me like a warm wave of nothingness, an orgasm of oblivion, as I hop down to boomerang the tire iron up over three rows of cars and into the front window of the dealership. A huge pane the size of a soccer net smashes instantly, and I flinch as it falls gloriously to the ground like a glass waterfall.

An alarm goes off, finally, and I run for it. Scampering up the fence, falling down over it, then scrambling up the hill in a furious, almost maniacal manner, I'm back in my car within seconds. Moments later I'm speeding out of the parking lot with squealing tires, out onto the highway, back into the inconspicuous night.

I laugh a while, take some deep breaths, then have another beer and a smoke while periodically checking the rearview mirror for flashing lights. No sign. Still clutching my beer, smoke dangling from my mouth, I turn on the satellite radio and check myself in the mirror. My eyes are so wide open. James Brown's *This is a Man's World* comes on. I crank it and start to sing along.

~

The next day I stagger out of bed at about three o'clock. I've been writing all night, into the early morning, and the rising sun finally sends me packing. The words come pouring out of my fingers, dancing like little spider legs across the keyboard—I can barely keep up. I've started writing a novel where the line between fiction and reality has become so blurred the writer has completely lost his handle on sanity. He's gone so far into his imaginary story he can barely distinguish truth from lie, fact from fiction.

My publisher has come over today as well. I'm relaxed, nursing some liquor in front of the television, when he waddles his way in. He's a heavyset guy, almost fifty and a failed writer himself, who self-published his first four books, mostly science fiction, before starting a publishing company. In this way he tried to publish more of his work, including a silly memoir about growing up in Winnipeg, but it barely kept afloat. Eventually he gave up writing, but kept the house running, signing a lot of first-time authors, making ends meet through government grants and modest sales. He was actually a decent publisher, just a terrible writer. I'm sure nobody had the heart to tell him though.

But now things are different. He's about to move into a new office building, hire seven more employees, and sign fourteen new writers. The fact a lot of this expansion comes as a direct result of the success of *Bending Light* is not lost on either of us. Still, I'm happy for him. He has a habit of adjusting his glasses and playing with his beard when he speaks, his second chin hanging under the first one like a wattle, and I like him, despite myself.

"So we finished the French translation," he says.

"Oh yeah."

"*Lumiere Oscillante*," he says in a truly awful French accent. I wince ever so slightly.

"That's *Bending Light* in French, I take it?"

"Oui, monsieur."

I take a sip from my drink.

"You don't like it?"

"Naw, it's fine. Doesn't sound right, I guess. Whatever. I don't speak French anyways."

"I can assure you the translator we got is the best. He did Chuck Palahniuk's latest novel."

"I hated Chuck Palahniuk's latest novel."

He looks at me.

"Anyway," he continues, "you're all filled in on figures and distribution, so you're good to go?"

"Yeah, I'm okay. Thanks for stopping in."

He adjusts himself, his glasses, and strokes his beard.

"So have you been writing at all?" he asks eventually.

I inhale, and exhale very slowly.

"A bit," I tell him.

"That's good, good, anything you want to run by me?"

"Naw, it's pretty rough right now."

"Okay, how about you read me a couple paragraphs, wet my whistle a bit. I'd really like to hear it."

I nod unconvincingly. "Sure."

I get up and grab my laptop, and place it on the coffee table. I open up the file I started working on last night, *Random Acts of Vandalism*, and start to read. I don't tell him the working title.

"'In essence, in absolutes, I guess all art must come from some form of reality, some degree of truth. Its roots must form somewhere in experience, however fantastical or absurd the finished product . . . but where does fact become fiction, where do art and life intersect? I don't know, I don't think anyone knows. It's less a question, and more of a statement, of the nature of who we are, artists in reality, or real life artists . . .'"

I look at my publisher, he smiles.

"Good, good, I like it. More, though, I want more. What else do you have?"

I scroll through. There's a passage about witnessing a friend go through a coke addiction. In actuality it's me, but I tell him it's about someone else. Then I start reading: "'Watching someone search for rock bottom, it effects you. They dig, ripping out morals, ethics, standards, dreams, goals, ambitions. They're deconstructing, backwards, unwinding everything they've built up. They're soaking up all the negativity and terror they can, determined to see how much they can really take, and how low, how utterly low and disastrous things will become before the void is filled. The problem is, they hover, somewhere above sustainability, and below productivity. A rat, a cockroach, feeding only to stay alive, breathing only to inflict more damage, the antithesis of life. Most wait, telling themselves salvation will come. . . . They become accustomed to waiting, not seeking. And every time their saviour passes them by, they become increasingly blind to that very search. . . . Death for these people is not a roar, although it may look like a spectacular finish. No, death for these people is a whimper, a fading, like morse code from a submarine slowly sinking into the abyss. . . .'"

He signifies he's pleased.

"I like, I like, but no suicides, okay. No more of those," he says, and then laughs his Santa Claus-like laugh.

I give him a smile, then there's silence. I take a sip from my drink. I feel raped now. Violated. I hate reading my work before it's done. It's like someone taking a cake you put in the oven, and eating it when it's only half-baked.

"So," he says, clasping his hands together. "How are you?"

"Me?" I respond, sarcastically, pointing at my chest.

"Yeah, how are you doing?"

"What do you think?"

"I dunno, that's why I'm asking you."

"I'm shit."

"You're shit?"

"Yeah. Shit."

"Okay, anything I can do to help? I'm here for you now, so anything you want you just say the word."

I rub my face, staring off at the wall. "Well . . ." I begin, but stop myself, clearing my throat before taking another sip of alcohol. I light up a smoke while my publisher waits patiently.

"Well when you can tell me how to function when half of me feels just fine about this kid copying the suicide in my book because it's making me rich, and the other half feels genuinely sorry and guilty about it, then I guess you have something I want."

He nods understandingly. "I know this is a tough, confusing time for you."

I cut him off, waving my hand in a dismissive manor. "Yeah I'm fine, I don't need any more advice. You find someone who went through this, you give them my email. Everyone has fucking advice for this. No one is in my shoes right now. No one has to sign cheques with blood on his hands."

He motions with his hands for me to calm down a bit.

"There's blood on those hands too," I say, closing my eyes and narrowing my gaze on him.

"I understand, believe me. I'm struggling with this too. This isn't how I wanted to grow my publishing house, on something like this."

I wave him off. "Don't even try. Don't even try to *think* you're going to wear this as much as I am."

He looks flustered. His cheeks start to show a tinge of red. "What do you want from me? What do you want me to say here? I'm trying to help you. Do you want to pull the book? We can pull the book. What other option do we have? We either learn from this, use it to our advantage, move on, or we let this destroy us."

I'm tired. I don't want to talk to him anymore.

"I'm tired. I don't want to talk to you anymore."

He sighs. "Okay, I'll go. You call me, email me, tell me what you need."

He stands up and shakes my hand while I'm still sitting down. Then he pats me on the shoulder as he walks by, waddling up the stairs and out of the house. I sit and ferment. Then I turn the television on and drown out my thoughts, quickly, like a skilled assassin holding his victim's head under the water as it surveys the landscape for any possible threats or witnesses.

Intervention is on, I'll be fine. I'll wallow in someone else's pity porn awhile.

~

Tonight I have a plan. I've done a bit of field work, made some rounds. Just off the end of the Skytrain in Coquitlam there resides a strip mall on the very edge of the suburbs. The iceberg tip of urban sprawl, gas stations abutting chain restaurants—highway runoff like a dirty slug, everything is always on sale out here. And the centerpiece of this strip mall is a Sony Entertainment store, around the bend slightly, just before the highway. Secluded in the dark at night, there are no stores around it open past 11.

Tonight at 12:30 exactly I'll break into the Sony Entertainment store with a crowbar and baseball bat, and have four and a half minutes of play time before I have to be out the back door, over the fence and up a small hill to the nearest Skytrain station. In the span of twelve minutes I'll go from criminal to public transit passenger, unbeknownst to the police. Either way I'm not stealing anything, not really, just damaging it beyond repair. That is my spontaneous justification for it all. Besides, I'm sure they have insurance. Everyone needs a little chaos in their lives once in awhile, if only to wake us from sleepwalking through school, nine-to-five, kids, mortgage and into a pension and incommodious deathbed.

It is now 12:15, and I'm sitting in the parking lot across the four lane street from the store. Seven beers inside my stomach, and half a pack of smokes swimming around in my lungs. I'm dressed in my black Gucci pinstripe suit, open collar white shirt, my dark brown alligator skin dress shoes. Style without substance.

12:20. I drink another beer listening to satellite radio in my Porsche. I've taken a liking to Rush Limbaugh. I hate everything he has to say, mind you, but it's nice to hear his husky baritone voice splatter fear across the American psyche. His voice is soothing in a way, a psychotic lullaby for the impoverished mind. This man speaks to me in my native tongue of over-informed, under-appreciative asshole.

12:25. I pull my Louisville Slugger up front with me, along with my crowbar borrowed from my father's tool shed. I don't think he'll mind. I have one more beer, light and suckle a smoke.

12:30. I'm out of the Porsche with crowbar and bat in hand, smoke dangling from the corner of my mouth. I'm across the road devioid of cars, and across the barren parking lot and its random oil patches and skeleton shopping carts. Multi-coloured fliers become tumbleweeds in the tar, unlit-neon-sign-blackness of this night.

I walk with confidence, with swagger, feeling like a character in a Guy Ritchie movie. In the moment, blood swirling around, oxygen rushing in and out. The air feels more vibrant, the lights more bright, the present more . . . present. It's times like these you wish you had a soundtrack. Maybe some *Hot Pants* by Bobby Byrd.

The door opens with one quick forceful pry. No alarm though. Strange. I'm guessing it's silent. I take two steps inside and then the alarm goes off. I nod to it in some weird kind of acknowledgment. Then I place the crowbar down the back of my pants, swing my trusty wooden bat up, and hit the first good, large LCD screen I find.

They don't break like windows, these things, the screens crack like flimsy plastic. If you hit them dead center for instance, the whole monitor will almost envelope the bat, wires and computer chips bursting forth like candy from a piñata.

I imagine the store owner tomorrow, watching this yahoo dressed in a full suit vandalizing the fuck out of his store. Staring at the tapes with the police, looking precisely flabbergasted. He's running through his mind the question of who could've possibly done this. As something this senseless, well, the perpetrator must have his motives. Old disgruntled worker? Family friend who never really liked him? His mistress's boyfriend? He scratches his head with the most perplexing look as some dickhead who looks like he's on his way to the lounge at Chili's bats for the cycle in his store.

I rapidfire my bat through a succession of screens down the side wall, then bust up half a dozen Sony camcorders, smacking them like Whack-A-Mole.

I glance at my round face silver Richard Mille watch: two minutes in, two minutes left.

I start to swing at a few more screens when I spot the pièce de résistance in the back of the store. A small room with sliding glass doors houses a Sony LCD Bravia XBR9 Series mounted on the wall. Fifty-two inches, decked out with surround sound. A plush leather couch beckons me in. I salivate.

The glass doors break easily enough with my crowbar. Then I give the garden of mounted speakers a good trimming. Finally I approach the television, take in a deep breath, and with one mighty side-hand swoop let all my fury come at her. A noise comes out of my mouth, half Bruce Lee scream, half female tennis star grunt.

I stand there in a state of accomplishment, huffing and puffing. The store's inventory is destroyed. Then I pee while standing on the couch, and check my watch. Time is up.

I unlock the back door, rip out through the alley, past the huge garbage cans, and up a small hill. I emerge at the Skytrain station, cross the street, up the stairs, and onto a train as it rolls right in. I'm exactly on time.

I sit down in a heap of exhaustion. There's only a few scattered passengers in my car. I take the baseball bat and place it between my legs, receiving a few stares in the process. I light up a smoke. A middleaged man dressed in a windbreaker looks at me.

"You can't smoke in here," he says.

I take a drag and blow it out. Then I wince at a pain in my back, pull the crowbar out, and place it on my lap. He looks at it with his concerned wrinkled face as though I pulled it out of my ass.

He wants to say something else, but he's looking at a young man with bleached blonde spiky hair, dressed in a suit with alligator skin shoes, sporting a bat and crowbar and smoking a cigarette, looking as though he just beat the shit out of someone. He hesitates, then closes his mouth, gets up, and proceeds to move down to the end of the car, keeping a sly eye on me as he goes. He's decided he's not going to be a hero tonight.

~

As soon as I get home I vomit out almost fifty pages, waxing poetically-charged literati gold. I'm dreaming up characters, all extracted from the past in some way, shape or form. I write until the sun comes up, peeking her head over the apartment complex, a beam of sun-dried orange and smeared yellow. The vampire heads to bed.

I awake early in the evening, full suit still on. Underneath it there's a layer of sweat encasing me like a cocoon. I cough a few times, roll over, then find my way to the bathroom for a very healthy piss.

I take a cab back to the mall to grab my Porsche, survey the cop cars and police tape, even make eye contact with an officer as I drive by on my way out of the parking lot and back home. I feel incredibly empowered.

My agent is over again—important, he said. Just had to see me. The publicist has been contacted by *Vanity Fair*, and they're doing a piece on the story. My story. Michael's story. Michael's parent's story. Whoever's story it is.

Apparently it would do more harm than good to turn down *Vanity Fair*. All they want is a reporter to come by, do an hour-long interview, talk about everything. I'm told it's been a long enough time since my appearance on *The National*, and this would be legitimate, respected exposure. It would be a story in a magazine sold and read around the world. This would be the most legitimate chance I would get to have my say, to stand atop my soapbox and tell everyone how I felt about the whole mess.

They've already lined up interviews with Michael's parents, my publisher, a few literary types, university professors, a psychiatrist who deals with copycat suicides. But they need me for the article.

They need their little pariah boy-toy to splash all over the pages like Pollock paint. They'll no doubt use me as the framing device, start off with an anecdote, something about my checkered past of dead friends and lost job, or my writing style.

I cough, hack out some phlegm onto the glass coffee table. My agent just looks at me, waiting for an answer.

"When would they want to do the interview?"

"A few days from now, maybe over the weekend."

I nod, run my tongue against the inside of my teeth, mulling. What am I supposed to do here? Say no and look dismissive? Say yes and look eager? Either way I fail.

I get up, head over to the impromptu bar I've made on the waist high book shelf in the corner of the den. I make two vodka-waters, handing one to my agent.

"Have you been seeing a psychiatrist?"

"Not really."

"So no?"

"Yeah. No."

"You sure that's a good idea?"

"Dunno, is it?"

"I dunno, kid. I'd be looking for any help I could get right now."

"Would you now?"

"I would."

"Okay then."

My agent swirls his drink a bit, stares blankly at the melting cubes, then speaks. "I'd do the interview. You're better off doing the interview. Michael's parents are doing the interview. You need to tell your side, because everyone else is going to tell their side."

"And what is my side?"

He shakes his head ever so slightly. "I think that's for you to figure out."

"Huh."

I take a healthy pull from my drink, then rub my face all over with my hands, like trying to clean off a layer of topical filth.

"Sure, let's do it."

My agent claps his hands together. "Great, I'll set it up. You're open this weekend then? You don't have any plans?"

"No, no plans. I mean I was thinking of lighting a McDonald's on fire, but I can reschedule."

He laughs, chuckles, it's not a funny joke to him, but he's humouring me. Must think I'm making some type of quip, and needs to validate it somehow by laughing.

I clear my throat as an awkward silence arises between us.

"Okay then, I'll set it up," he says, standing up to place the drink I made for him on the coffee table. He didn't even take a sip. He stops and looks at me. "You'll be fine. Just be yourself. Don't drink too much. We'll stop by beforehand and brief you a bit on what to say."

"Brief me? Are we in the army or something? I thought this was for me to figure out."

"We'll just go over some of the things they might want to talk about—your past, that kind of stuff. There's going to be some hard questions."

"I see."

I sit back on the couch as he leaves, take another drink, light up a smoke and turn on the television. I flick awhile, trying my damndest not to think, but it's futile. My phone starts to vibrate. It's my old friend Ryan. He's going out tonight to some lounge for drinks with a few friends, he texts me, and wants to know if I'd like to come along. Tells me it would be good for me to get out and meet some people. Would it now. We haven't seen each other in years, Ryan and I. Don't even know how he got my number. Whatever, he's an old friend, and I feel as if I have an obligation to my past.

'Sure', I text back. 'Sing when you're winning.'

I shit, shower, and trim my beard—the holy trinity—then throw a bit of gel in my blonde spikes. Pull out a suit, my Givenchy navy blue thin cut, and a hard pink shirt, open. Dark brown loafers, matching pink socks.

I decide it might be good to eat a full meal, considering the last time I ate a full meal was in Toronto almost two weeks ago. I head out to a newly opened restaurant, a quiet one down by the docks. Overlooking the river, sparse lighting. One of those one-syllable places, spelled with an umlaut.

I order a steak, some fries, and a bottle of wine. My pink socks are sticking out of the end of my dress slacks, I can tell, because I keep catching the waitresses looking at them. They giggle, looking more intrigued than scared. I'm passing as a respectable, responsible guy with a rakish taste in underwear.

One of them comes over, a tall blonde with a caramel tan. She offers to refill my wine.

"Of course," I say, holding up my glass.

She pours, a smile sliding across her face. I look at her.

"We all wanted to say we like your socks."

I glance behind her, to the three other waitresses standing by the bar. They look over and giggle slightly.

"Tell them thank you, from the bottom of my heart," I say, palm over chest.

She smiles, finishes pouring.

"And what's you're name," I ask.

"Deanna."

"Nice to meet you, Deanna. Thanks for the wine and the compliment."

"No problem, anytime," she says, then walks away after having another good look at me.

Sharply dressed, psychotically pretentious, hiding a viscous, terrible secret. I am Patrick Bateman. Dress me up, but don't dare take me out.

Deanna writes her name and number on my receipt. Probably after she saw the $100 tip, I'm thinking. Folding the receipt away, I head out to meet up with Ryan and his scattered acquaintances.

Ryan looks good, healthy, dressed like a banker just finished work. He is actually. He's cut his hair short, almost shaved, his spiky blonde Japanimation hair long gone. Long gone are his drug days too, it seems, he's more of a catalyst, an update, a newer version of the troubled young man I once knew. Ryan 2.0.

We catch up on old times, talk about the drug binges and the debauchery. It's warming to see a familiar face.

Drinks are good, conversation is good. It's dark, candle-lit in the lounge. Nobody seems to recognize me, or care, or want to bring *it* up. I'll take it.

One girl takes a liking to me. A brunette dressed elegantly in a dark cocktail dress. Amber. Green eyes, looks a bit like Alyssa Milano. I tell her I'm between jobs. She understands, she says, adding something topical about the economic downturn. She's a legal assistant about to take the bar exam. Has her own car, her own place. A well-adjusted woman, Amber is, one who happens to be intrigued by me for some reason. She likes to fish for compliments. I tell her she looks stunning tonight, like I'd seen her some other night, and she was only radiant.

Amber tells me her parents just retired, finally. She's hitting the glass ceiling at the law firm though. Older employees not looking to leave the workforce just yet, willing to hold onto their jobs a little while longer until the hurricane quiets to a tropical storm. I concur with her dilemma through a telling nod. We're the generation waiting for the keys to the car, for the right to take the controls. Patience is our virtue, our curse, our conundrum.

I head outside to the deck for a smoke. Thunder clouds are moving in from the west. Dark skies hovering. It will rain tonight.

I head back inside just as a few people leave. Amber comes and sits beside me—we chat for a bit, mostly about school, and jobs, and life and whatnot. She's a nice enough girl, smart, head on straight, seems cultured.

Another couple leaves and I think it's time for me to go. Six drinks in and I'm starting to unravel, chatterbox. I tell Ryan I'm thinking of going home. Amber looks at me.

"You heading home?" she asks.

"Yeah, tired, you know."

"You wanna go have a drink somewhere?"

I look at her. She looks . . . something. I have no idea. Women are a strange, alien species to me. I haven't been laid in close to a year. I can't read her at all.

"Yeah, like at another bar?"

"I know this place by my house, it's quiet."

I nod. "Okay."

We head out, and I follow her car, a brand new black Beemer. She leads me down to the water, off to the west of the city, into the parking lot of a funky little bar off the main drag. They serve dinner late, then people hang around until closing. More of a hangout for people who know people who work there. It's nice though, and we sit in the corner, looking out over the beach onto the ocean.

Amber is a bit out of my league, but my Porsche tells her otherwise. She looks like she could have come from money—nice ring, nice purse, nice car—she takes care of herself, or someone does, financially. But then again I could be wrong. I really have no fucking clue. I'm guessing, and I usually guess wrong.

"So you're quite the mysterious one," she says to me after our drinks arrive. Her legs unfold slightly from the side of the table. Smooth. I don't know what I'm doing, or what I'm supposed to say here. She's obviously not humouring me, but finds me somewhat appealing or attractive in some way.

"Yeah, mysterious sounds good."

"No I mean you're hiding something."

"Hiding something?"

"Yeah, I can tell. I'm good at reading people, my Dad was a psychiatrist."

I cough. Take a long pull from my drink. I go to open my mouth, but stop, playing with the straw in my drink instead. I look out the window. "Look," I say, "I'm not big on interrogations or anything. This secret, it's not something cool, okay? You invited me here."

She smiles. "I know, I'm sorry. I just had to point it out. I have secrets too, we all have them. I want to tell you something, and you seem like you're a good listener."

The word comes out of my mouth hesitantly. "O-kay?"

She adjusts herself, looks me in the eye. "I was dating this guy, he was a great guy, and we'd been going out for over a year. But something always put me off about him. I didn't know what it was. . . ."

"Okay. . . ."

"Anyways, so one day he just leaves me. He didn't give any reason other than he was into this other girl. He just left me, alone. Wouldn't return my phone calls, wouldn't give me any type of explanation."

I lean back in my chair as if she might pull out some type of weapon at any moment.

"So the strange thing is, this has been happening to me all my life. Every boyfriend I've ever had has just left me. No real reason, sometimes they just move away, or cheat on me. I've got all this baggage, and I never brought any of it on myself. I'm a good person. I don't lie, I volunteer, I've never hurt anyone."

She ends the last sentence as if I'm supposed to respond. I don't.

"These guys, they're all just assholes," she goes on. "I've never had a one night stand. Never cheated on a boyfriend. I mean am I not good looking? Tell me honestly."

I'm sitting there, leaning back to keep my distance. I don't answer, but take a sip from my drink instead.

"It's a simple question."

In all actuality, she's quite attractive. Good body, no fat on her. Nice face, good fashion sense, she's easily well above average. An eight. The type of girl that doesn't have to chase guys, if she waits long enough they'll come to her.

"You're good looking, so I'm not sure what you want me to say here."

"Just answer honestly."

"You're hot. I mean you're not drop-dead gorgeous, but you're good looking enough not to be too worried about your appearance hindering you or anything."

"Would you sleep with me if you had the chance?"

I take another sip from my drink, but I don't take my eye off her at all. I'm getting the sense I'm on candid camera or something, like this is some fucking hoax.

"I don't understand this at all. Is this why you asked me here?"

"I asked you here because I wanted to get an honest male opinion. You seem like a guy who's been through a few things. I just want to know what you think."

"What does it matter?" I say, my voice becoming a bit harsh. "Go ask some other guy. Go ask the bartender," I say, nodding towards the bar.

"I want to ask you."

I shake my head, about done with this. I lean forward. "Look. I've paid for my sins, and now I just want to be left alone. I don't owe you, or women, or anyone, a God-damn fucking thing. So if you expect me to sit here and defend the male species. No, not going to happen."

She comes back at me, accelerated. "Did you come here because you think you might get laid?"

I lean forward, rub my eyes with one hand. I'm not doing this shit, not tonight.

I stand up, pull out my wallet and put down a hundred in twenties. "Thank you for the drink, it was nice to meet you."

I walk out of the bar, shaking my head in disbelief. I head up the street to my car, hearing high heels behind me, speed-walking.

"Wait," says Amber.

I stop, wincing first before I turn around, expecting some sort of retaliation.

She comes up close, her perfume following in slowly, into my nose. She holds my hand. "Look, I know you're hiding something, it's weighing on you. Maybe an ex too, I think, but I don't know. I don't want to know. I just know I haven't had sex in quite a while, and I was just wondering if you could help me with that."

I can't help but laugh. I look around to see if any other human being might have heard what she just said.

"You're fucking joking right?"

"No, I'm not. Look, if you don't want to, that's fine. I'm just attracted to you, and I'm really stressed out lately—I need a rebound lay or something. And you, you look like you might need the same thing. A . . . release."

I still don't know what to say. I'm flabbergasted. This must be what the Sony Entertainment store owner is feeling right now.

"Sex? You just want to have sex with me?"

"Yes, and you can leave in the morning. Actually it would probably be better if you did. If you don't want to do this, it's fine. I'm just offering."

I take a breath in. I'm incredibly turned on. However I'm a man, so the bra section in the Sears catalogue turns me on.

"So, like at your house?"

"I only live a few blocks away."

I just look at her, still unsure if I'm getting duped. I feel now as if I have the right to ask a few inquisitive questions.

"Are you a prostitute or something? I'm not paying for sex."

"No, I'm not a prostitute. Look, I'm not going to wait for an answer, it's starting to rain."

She's right, it is. Thunder grumbles across the bay, faint sheet lightning off to the west.

"Okay, Amber, you got me. Where's your house?"

She looks at me, and smiles.

~

Sheet lightning. Lighting up the sky, an excess of oxygen white, a camera flash, hills and mountains exposed in the obsidian panorama. Thunder erupts, barrels overhead and into the eardrums, a peripheral ignition.

She comes into the room wearing only her panties. Slivers of light spill in through the blinds as she pulls off my clothes, runs her nails over my chest and arms. She doesn't look me in the eye. I'm to remain anonymous to her. She just needs to feel sexy, feel wanted, turned on. I pull her in tight, willing to oblige.

Grunts and gasps join the thunder. I wince out a noise that grumbles from my throat. She grabs my shoulder blades and tries to rip them apart as I cough, pull out, collapse beside her. She rolls over onto my side, her pubic bone pushing into my ass.

I relax so much I start to free fall into the bed sheets. Unaware of anything other than the physical, unable to think about anything but the present, I close my eyes and sink into a deep unconsciousness, a beautiful opiate slumber as the thunder keeps us company in the dark.

It's the first time I've slept without dreaming in months. Deep, black, blissful sleep. Nothing, no consciousness. No thoughts. A blank page that remains unwritten until I awake a few hours later. Amber is fast asleep, snoring quietly. Cute.

I get up, get dressed and get out as we discussed. Breakfast would be simply awkward. I don't leave my card, or number. I figure I'll just leave, as planned. Don't fuck up good sex with bad conversation.

I go home and take a shower, and then a nap. When I awake, I turn to my laptop, spilling more characters onto the page. Story lines take form. After a few hours I pass out again with the laptop on my stomach, feet on the coffee table, my hands exhausted from hours of typing.

~

I'm awake. Startled, by a pounding at the door. The doorbell ringing incessantly. It's my agent, and publisher, along with a publicist, here to brief me for my *Vanity Fair* interview. An unbearable stress, almost forgotten, gallops up behind me.

"Remember, you want to seem like you're dealing with this—not too well, it's hurting you, but not destroying you. You don't want to seem like it isn't affecting you at all, but then again you don't want to seem like you're totally immersed in it, unable to let it go. Understand?"

"You want to remain humble, so keep money and book sales out of it. Don't talk about how this has made you a much sought after writer. But then you want to let them know you're a skilled writer and that you have talent, ideas, a second book well underway. Focus on this second book, but not too much because then you'll look like you're peddling, trying to drum up press."

"Offer him a drink, but don't drink too much. You need to be relaxed, seem confident, but not cocky. Try to divert the conversation away from Michael as much as possible, but don't make it seem like you're trying to divert the questions away from Michael. Try to be coy about it. Seamless."

I just stare at the three of them, these three censorship monkeys staring inquisitively back at me.

"Anything else," I say.

"Try to get out of the house. Go for dinner. Maybe introduce him to your father. You need other people to show that you're stable. He's going to be watching you like a hawk—it's all going to be on the record right from the get go—you know how it goes."

"I know how it goes?" I say, taking a deep breath in. "Okay, can you guys get out now?"

They all look at one another, nod and leave shortly thereafter.

I shower, trim my beard, and take a nap. I change into a black short sleeve dress shirt and tapered jeans. I'm supposed to look casual but not too casual. Not over or under-prepared. Ready but relaxed. I'm supposed to balance, hover, between a million different things. Untethered, I've lost all sense of gravity.

The journalist shows up on time. He's in a rented four-door car. Mid 40s. Glasses, short hair starting to thin and grey. He's probably done over ten thousand interviews in his life. I am simply the next one on the ever-growing list.

Steve Machin. That's his name, pronounced "Mash-in." He tells me a little anecdotal story about taking his American money to get it exchanged into Canadian. That's what you do when you come to Canada from the United States, you change your money. Because you usually get a bit more. Not this time though. The exchange rate is zero. He thought that was interesting. I smile politely.

He's been on staff at *Vanity Fair* for eight years and mostly covers lifestyle stories. Entrepreneurs. Artists. Public figures, that sort of thing. The occasional political story.

Columbia, where he did his master's degree. Where he worked on the desk at *The New York Times*, some other magazines—I'm zoning out. I stand up and head to my bar for a drink, asking him if he wants one. He declines, asks for water instead. I get him water.

He turns his recorder on, so I guess we're starting right away. He wants to talk for an hour. He's already done all the other interviews for the story.

The first ten minutes of the interview are the usual, trying to get background on me, filling in all the blanks. He's massaging my vocal chords into coherence, so when the juicy questions arise I'll be lubed up properly for that brilliantly placed pull-quote response. I know this drill all too well. He also notifies me that a photographer will be coming tomorrow. Drops it into the conversation casually, this bit about a local freelancer meeting me to take a few photographs. Fantastic, I say.

The usual suspects of questions start to roll off the conveyor belt. What was my initial reaction? How do I feel now? Do I feel responsible for his death? What would I say to Michael's parents if I got the chance?

He asks me if I blog, or Twitter. I don't. I have a Facebook account, an email. He asks me if I feel as if I think young people don't read books anymore. I say one young person read my book. He asks me if I feel a part of a new breed of Gen Y writers. I don't. Do I feel a part of any movement? I don't. Am I rebelling against technology, the global village kids are growing up in? I'm not. I download music all the time, spend a lot of time on the internet. I am not a part of the new scene, but I do participate in its recreationally from time to time.

I tell him I feel like I'm in between generations. I had no internet or cell phone in high school, but now I spend just as much time in front of a computer as I do a TV. I was here before the revolution, and was converted by proxy. I represent the last remnants of a generation raised in a de-globalized world.

He asks me some of my influences. I rail off some notables. Movies? Sure. Music, yeah I listen to it. I'm not cutting edge, I follow the trends, pick which ones I like. I tell him I can remember a time in high school when I listened to music on a cassette player. He smiles, and I suddenly feel very old.

He asks me about my writing style. At night, in the morning, strict regimen? I tell him I write in spurts of inspiration, leaving out the detail that random acts of vandalism and sex have become my primary muse and motivation.

The comparisons to Douglas Coupland? Flattered, sure. For "The iPod Generation," as *The Globe & Mail* put it? I wince, and say nothing.

He asks me about my second book. It's coming along, I say. He asks what it's about. I tell him it's about art imitating life, but other than that, it's too early to tell. Working title? No, don't have one.

I'm being more than amicable. He's trying to soften me with each blow, work the body, get me to open up and drop my guard. He's good at what he does, and he's trying to make me feel comfortably confident in hearing my own voice.

He slyly lets the conversation veer off-topic a little in order to feel natural. We talk about *Oldboy* and the Virginia Tech massacre, those kids who lay down on the highway and died after watching *The Program*. John Hinkley Jr. and *Taxi Driver*, the rash of fight clubs in Silicon Valley after *Fight Club*, and *Futility, or the Wreck of the Titan* and the Titanic.

But the life imitating art discussion wears thin quickly, and he veers back to me. My past, my parents, separated, one left. No siblings. Grandparents? All gone. High school? I tell him I slept through most of it. What did I want to be when I grew up? A rugby player.

Then he goes back to *it*, one last time. I give him something.

"I had this dream a few weeks ago, I'm walking down the street and it's dark out. I go to cross the street, and as I do, I get blindsided by this car speeding down the road. No warning, no anything—I barely even see the headlights before it rams into me. I hurl around, feeling like I can't breathe, my lungs shrinking. Then

I hit the ground and everything goes quiet. . . . But then I get up, miraculously, unhurt. Completely shell-shocked, yes, but unhurt. I walk over to the car—it's just sitting there in the middle of the street, front window smashed, headlights still on, engine running. I look in the driver's side window, and I see myself. I see myself sitting there, staring straight forward, frozen—and then I woke up."

I look at him. He's ever so slightly nodding.

"Honestly," I say, "that's about as close as I've ever gotten to understanding this whole mess." And I leave it at that.

He senses I've had just about enough. It's only been about forty-five minutes but he calls it a day. I walk him upstairs to the door where he gives me the card of the photographer looking to stop by tomorrow for photos. He leaves, gets in his rented car, like a burglar who broke into my house and rummaged through all my shit without stealing anything. I feel violated in the most passive-aggressive way.

I head back down to the den, and my father comes home a little later after a long shift. We eat dinner, watch sports highlights together, then have a beer. We talk to each other in single syllables, but it's comforting after having talked so much earlier.

I try to write later, but nothing comes. So then I do the next best thing and pump myself full of chewable codeine. I take four, with a shot of tequila chased by children's cough syrup. The most I've ever taken is two, so this should be interesting.

I watch television for a bit in the dark, *South Park*, followed by some European soccer. Then I turn the channel to static and press mute.

Time slows, then drags, then starts to flow like mud. My eyes begin to water, my head weighed down by my chin, and my mouth starts to dry up. I take a few sips of water. Each joint of my body starts to fabricate a soft glow around it, and I chuckle quietly to myself. My weight cuts in half—I'm barely pressing into the couch—as each valve of my heart pushes blood more slowly, transient white blood cells wallowing in the gridlock. I'm starting to worry about overdosing, but I'm way too relaxed to care.

Death has no relation to fear now. A somber reckoning, a comfort in the unknown, that's all. I know this feeling. An old friend returning to familiar places. I feel ready to die at this moment, ready to leave the absurdity of this life behind for the reality of another unknown. I'm at ease with the knowledge of an afterlife. These drugs are doing more than their job right now. I could enjoy rape, I decide.

I have a sudden urge to fall asleep in a McDonald's ball pit, but it passes and I'm out.

~

I feel like shit. My insides are grumbling a nasty conversation, the medication having spilled out from my stomach and all over my internal organs. Liver, intestines, colon, lungs—it's a hangover without the headache. I was probably two, maybe three pills from an overdose or a life-threatening trip to the hospital.

I spend most of the early morning on the toilet. I vomit, I have diarrhea, and my urine comes out endlessly, everywhere, leaking all over my pants. I endure a constant perspiration from my face and armpits, but eventually it passes once a new wave of fresh medication takes over.

The photographer shows up—I completely forgot. It's raining outside, I invite him in, ask him if it's okay if I have a shower before we go out. He's okay with that, this is all he has to do today as well. We are the only entry in each other's schedules.

I throw on my black peacoat and some dark jeans, and a dark toque over my stained blonde hair. I light up a smoke outside the house, and the photographer stops and looks at me. "So I was wondering if you'd be okay with maybe taking some pictures in front of the bridge?"

I'm not.

"Naw, I know," he says. "Had to ask though, it's my job."

I understand, sort of.

"So do you just want to follow me? I've got a few other ideas."

I stand there, hands in my jacket pocket, smoke dangling from my mouth. "Any chance I could just go with you? I'm feeling kind of sick today, not really in any condition to drive."

He nods, seems to understand. "Sure."

We get in his car, an older BMW. Slides of negatives, photo albums, yellowing newspapers everywhere. He apologizes for the mess.

His name is Wayne. He's actually only a few years older than I am, just turning thirty. This is his first gig with *Vanity Fair*, and he admits he's fairly nervous about this shoot. About me, about the story, he wants everything to go off without a hitch.

He has that photographer look to him. Half bastard son of hippie parents, half entrepreneur and self-made business man. He has great style, with short curly dirty blonde hair straight from a Commodore show, indie-hipster splashed all over his tight-fitting jeans.

He's cool with me smoking in his car, as long as I keep the window down. I keep it cracked only a few inches though, the rain is everywhere. Fat, disgusting rain. He wants to stop by his studio for a bit, then maybe if the rain stops head outside for a few photos.

We head into the city, skyscrapers piling up in the peripheral vision. Massive grey obelisks guarding the horizon. They stand tall over the plush green tree line, the windshield wipers letting us see them only in short three-second intervals.

Wayne's studio is a small space just off the back of the busy retro retail street that is Commercial Drive. There's a McDonald's within smelling distance, a bus route nearby. We're up high, second story, above a Chinese restaurant.

The walls are a hard white. Most everything is a hard white. His girlfriend is there, she's also his receptionist, runs the office, equally indie-hipster. They're a lovely couple together, they hold themselves well, however they seem tense around me. It makes me tense up. This is what it must feel like to have an aura. Or be O.J. Simpson.

The main room is already set up, black background, lighting everywhere. He tells me he's fine if I want to keep my jacket and toque on for now, he's going to take a lot of pictures. There's a bathroom off in the corner of the office space if I want to check myself out. I don't.

While he sets up, I ask Wayne how he got the job.

He tells me he'd done a bunch of shots on the downtown eastside. They won a few awards. One in particular, a junkie literally shooting up on camera in a downtrodden alley, the needle pressing into his vein. The junkie is shirtless, and it looks like he's staring off into the night sky, which is perfectly lit, stars scattered across the top of the photo.

He stops, asks his girlfriend to get the photo.

He's right, it is an amazing shot. A million words. In actuality the junkie heard a noise that turned out to be someone yelling from a third-storey window as he was shooting up. But the way the photo turned out it appears as if he's looking up at the sky for God, a slight glaze on his eyes suggesting he's about to cry.

The shot bolstered Wayne's career. Until then he'd mostly been making a living taking concert photos and shooting weddings. He fucking hates weddings, loathes them with a passion, but they allow him to be a full-time photographer. He seems okay with this deal, although you can tell it's something that isn't, and never will, sit right with him.

Anyways, he says, so someone who knows someone who works for *Vanity Fair* saw the photo, and he got on their freelance list. This was almost two years ago, and this is his first call. He's been waiting two years for them to phone him. If they run one of his photos for this story, the phone will start ringing off the hook. No more fucking North Van IKEA weddings where the bride's mother runs the show like a psychotic, slave-driving Neo-Nazi dictator pumped full of botox, prescription medication, red wine and barely hidden depression.

He also mentions to me the fact that he took shots of Michael's parents yesterday in their home. I just nod and stare off at the ground until he feels uncomfortable enough to change the topic.

His girlfriend helps him set up some more lighting. He senses I feel a bit awkward just standing around. I can smoke if I want. I will. His girlfriend asks me if I'd like anything to drink. Beer? Yes, they do have a few. She brings me a cold Heineken. I don't drink Heineken but I will now.

He takes some test shots with me smoking and drinking the Heineken, trying to make sure the lighting is good. I take a long drag from my smoke and exhale it down towards the ground. I feel like a circus act. Just stand there and be yourself, people will pay to come look at you, you don't have to do anything. Like the lizard lady, or the wolf man, they just have to stand there. The patrons fill in the story just fine.

We take a bunch of shots, chat a bit more, I have another beer. We even crack a few jokes to break the tension in the air. Wayne's girlfriend is very pleasant, they're welcoming, like an old couple who've invited you over for tea. I feel for Wayne a bit, this situation, the pressure of the shoot. This probably wasn't the call he wanted to get from *Vanity Fair*, depression porn story. He tells me he spent all weekend taking shots of the bridge from various angles, out in the rain with a plastic cover over his Nikon.

He said he read my book too, actually before he got the call, noticed a review of it in a local rag. He liked it. But I've found everyone says that when they talk to you in person about your art. If they don't like it they just won't talk to you about it in front of you. Fair enough.

We head out after an hour or so, the rain having subsided momentarily. Wayne takes me downtown to his favourite alley, between tall office buildings just off Robson. Graffiti covers one wall, a huge spastic mural of colours and shapes and sharp paint edges. It's gorgeous in the ally actually, the light coming in perfectly parallel, making you feel like you're standing in one of those deep trails between ominous cliffs, like a modern day *Lord of the Rings*.

But the feeling passes after a few minutes. That incessant clicking noise, shutter closing, a spastic eyelid stealing my soul over and over. About the time I've had enough he tells me we're finished. He's happy with them. Asks if I want to grab a quick coffee on the way back. Sure.

We sit outside on the deck. A few people seem to notice me, they don't say anything, just whisper and look over periodically. It's intrusive but I can't do anything.

"Man, I'd say I feel for you, but I have no idea, I've never been through anything like that. Except maybe with that photo I showed you."

I nod. He's being refreshingly candid. It's like when someone dies in your life, and others tell you they send their condolences. They feel for you. Sure, maybe they do. But this wasn't their blood that died, so in actuality they don't physically know how to feel for you at all when it comes to something like this.

"It is fucked though," he continues. "I mean he's still on the streets. I go and take this photo of him, supposedly because I'm trying to shed light on the situation down there, that whole mess, and what the fuck did it do other than accelerate my career? I have trouble looking at the photo now, at all. I don't have it up. I have like a hundred prints of it sitting in a desk."

I nod knowingly. Wayne has faced a similar conundrum of his own. He's living with it.

"So how do you deal with it?" I ask him in all seriousness. I'm actually intrigued to hear what he has to say.

"To be honest," he says, then he stops. "To be honest, I don't."

There's a brief silence between us.

"I ignore it," he eventually goes on. "It's not something I'm going to get over one day. It's a scar I'll live with the rest of my life. It'll fade, and yeah it's faded. But then I saw the guy again a few weeks ago. And it's all right there back in my face fucking up my whole life. I mean I want to take him in and shelter him, I feel so bad, but I know I can't do that. He's a junkie. I can't afford to take the time out of my life to try and fix a junkie. We're both just fucked, forever tied together by that photo. I mean every time I see him from now on I'll empty my wallet for him, buy him lunch, whatever. But it's fucked. I mean we can't go for beers or anything or be friends, he's a basehead."

Wayne and I sit there sipping coffee, me smoking, in some weird ritual of camaraderie. It's a telling silence, two guys crossing similar routes in life, a simple nod of acknowledgement. A tap of swords as we pass.

I won't let Wayne drive me home, it's way out of his way, I take a cab instead. I tell him I've got lots of money, no worries. I do ask him if I can buy a print of his photo. I ask him what it's called. He says he left it untitled, he could never seem to come up with a proper title. It seems fitting. Wayne takes my address and says he'll send me a free print of it. I tell him no, hand him a hundred, he tries to turn it down. I push it at him, he takes it—he is a photographer after all.

We shake hands and I leave, feeling a bit better knowing at least the photos of me will have a hint of connection to them. My photographer has a few scars too.

As soon as I get home I'm ready to write. It's a feeling of anxiousness, a junkie looking for his own unique fix. Just get me in front of a keyboard and I'll be fine.

I head downstairs. The television is on. I look at the screen as I go to grab my laptop and head to my room. Michael's parents are being interviewed. What are the fucking chances. I stop dead, standing there, holding the laptop.

"Fuck me."

Michael's parents sit close together on a couch. It's a nationally syndicated talk show, and some older heavyset woman interviews them. As soon as I hear Michael's father speak I have to hit the mute button.

But I can't seem to leave the room. I stand there, frozen, watching their mouths move against the absence of sound. I am stuck there until the interview breaks for commercial, at which point I put my laptop down, defeated. The ideas have all washed away.

I go make myself a drink.

~

It's been four days and I haven't written a thing. The *Vanity Fair* article is apparently coming out in a few days. I'm imprisoned in my own depression now. Infamy and depression sit on either side of me on the couch, one hand on each shoulder. The devil and another devil, by my side.

Listening to their sage advice, I decide that tonight I will light a McDonald's on fire and burn it to the ground.

~

I am about to light a McDonald's on fire. There's a new one in the high-end neighbourhood near my father's house. It closes early, doesn't have a 24-hour drive through.

Tonight I've chosen my D&G beige suit, two button, with a yellow cream shirt, and black tie and shoes. I've already put back about a third of a bottle of 151-proof rum, the remainder having already been allocated. I've also got a jerry can full of gasoline.

I park my car at the end of a street way up past the restaurant, so I can scramble back here to watch it burn from a safe distance when it starts to light up the night sky. I can already imagine the stench.

I start out back with the jerry can, making sure to pour some on the drive-through order receiver. Then I quickly do a full lap of the perimeter, followed by a line out the back alley, ending a safe distance away. I pick up the bottle of rum and stuff a ripped-up rag down into it with a bent coat-hanger. Then I turn the bottle upside down for about a second, and pull part of the rag back with the hanger. A bouquet of fabric sprouts out.

I head back out to stand in front of the McDonald's—its yellow lighting and $3.99 Value Meal posters stare at me blankly. There's something eerie about it, this place all closed up, lights extinguished inside. I have a small epiphany, realizing that all the horror in our lives is mostly man-made. We bring it on ourselves.

I light my makeshift Molotov cocktail with a concentrated look, then watch it burn momentarily before heaving it aloft with some serious might. I almost fall face first into the parking lot I throw it so hard.

The bottle smashes through the large front window, skidding right up to the till like it's ordering a Big Mac. The glass is obviously cheap because it smashes immediately, another percussion of shattering reminding me of the BMW dealership. Large portions of glass falling like a waterfall is something everyone should hear. It's beautiful, like electrified water.

I watch as the fire spreads all over the floor and up the front counter, an amber tint of blue at its base. Then I run around back and take out my Zippo and light the end of the gas line. It slowly creeps up on the building, a wandering drunk knowing exactly where he's going, before suddenly splitting in two. The twin trails of flames race apart, making their way around the building and out of view.

Off I run, into the bushes and beyond. I hide in an alleyway, huffing and puffing, some eight or nine blocks away before I hear the sirens start to wail in the distance. Occasionally smelling my hands, I enjoy one of the greatest smokes I've ever had. My hands smell like gasoline, and it's intoxicating.

I head up to my car and sit on the hood on the street overlooking the McDonald's. Oh yes she's burning nicely now—the whole thing is on fire—flames licking up the side walls. A crowd has started to gather a safe distance away. One of them, a young male, is continuously clapping.

I smile, sitting on the hood of my car drinking beer and smoking. People appear on their patios, one after another, eager to watch the blaze. The sirens have now turned into flashing lights, but it's much too late. This McDonald's will burn straight to the ground.

Finishing my smoke, I get in my car and head home.

~

Nothing. I've got nothing. I burned a McDonald's to the ground, and nothing comes—I'm still blocked. I pace around the house a bit, have a smoke, make a drink—nothing. I watch some television. Nothing. Then I go and lie in my bed, trying to figure out what I can do to start writing again, and I fall asleep.

~

It's been almost over a week and not a single word written. I tried forcing myself, pumping out words in succession in an effort to jump-start some semblance of creativity, but nothing, it's dead. The battery is shot.

The burned down McDonald's is all over the news. There's a video of it on YouTube, and really grainy security footage of me lighting it on fire. You can't even tell it's a beige suit I'm wearing. The video is so poor it looks like a naked guy with baggy skin in black tie and shoes doing the damage. That's what happens when you're McDonald's and you get cheap cameras.

Apparently the police are investigating the fire. I can feel the heat, so to speak, so any further criminal activities should probably be put on hold for the time being. The downside of course is that I'll be unable to write, or even inspire myself to write. Creativity through destruction—the irony is not lost on me, if you were wondering.

One afternoon a few days later, in the midst of a somewhat overdue wallet cleaning, I find the receipt from the restaurant on which Deanna, the tall blonde waitress, scribbled her number in looping feminine lettering. I call the number, get voicemail, and explain to the ether that I'm the guy from the restaurant with the pink socks who gave her the big tip. Apparently I'm wondering if she has plans this weekend. Deanna calls me back about an hour later, says she'd love to hang out. She's going to a party tonight down by the docks just east of the city, and I should stop by. I tell her I will stop by, with a buddy. She tells me she'll text me the address.

I call up Ryan, ask him to join me this time. He's single so he's down. Tells me he's going to wear a suit because he's not getting upstaged by my socks again.

I throw on my Dior Homme black pinstripe suit with a Tom Ford checkered dress shirt. Matching low-neck cardigan, some skinny-toed dark dress shoes, matching checkered socks.

Ryan is wearing an ash grey suit, an open flower-print dress shirt. He looks hideous in the most stylish of ways.

We pick up some booze, drink and drive for a bit, chatting about the old times. Then we park the car and walk to the party. It's off the main drag, just up a small hill. A three-storey condo, we can see people milling about on the deck a block away. It's

good the party is crowded, we'll blend into the scenery incon-
spicuously. We probably know no one there.

The condo is new, built within the last five years, the paint
still plush, the kitchen counters still gleaming, the art still JYSK
contemporary. It's a fairly dressy affair, we don't stick out all that
much, maybe a bit but not enough to get more than a few sideways glances.

Deanna finds me quickly. She's a tall offering of MTV priss,
a wine glass dangling from her tanning bed hand and designer
jewelry. She's already drunk. Not glassy-eyed drunk, mind you,
but getting there. She's happy to see me, didn't think I'd come or
even call. She thanks me again for the tip, tells me she bought the
dress she's wearing with it. I smile approvingly and tell her to forget it.

Deanna introduces us to a few of her friends, and before I
know it Ryan is off with one of them, suit and all, deep into the
bowels of the house somewhere. He always knew how to facili-
tate a proper transaction.

Some guy makes me a drink in the kitchen, a Mojito. Deanna
starts going off about her job at the restaurant and how she hates
her boss and most of her co-workers and her mom won't shut up
about her finding a husband and having kids. And she just bought
a new car and needs to go to the gym more because she's getting
fat but she really likes chocolate. And she wants to move into a
new place with her new friend but she's not sure she can afford
it on her salary so she's going to have to ask her dad to co-sign
for a loan at the bank. She's thinking about going back to school
to become a dental hygienist because they make good money, but
she's not sure about the hours and she also doesn't know if she
can work on teeth all day. So she might try to go to school and
become a pharmacist but that would be really tough because her
grades weren't the best in university and apparently it's really
competitive here. That and she has a dog named Russell. I'll let
you guess what kind of breed it is.

I'm looking for a balled-up sock to shove in her mouth. Here
I am, sipping a drink in the kitchen, and this girl is literally telling
me her entire life story in the span of twenty minutes. All I can

do is nod and get the odd word in, which only serves to launch her off in another tedious direction.

Oh yeah, she wants to go to Australia for a year, or maybe teach English in Asia. Either that or maybe move to Banff and work retail in a clothing store. Always seeing everyone else's Facebook photos taken in exotic locations has given her the travel bug evidently. She's been to Mexico a few times, Cancun, but stayed in a resort. Wants to backpack this time, soak up some culture. Sh's a big fan of indigenous culture.

I can't even fathom spending more than two hours with this woman, even with the promise of sex at the end of it. Before I tell her this, however, I excuse myself to the bathroom. Deanna says it's down a floor. Breaking free of the kitchen, I shape my hand into that of a handgun, stick it in my mouth and pull the trigger. Some girl notices me, gives me a weird look—I shrug and head down a flight of stairs and onto the balcony for a much needed smoke.

There are lines of street lights and lit windows out across the way, apartment complexes and restaurant billboards. I can see a few pools and backyard gardens. Nice neighborhood.

I flick my smoke out onto the alley and head back into the confusion. There's an English rapper playing on the sound system, I can't place who it is. People dance on the second floor. Some drunk girl in a cheap tiara knocks over a lamp, spilling her drink on the couch. Nobody seems to notice, or care.

I take in a deep breath and locate the bathroom. There's no line up but there's someone inside. I knock. "Just a minute," says a female voice.

I wait there, standing right in front of the door, Mojito in hand. Eventually I hear the toilet flush and the door opens. It's Robin, and it's been almost a decade since I've seen her. She's definitely older, filled out a bit, but there's no mistaking those eyes.

Her father is Italian. Straight from the boat Italian, barely speaks a word of English. But her mother is Swedish. She's got her father's dark complexion, dark hair, tanned skin, thick yet slender eyebrows, and light blue eyes.

She just stares at me. "Eli?" she says quizzically, as if I might be Eli's older brother.

"Robin?"

"Yeah," she says, coming closer. "Is that really you, Eli?"

"Yeah, I'm older though."

She smiles, then moves in and hugs me. It's a long hug, and her perfume lifts off her hair and into my nostrils.

She leans back, runs her hand through my short beard, my spiky blonde hair, the dark roots starting to peak out. "Oh my God, you look so different I barely even recognized you. And the suit?" She looks down at my suit, running her hands across the insides of each notched lapel. "And the suit? Wow."

"You don't look so bad yourself," I tell her.

"Who are you here with?"

"Um, Deanna. I came with Ryan."

"Ryan, wow, there's another blast from the past. How do you know Deanna?"

"Friends of friends type thing."

I realize right there I don't want to be at this party anymore. I'd rather just hang out with Robin.

"Who are you here with?" I ask.

"Oh a few friends, I haven't been home long."

"That's right, you left. How long ago was that?"

"Seven years."

"Seven years. . . . Italy?"

"Yeah, for school. I just finished my Master's."

"And now you're back?"

"Yeah, well, for only a few weeks. I'm off to Japan to work at the Canadian Embassy."

"Wow. So you speak Japanese too?"

"And French."

"Jesus, so what is that? Quadra-lingual?"

She smiles. "It's just multilingual after two."

We stand there together, staring at one another a while. I feel like I've seen a ghost, and shake my head a bit.

"So what have you been up to?" she asks. "Still out partying like mad? You were such a wild kid."

I grin a crooked grin, sheepish, looking down at the ground. "I, uh . . ."

I look at her, and she senses my nervousness.

"How about we go for a walk? You can tell me all about it. You're not selling drugs are you?"

"No," I say, smiling.

We head outside. The cool night air feels good on my skin, and I breathe deeply to take it all in. I can scarcely remember ever feeling so smitten. Other than when I first met Robin herself, that is, and something about me actually interested her enough to keep me around. We enjoyed a few blissful months together before she left for Italy, and we in turn left it at that. I told her I didn't want to keep in touch—no email, no phone, nothing. It would be too tough for me, we decided.

I want to tell her that after she left me I cleaned up, got my shit together, and went to university, but I hold off. Instead I keep the focus on her. She tells me she dated a few guys in Italy, but nothing every really amounted to anything. She's got no baggage apparently. No hang-ups. And now she's off to Japan to assist some fucking diplomat. Just my luck.

Most of the time I spent with Robin I was fighting off other guys. They came in droves, all the time—I knocked one out, and Robin told me to never do that again, later admitting she found it chivalrous.

Robin was the type of girl that made guys do incredibly stupid things—lose all reason, forgo all logic, empty all bank accounts— and for a few short months that was me. For a few short months I knew I was something because someone like her returned my phone calls. She was the utmost validation any guy could have.

I tell Robin my life since she left—school, work, the book. Sitting outside a Starbucks on a bench near a park I tell her everything. I have a venti something or other, and later a smoke. Robin frowns at the latter, but not in a vindictive way.

"Well it's good to hear you're at least on your feet financially now." Robin holds her coffee in both hands as she speaks, but it's not cold enough to cozy up to each other for warmth. I curse this heat.

"I thought about you once in a while. Wondered what you were up to," she says.

"Did you ever Google me?"

She smiles, laughs a bit. "Maybe, a few years ago. Did you Google me at all?"

"Psshf. Hardly. Only like four hundred times, not that much."

She laughs again. "I can't believe you became a writer, that's so cool. How's the second book coming along?"

"Good. I mean, it's okay. Everyone is telling me to write another one, but I don't really think I want to. It feels so forced."

"Why don't you travel a bit, see the world?"

"Where, like Japan?"

She smiles. "I'm sure you could come visit me, once I'm settled."

"How long are you going to be there?"

"I'm not sure. It's a year-long internship, so at least that long. I'd like to come back here, be with my Mom and Dad. I've been away so long, I feel kind of rootless."

I lean forward, staring into my coffee cup. "I'm just really glad I saw you again," I say.

"Yeah, it's nice to catch up. We had a cute little thing there for a few months."

"Cute?"

"Yeah, you were such a cutie. You'd always buy me flowers, or steal them from someone's yard. You're the most romantic drunk I know. You remember that night you slept on my lawn because my parents wouldn't let you in the house? You woke up in the morning with hypothermia, and Mom had to take you to the hospital. You shivered the entire time, like a little puppy dog, apologizing over and over."

We share a laugh, then drift into a prolonged silence. I'm worried she's going to get up and leave. This is a woman, after all, and I need to be a man to get a woman. But I don't feel like a man yet.

We chat a while, laughing at the old random memories that arise. I could sit here on this bench and talk for hours, but I can sense it's getting late. Deanna texts me, asking where I am. I tell her I was feeling sick and went home.

"So," I say, "maybe we could get lunch sometime, or dinner."

She arches an eyebrow suggestively. "Are you asking me out on a date, young man?"

"Maybe. Do you have a boyfriend?"

"No."

"Then yes, I am."

"I am moving to Japan at the end of the month though."

"I can't come visit you?"

"Well of course you can. That would be lovely. It's just . . ." Her voice trails off. I intervene.

"Well let's just go for dinner. No expectations or anything, just dinner. Two old friends having dinner."

She seems pleased, answers genuinely, "Sounds like a good idea. I'd like that."

I walk her back to her car where we exchange numbers. Then I head home, listening to Sade on satellite radio in a silly romanticized trance.

When I get home I don't write. Instead I lie in bed for hours trying not to text Robin out of blissful stupidity. I awake the next morning with my cell phone still in hand. It's ringing. Robin? No, my agent. He tells me the *Vanity Fair* article is out.

I get dressed and head down to 7-Eleven. Johnny Depp is on the cover. The bottom right corner reads: "Life imitating art. The world of literature rocked by copycat suicide. Page 98."

I turn to Page 98. The lead photo for the article is a time-lapsed shot of the bridge streaked with rain and smeared head-lights. Then there's one of Michael's parents sitting in what I assume is their living room, holding a portrait of their son. Then there's me, in Wayne's studio, blowing smoke down and away from a lit cigarette, clutching a beer, toque and peacoat on. One of the test shots made *Vanity Fair*. They're all Wayne's photos, every one. I smile knowing he's probably very happy right now.

I purchase a copy, read the article in the parking lot sitting in my car.

I'm painted as a victim, as someone not to be blamed. Just a young, slightly naïve artist and sympathetic character who's tried to hold himself with dignity throughout this ordeal. Apparently

I'm a young writer now forced to live with a very heavy burden. Fair enough.

I breathe a little sigh of relief just as my phone starts to ring incessantly. I turn it off, and head home for a nap.

~

There's two important messages on my phone when I awake. One is from Robin telling me Friday is a good night for dinner. The other is from Michael's father. They read the *Vanity Fair* piece and they want to meet me.

My father hovers around the house. He hovers around my proximity like he wants to tell me something, but doesn't dare. I notice *Vanity Fair* on the table beside his chair.

~

When I was a kid, my Dad told me it was good luck to hold your breath while driving over a bridge. I can't remember why. We used to do it driving through tunnels as well, my cheeks bursting with air as I held my breath as long as possible trying to impress my father.

I try to hold my breath while driving over the Lions' Gate Bridge, but it's too long. I only get about three quarters of the way. I don't look at the flowers and shrine left for Michael midway across.

Michael's parents' house is a quaint little suburban two-storey place just past a high school. You can see a soccer field from the street outside, and I stand there a moment, completely unsure of the foundation I'd built up on the way over here.

I ring the doorbell. Michael's father answers with a handshake. Michael has his father's eyes. Had his father's eyes.

Michael's mother greets me inside the foyer as I take my shoes and jacket off. Michael's father asks me if I'd like a beer. I would.

We head into the living room. I can sense the presence of photos of their son hanging on the walls. I don't dare look at them.

We sit in the living room. Michael's mother sits beside her husband. I sit across the coffee table in a single seat sofa.

Small talk ensues, mostly about the weather. Michael's mother remarks on my hair. I said I shaved it and the beard yesterday, looking for a bit of a change.

"Eli," says Michael's father. "We asked you here today because we feel as if we've neglected you throughout this process. And when we read the *Vanity Fair* piece we realized we wanted to speak to you. We wanted to say we don't blame you for our son's death."

I nod, once.

"Thank you," I muster.

Michael's mother looks emotional. "We read your book," she says. "And we saw how much Michael must have identified with the character, the character you created. He was so much like our son—talented, introverted, conflicted. He always struggled so much, he was a very sensitive boy."

Michael's mother starts to cry softly. Her husband embraces her, then speaks. "We know this wasn't what you'd intended at all with the book. You didn't ask for this, for any of this. We wanted to extend our sympathies for you during this whole ordeal, this must be tough for you as well."

I pick at the label on my beer, unable to take a sip.

"Our son," continues Michael's father, "he was being ripped apart. And that was in no small part because of us. Our marriage wasn't great, and he felt like he was stuck in the middle. He felt the world on his shoulders being an only child, and one of the things he found solace in was art. His piano playing, and his books. We got him a copy of your book when we saw the cover, of the bridge, and he loved it. Kept it by his bedside. Talked about the character in it all the time. We never knew he would do what he did."

Michael's mother speaks, wiping a tear from her eye. "Eli, we don't blame you for anything. We don't want you to carry this burden anymore. You've done nothing wrong. You're such a talented writer, and you have so much promise. The last thing we want is any more pain or suffering for anyone. We want to start the healing process, and that begins with you."

I don't know what to say. All I can say is exactly what I should.

"Thank you."

Michael's father speaks again. "We all carry our burdens. You don't deserve to carry this anymore, we just want you to know that."

~

The Lions' Gate Bridge now has four 24-hour security cameras watching over its pedestrian crosswalk. I can see them up there, perched above the passing traffic like eagle's nests. I walk with my hand on the green railing, sliding it across the thin film of fallen rain.

The sun is out, showing itself through fresh white clouds. Water drips, cars roll by, and I get about fifteen feet from Michael's shrine before I'm forced to stop. I feel drunk. I can barely stand. But I haven't been this sober in what feels like a very long time.

Flowers wilted from the rain. Wet paper scribbled with condolences and compassionate thoughts. A framed, sun-bleached photo. I look at it almost out of the corner of my eye, trying to think of something eloquent someone told me at some point. A quote or small blurb about life and all it has to offer.

Nothing comes, but I'm okay with it.

DAY I

Flakes of ash, adamantine grey against the backdrop of the day. It's light out but there is no sun to be seen across this dystopian beach. There is no horizon, simply an obtuse line that navigates my peripheral vision. A lake, muggy, dark, thick and green. Oil atop water. The trees are charcoal black, the sand gritty, a smear of achromatic colour, zero chroma.

I can't seem to properly formulate the state of my own mind. Nothing seems to be able to stick comfortably against the walls of my psyche. Something other than a lucid allusion, a parallel universe within myself, or some type, form, or make-up of another soul within a soul. My conscience lacks sense.

I walk, down the beach, barefoot and shirt removed. Tattered jeans, the white cotton unraveled at the seams around my ankles, dangle as chimes of fabric that move with the quiet wind across my toes. The air moves no higher than my knees, it's thick and dense at waist level, has the taste of aspartame and cold iron on the roof of my mouth. Thickset, clumped air, barely breathable.

I have a knife. A Rondel dagger, with ancient writing inscribed along the base. It's longer than usual, close to a foot. I'm not entirely sure if it's for me to use, or to use on myself.

I walk along the beach as it begins to darken. Distant lights across the bay—they could be ships, or homes of the damned. Part of me thinks I can hear screams from their vicinity. Part of me thinks I'm crazy.

I stop to turn towards the water. I can feel soot and grime on my face, dried sweat encased with alloy and minerals, as blue flame ignites a snake's path across the bay, about fifty metres away. It slides its way across the water's surface, zigs and zags as if weaving through an invisible maze. Comes close to shore and starts to head towards me. I can sense it's alive, has purpose, intent, as it approaches.

The heat pushes against my chest and face as the flames stop abruptly at the beach. At the water's edge, where a hush spills out of the fire in a combustible manner, bright red, no pollution. The purest fire, burning clean oxygen, the smell of calcining hydrogen.

I turn back towards land. Towards the forest. Where giant sequoias tower as skyscrapers, until they're so high they disappear into the dark light of the sunless day.

The forest pulses at me, the trees packed so tightly together they form their own backdrop. I walk until I can no longer see the beach. Noises, squeals, possibly a drum beat. The sound of distant chimes, or church bells. I can't be sure of anything.

Off down the path I see a large animal. A jaguar, its spots like freckles. Dark red ambient marks with deep hard orange, fluorescent, multi-coloured specs. Behind, holding the chain around its neck, my father, dressed in a green suit. The animal looks at me.

My father reaches forward and unhooks the chain, releasing the beast. I'm too far away to see his face, to comprehend his action, as the jaguar starts to run, towards me, much faster than expected.

Before I can pull my knife up to defend myself, the jaguar slices open my belly, scratching lines of blood across my torso. But I feel no pain. I stab it in the back, feeling my blade slice its spinal cord. In the side, organs burst and puncture, spilling out internally. Hard and fast I shank it, my teeth gritted with bloodlust. It growls in pain.

I stab it in the eye until it bursts, its pupil squirting out one side of its socket. I can see the dagger through the top of its mouth. Buckets of blood pour out onto me. I pull the dagger out of its eye and ram it into its mouth, so far up my wrists pushes its jaw open until it dislodges and snaps. I watch its tongue dangle off to the side, sliced almost clean through.

I pull the blade back. The beast slumps forward, lifeless. I cut open its stomach, my hand gripping its fur for traction as I plunge the blade deep and pull towards myself. I pull back its rib cage, hearing each of the bones crack in succession. Its organs spill out in a sticky bile, and I cut its intestinal cord as the slime slithers through my hand. I wrap the film-covered cord around my wrist.

Covered in blood, I start to walk back towards my father, pulling the cord along behind me, in a bloody mess. But with every step, my father's figure fades into a shady hush of smeared colour. Blackened by the night into near nothingness, unobtainable. I drop the dagger to the ground.

As I walk, I look back to see the animal has risen, trailing me as if uninjured. I look down at my hand. The cord is gone.

Its eyes remain on me.

The Journalist

I fucking love the wire. Each day you can sit at your computer and read shit that only cements the saying, Truth is stranger than fiction. And every once in a while you come across a story that literally stops you, and you're forced to sit back and revel in the chaos.

~

Tom Billinger is a North Texas chicken farmer. He inherited the farm from his father Bill. His father was a bit out there—in fact before the year 2000 and all that Y2K hoopla, Bill sank his life savings into buying three full-sized buses and burying them ten feet underground as self-contained bunkers. Y2K came, and went, and Bill looked like a fool. He eventually checked himself into a home, and died shortly thereafter, relinquishing the farm to his son Tom.

Then over the course of five dusty, dry Texas days a terrible brush fire unexpectedly ripped through the county. Countless homes and farms were lost in what seemed like a blink of an eye. With less than two hours notice before the fire engulfed his property, Tom was able to move almost his entire chicken coop, some 1,500 head of ready-made KFC, and most of his family's personal belongings—pictures, mementos, basic household items—into his father's bunkers.

Tom visits his father's grave everyday. Tom is not the son of the laughing stock of the local chicken farm industry. Tom goes to church and does not pray, he gets up and sings when the preacher tells him to. He belts that shit out like Christina Aguilera.

The story goes something like this. Matt O'Connor is twenty-six years old. He's a second-year apprentice electrician. He works in Fort McMurray, two weeks on, one week off. The money is pretty good. He has enough to keep a nice apartment: two bedrooms, small deck, a barbecue, nice TV. He doesn't have money to throw around, but he makes rent, he always has cash to take his girlfriend out for nice dinners. He was born and raised in the same town, and still lives just outside the city.

Matt's parents are split up, both on second marriages. He has a few half-brothers and sisters he sees once in a while—at gatherings, holidays, the usual. He's amicable with both his parents, largely because he doesn't need to borrow money off either of them anymore.

He graduated from high school, worked a bunch of low-paying labour jobs, drank hard, dabbled in a bit of coke, had a few years where he was getting high on pot a lot, but really nothing out of the ordinary, not for here. He blended in like scenery. Matt went to the gym, hit the bag, sparred a bit. He didn't train other than to keep in shape, more or less to look good for his girlfriend and keep his ego sufficiently fed. Matt, it appeared, was going to be okay. He would be an electrician soon, and sooner or later he'd land a good job in town, union, full benefits. He wouldn't have to travel to northern Alberta for work, and he'd be climbing the ladder every year. Before he'd know it he'd be moving into a house with his girlfriend and having two kids, both boys, playing hockey. He'd be making mortgage payments, taking a nice vacation every year, and sometime down the road he'd be sinking his ever growing slush fund into a bit of real estate with his uncle. Not much, maybe own a few condos, rent them out, watch the money stream in.

Sure he had a past—a DUI, thrown in the drunk tank a few times, questioned by police one time when his buddy went down for dealing drugs—but in all respects, given the circumstances and the environment in which he grew up, this kid was going to be successful. He wouldn't be running for mayor anytime soon, but he'd be raising two kids with a solid roof over their head and food on the table. They'd have the money for sports, and he'd be able to buy them something nice at Christmas, maybe a dirt bike or an ATV.

I'd tell you more about Matt but I'm sure you can fill in the blanks from here. Good guy. Not a great guy, but a good guy who slowly got his head about him and walked away from what could well have been a shitty life. No fucking medals. No speeches and praise in the vanity pages. Maybe a pat on the back from his father from time to time, or a growing respect from those around him. He'd get no parade, but he'd be okay with that.

But that all changed one fateful night, and now he's somewhere he never thought he would be, but always kept in the back of his head as a serious possibility.

Matt came back from a two-week stint up north. He got into a fight with his girlfriend—she was upset he didn't call or text the last few days he was working. Truth is his cell phone just stopped working, and he couldn't get to a computer in time to let her know. No biggie, she'd be over it in a week. Any young relationship deals with trust issues. Matt was a good guy, hadn't cheated on her other than some dirty dancing at a club in Edmonton, maybe a few kisses. Nothing to shake a stick at.

So Matt's first night back he's out with his buddies, and his girlfriend is out with her friends. They've been texting all night, chances are they'll meet up sooner or later in the evening, or early morning, and have some well-deserved make-up sex. She'd let him try anal, and it'd be all good.

Matt heads to the Blue Fox Pub with some buddies to watch the UFC fight. Everyone gets riled up, has a few drinks and shots to wash down the dirty disgusting pub nachos. They meet some other friends who happen to be there and more drinking ensues. By the time they leave the pub Matt is good and drunk.

They get to this house party just off the block by the strip. It's way out of hand, people fucking everywhere. They know a few people, fit in nicely. Chances are the cops would show up within the hour and they'd be at the club. Until then they'd finish the beers someone brought in the back of a truck and smoke a bit of pot.

They hang out in the backyard, chat up some girls, Matt texts his girlfriend, she wants to meet at the club later. Plans are coming together.

Sean Smith is at the party too. Sean is not far removed from Matt. He works construction in town, usually making decent coin. Sean, though, is having a rough time lately. Construction in town isn't what it used to be, and he's buttressing each new job with EI, and he's about three months into a healthy coke habit. And to top it all off his new girlfriend is just fucking crazy, and he's only finding this out now.

Sean knows the owner of the house, so he's more comfortable at the party than most. He's also pretty drunk, and about two lines into an eight ball. But after a few more months he'll kick his coke habit, break up with his girlfriend and get on with his buddy's roofing business. In five years he'll be partner and this whole dark phase will be something he'll look back on and chalk up to experience.

However, Sean's girlfriend, Amy, is going ape shit tonight. She's all up in a fuss about something, not enough attention I'm guessing, from a boyfriend tiring of her mouth and crazy-ass ways.

Amy comes to talk to Sean, and she gets nothing from him. He's not starting a fight at a friend's place and tries to brush her off, let her cool down with her bitch drink, hopefully she doesn't do anything stupid.

But Amy does. She goes wandering around the party and finds Matt, who appeals to her—she likes his eyes, he looks like a good replacement boyfriend, or at least an invigorating hate-fuck. Matt is taken back a bit because, truth be told, Amy is hot. Not model hot, but hot enough to turn a few drunkard heads at this party.

Matt's friends think he has won the lottery, but Matt is not having any of this. He waves her off after a while, tells her he has a girl, and when she advances more, tells her he's just flat out not interested. Sex, yeah, it would be nice, but Matt is starting to think longterm more and more these days, and this bitch just ain't worth it when he can wait a few hours, butter up his girlfriend, and have steaks from the freezer. Going out for this burger is nothing but a bad idea.

Amy is upset, livid, and storms off to snickers from Matt's buddies. Being the manipulative bitch she is, she lies to Sean and tells him some drunk fuck was hitting on her. She told him she had a boyfriend, but he wouldn't leave her alone. Sean, trying to be the good boyfriend he is, calms her down. She doesn't relent, though, she wants vengeance. She wants her man to kick some ass in her honour, be her knight in shining armour.

Sean relents and goes looking for the guy. Matt is easy enough to find, he's out in the driveway where some people are passing around a joint.

Sean confronts Matt, and before you know it everything has escalated. The explosive mix of the UFC event a few hours prior, the coke in Sean and the booze in Matt means verbal disagreements just can't be sorted out by walking away. Plus there's a small crowd growing, starting to bark for a dick measuring contest.

Matt is confident with himself physically. If the two were in the ring together for instance, he'd hand Sean his ass on a platter. He's got an inch or two and maybe ten to fifteen pounds. Sean would be beat like a red-headed step child.

So Matt doesn't back down, simply stands his ground, sticks by his story. His friends back him up, tell Sean it was his girlfriend doing the hitting and all that shit. But when Amy comes up and hears this, it only stokes her fire even more. She spits on Matt's face, at which Sean laughs. There's a few pushes and before you know it, the two are throwing down in the driveway.

Sean takes a few good shots, and Matt keeps him pinned against a car. It's only fifteen seconds into the fight when it looks like it's a done deal. Sean, bloody nose, stops throwing and simply starts defending. Matt feeds him a succession of jabs and uppercuts which sends the crowd into a tizzy.

Matt pushes off him, signaling that he's done if Sean's done. But Sean's ego is bruised and he decides to come back at Matt once more. And Matt responds with another punch.

He cracks Sean off the left-hand corner of his jawbone with an over-the-top-coming down right hook. The kind of knockout punch that takes everyone by surprise.

The punch hits Sean's mandible on its sweet spot, instantly dislodging it from the maxilla. Like a hanging punching bag, the ripping mandible sends shockwaves up both sides of Sean's face, forcing him to instantaneously blackout.

So when Sean falls, he falls freestyle, no control as he's already asleep at the wheel. His neck hits a corner of lifted pavement at such an angle that the small portion of his cervical spine not covered by bone or muscle breaks one hundred percent of his fall. All 195 pounds of unconscious Sean falls directly on exposed spinal cartilage. He's dead within sixth tenths of a second.

I'm sitting here in the courtroom, dressed in my blazer and tie, watching Matt. He's sitting behind a glass casing that holds defendants. Matt couldn't make bail, he's spent the past three weeks in community prison. He's being charged with manslaughter, largely because Amy has no problem lying in court about what happened between her and Matt prior to the fight.

I've only been covering this story for three days and already I can see everyone hates Amy, including the crown, including the judge. She waltzes into court dressed way too provocatively, her cell phone has gone off more than once, and she makes exaggerated gestures whenever she hears something she doesn't like. She acts like a white Latino girl, straight out of high school. It's fucking embarrassing being within striking distance of her.

Amy is hanging around because Sean had life insurance, and she wants a piece of the pie for her supposed grief. They'd only been dating two months, but chances are she is going to milk this cow for everything it's worth once she hits the stand.

I was never one to slant articles, I was usually right down the middle for most cases. I might let a bit of colour seep into a positive light for a witness or defendant I liked, but those were few and far between. However this trial was different. I was going to slant my articles like a motherfucker. Not sure what it would do other than possibly paint Matt as the victim rather than the accused. Maybe I'd pop my cherry and get called with contempt of court.

That and I'd been working this fucking job for years and really needed something to reinvigorate myself. Tampering with the justice system just seemed like a good idea at the time.

While shooting a documentary in Colombia about abduction, American filmmaker John Guarez and cameraman Mike Burrows were, ironically, abducted.

The pair were held for two weeks by a small group of Colombian criminals, who recorded the entire ordeal on a hand-held camera, including the actual abduction. They interviewed the filmmaker and his cameraman, placing guns to their heads and threatening their lives. They also used the camera to explain why they were abducting the two Americans, and what had led them to do such a despicable thing. They planned on sending the videotapes to the victims' families in hopes of getting a fifteen million dollar ransom.

Then a rival gang bombarded the house they were being holed up in, killing the abductors and taking John and Mike hostage themselves. However, on the way back to their safe house their car was the victim of a drive-by shooting by yet another gang, killing all of the men except John and Mike.

The pair were taken into custody by the police, questioned and then released. However in a mixup at the local station, the abductor's video camera was mailed back to John and Mike after they had returned to America, instead of their camera they had been abducted with. All the footage on the camera was completely intact.

The film opens next week at Cannes.

I head back to the newsroom after the trial confirmation hearing, then out for lunch down the street. Pizza, pop, another slice of pizza. I sit by the window and stare out at the street. A hot chick strolls by, I watch her ass wink at me until she's out of view.

Some guy accidentally bumps into my back trying to get a napkin. I turn around, he takes one look at me and gets all apologetic.

See the thing is when you look like a college football lineman, people think fucking with you is a bad idea. Little did they know I'd just packed on about twenty-five pounds in the past few years. I still felt skinny, but I looked like I could handle myself. I used to be tall and lean, but now I'm tall and husky.

Of course it has its downfalls. For instance, I can barely run a block without wheezing up a storm. When I cover trials in the courthouse, the rickety old court room seats creak when I sit in them. They cry almost.

I head back to the newsroom, file a brief and another eight inches on a drug charge, and wait for a call back from a defense lawyer on my third story—a civil case involving millions of development dollars that just disappeared. I zone out through an afternoon editorial meeting, as all I can really think about is how much I feel for Matt. He sat there in the defense box like a criminal, tired and worn down from prison. Part of me can't help but see myself in his place in another life, and it's starting to make me think.

Ralph Youmous was obsessed with aliens and UFO's. And he had good reason to be, as mysterious crop circles had begun to appear on his property in North Dakota. Ralph got so scared that he started wearing a huge metal helmet on his head pretty much all day, everyday, in hopes of keeping the aliens from reading his mind.

Then one night he went atop his roof to catch the aliens in the act. He was subsequently struck by lightning and died. Three local teens were arrested for trespassing after admitting to doing the crop circles as a harmless prank.

A newsroom is a beautiful place. If you love longwinded discussions about protected sources and federal politics. A place where morals and ethics are discussed as part of the job, a place where you can actually feel like you're making a difference once in a while. They're hotbeds of thought, of proper discourse and responsible reporters living according to codes born of human decency. Most reporters simply want to ensure any faults within the systems in place to govern and protect are exposed for the good of the people. And oh were the systems broken. From ICBC and Pharmacare to the provincial government and Employment Insurance. Health sectors, private enterprise, and public works. The inner workings of each had been created by the cream of its respective workforce. The ones who didn't care about things like medical premiums and insurance deductibles. They were set up to create an illusion of safety, one only really applicable to the super-rich or the super-connected.

And it is also a world of complete and utter chaos for journalists. Yet another system in a long line broken from within, where the most important employees—the editorial staff—were paid the least and treated even worse. It cultivated a hatred towards the private sector already boiling to begin with. Ask any reporter who has worked for a major media corporation for more than a few years and the one story they'd love to write is the one they never will—about their own company.

From the first day I started, to today, I've been bombarded not only by this helix, but one of sheer complexity, a world only understood after the damage was done and it was all too late.

A world of bylines, phoners, pull-quotes, sub-heads, sources, file under news—unedited. Youthful exuberance from the rookie reporters looking forward to changing the world, to writing the world, to writing the great stories. But they were beaten over the head with it from Day 1, the ethical conundrum: the story or your soul, kid. Detach from the situation. So you became like a boxer in the most drawn-out match of his life, getting beaten punch by punch, black eyes with a tint of jade. Graduation isn't so much a blessing as an infantry badge. I'd seen it happen. Fuck, it was happening to me.

There was next of kin, pressing charges, the department said Tuesday, would not comment on the situation, offered a plea deal, suspect in custody, alleged pedophile released on bail, community outraged once again, informants, freedom of information requests, the chairperson will be stepping down tomorrow due to personal reasons, family matters, unconfirmed, unpublished, erroneous statements, retractions, corrections, apologies, hate mail, nasty phone calls from irate conservatives or religious idiots.

Police press conferences, flashing camera lights, no further information, leads are being followed up, suspects in questioning, watch the faces of family and friends in the courtroom, dragged there everyday by tragedy gone public. Interview them about their dead son, the one who was a drug dealer but still a good kid. Executed in the back of a restaurant, mind you, but still a good kid.

Fundraiser photo ops, advertorial drivel, car ads and bullshit product reviews set for release nation wide, heralded as the next whatever, derives influences from whoever. Press pass plus one, release dates are subject to change, photo contributed, news services, column width, word count.

Then you write a story about a homeless man's sick dog who needs treatment to live, letters and money pour in, a vet offers his services. With sixteen inches, a column mug and a grayscale photo on A6 you've changed his life forever, made it worth living again, and it feels better, but it fades.

You start drinking and chain smoking on deadline days, making friends with radio reporters, spilling beer over shop talk—at least these guys know what it's like to cover an election pushing three in the morning jacked on caffeine and a daily byline.

Steal food from advertising luncheons, shovel it into your mouth quickly. You're broke, you're literally starving some days as the ads guys drive into the parking garage in Beemers and new model cars with drop-tops and sunroofs talking about making mad K. You tell yourself you're not in it for the money, because, well, that's about all you have.

You interview a four year-old boy who has a brain tumour, his mother cries during the interview when she talks about how her son asked her why he got cancer, does God think he's a bad person? Local groups raise funds for the kids, cops, firefighters, his school, they've pooled money for his hospital stay, bought him a brand new bike. This kid, he's still a kid, still loves to play around, goof off, and you think if God exists He's the biggest asshole ever. He tells you he likes *Transformers*, the movie, saw it at the IMAX with his Dad and you're speechless for the first time in your career.

He dies six weeks later, his obituary gets buried at the bottom of the page.

Apply for a human rights job in Mozambique teaching journalism to young local reporters, no call back. Apply to indie-hipster magazine in metropolitan area to review shows, call back, interview, no call. Watch interns crust over with a hardened black film, ready for rollover, for the turnover of burnt-out fifty year-old veterans who settle into comfy PR jobs with wives and kids and sports practices and summer vacations.

Planned issues, certain inches to fill, front cover photos, freelance to bridge the money gaps, weekend drinking binges to clear the mind, surfing the internet between story ideas, checking websites, reading real journalists from far-off internet publications. They seem like they're enjoying it. I should, I tell people. This is a dream job, still a job, different paper, different problems, union contracts, tighter leashes, canned copy, same shit different day.

You rumble on like a running back, bouncing off hits, spinning from trouble, grinding for every yard, every inch, you love this craft, you're sure of it, you just can't place it right now. You're too jaded, you've watched too many good editors fired for doing their jobs right, too much advertising influence sucking clean the marrow of editorial, too much trumping of content for sales pitches, too little journalism spread too thin over too many articles.

And then one day you wake up five years later, twenty-five pounds overweight, and think to yourself, Matt's trial is the last story you ever want to write.

Adam Borowitz and Eve Kissinger were a perfect couple. Aside from the fact that they had more compatible names than Romeo and Juliet, the two also had the strange coincidence of being born on the same day.

The two got married on their birthdays, and then headed out on their honeymoon to Australia. While out on a nature walk one day, Eve reached into a tree to grab an apple, and was subsequently bitten by a King Brown Snake. Adam was unable to get her to a hospital in time and she died.

Adam has since changed his name, and his whereabouts are unknown.

I head home around six. The sports guys usually show up around then and we like to sit and chat about sports. It's a good way to detox from the courts all day, talk shop about the NHL, or whatever's going on that day. Something is always going on in the world of sports. That and the sports guys seemed happier. I could write drivel about the Canucks too on game nights, except it would wear thin I'm sure like every other beat. They had their own problems to deal with just like we did.

I live in a one-bedroom basement suite. Tiny, as in if you leave the front door open, and the bedroom door open, and stand outside and look inside, you can see right through the entire place and out the window. The kitchen is also the living room, the living room also the hallway to the bedroom. The bathroom is about as big as a walk-in closet.

But I have enough. An old ratty couch, a few pots and pans, a bed, and my laptop on the coffee table. I kind of enjoy living a simplistic existence, it being easier to clean up at least. That and it is close enough to downtown that I can walk to work, across the bridge in about half an hour. It's the only exercise I've gotten in close to three years other than falling down a steep hill after yet another night of hard drinking.

I've been living here for almost five years, and the only tough part about it is the owner of the house. I've never said one word to him, though he looms overhead, literally and figuratively, like a silent spectre.

To make a long story short, Robert is the exact opposite of one of those LIFE channel success stories. Having long suffered from Tourette Syndrome, Robert Mitchem decides deep brain stimulation might be the answer. Meanwhile his wife Julie decides it is in fact the answer, as she's done all the appropriate research. And so, at the tender age of forty-three, Robert goes in for surgery and promptly comes out a vegetable. Deep brain stimulation has about an eighty percent success rate—you never hear too many stories about the other twenty—so now Julie is forced to wheel her permanently paralyzed husband around, and gaze deeply into his lifeless eyes, knowing she probably should've just learned to weather the constant swearing in the first place.

Now every time bad shit happens in my life, my mind is transported not to Robert but straight to Julie, and to her blank face staring back at me. As if anyone could ever know just what's going on inside that head of hers, let alone her husband's. It baffles me, and also reminds me that things really aren't that bad, and could always get a hell of a lot worse. Robert's wife has become not only my landlord, but a landlord of the mind. She reminds me, like a tattoo, of something I've experienced in my life, like a tragic loss of some sort. The random cruelty some people are dealt, like the one and only Blackjack hand they'll ever play in the game of life, always sets my mind to such contemplation.

So whenever I see her tending to her garden in the backyard, I offer to help. I take her two dogs, Bender and Casper, for frequent walks, and always run out to the car when she is carrying a load of groceries. It's the least I can do. All the shit that I've been through, it doesn't even come close to this woman's strife, and she's still here. The least I can offer is to be a considerate, caring tenant.

After his parents' divorce, 15-year-old Evan Koss began spending a lot of time on his computer. He gravitated towards chat rooms to deal with the fact that he was now forced to live with his mother, as his father had moved to California to marry another woman who already had kids from a previous marriage, and had also just divorced.

Evan fell in love with shygirl178. They talked for weeks, and soon Evan was making arrangements to head to California to meet her. They were planning on getting married in Vegas. So he stole his mother's car and set off across the country. However shygirl178's parents were privy to her plans with Evan aka emoboy12 as they had been monitoring her computer, and just before the two were about to meet at a hotel room, Evan was pulled over by the police.

Turns out shygirl178's stepfather was also Evan's actual father, and the two were technically step-brother and sister. They had bonded in a chat room about the fact that both their parents had recently divorced and remarried.

Opening statements. Theatre art. Performance lawyers. It's different when you see it in person. Perfectly crafted arguments from days on end of notes and strategizing and late-night coffee binges in the boardrooms of second-floor law offices.

There are two sides to every story, and each side has representation here. Each side, prosecution and defense, pump their story with cohesiveness, clarity and reasonability while injecting the other's with doubt, falsities and discrepancies. They jack their side with steroids for this judge, while deflating the other's, and vice versa. After a while their suits look like yin-yangs, two fishes eating each others' tail. The snake and the mongoose, prey and predator all dressed in customary Armani drags and seven years of post-secondary education.

We see two pictures of two characters: Matt and Sean, good and bad. Their faults pointed out, propped up, dressed in thesaurus-sculpted abuse. Their accolades painted with similar bright colours, exploited, put out on the windowsill for all to see.

After six hours of opening statements I have no idea who either of them are. There is so much said, in fact, that I am no longer able to filter any type of information. All I can do is watch Matt sit beside his lawyer, his suit wrapped around him like a straight jacket, paralyzed. He just sits there for six hours, hardly moving at all. Any life left in him is hiding somewhere beneath the surface—like my landlord's husband, he is more vegetable than human. His eyes, though, say it all. This is not where he wants to be. This is not *what* he wants to be. This is not what he wanted to happen in his life. He's been thrown the world's biggest monkey wrench, and as a result is now facing five to ten years in jail. Prison means no more electrician's ticket, no more of anything really until he can perhaps get a pardon a decade or two down the road.

I glance over to the jury to see if they are looking at Matt. They too sit there in a state of stupor—you can tell none of them want to be here. They look worn-out already, and opening statements are still being given. They say jury duty is an exciting life experience until you actually have to do jury duty. I wouldn't wish this trial on anyone. There really is no right answer. Both sides have a good argument, it was either self-defense or a consensual fight, and either way did Matt's punch intend to kill Sean? If not, then why would he consent to a street fight? Who was right is anybody's guess.

I head back to the office, transcribe all the notes from the opening statements. Then I start to weigh down Matt's side. I phone his boxing trainer, and his sparring partner, who offer glowing quotes of a gentle guy stuck in a terrible situation. His employer even speaks on record, saying Matt would never hurt a fly and that this was totally out of character for him. He would only fight Sean in self-defense.

I file the story, almost fifteen inches, which isn't long—well actually it's long in today's world of journalism. I haven't written anything over twenty inches in months, and I've seen twelve-inch features slashed in half. Whatever. They end up running it on A3 with a photo, and I pray one of the un-sequestered jurors slips up and reads the article. Chances are decent, what with ours being the only daily in the area. I know that if I keep my foot down on the neck of this trial I can possibly swing a few opinions, and in the process maybe get fired and go down in a beautiful hail of gunfire and flames.

While robbing a bank in Toronto in an attempt to pay off a gambling debt, former bank clerk William Baldwin tripped and fell to the ground, discharging his firearm into his stomach and killing himself.

Upon hearing of her son's death, Ms. Baldwin suffered a heart attack and died. Having been a government employee her entire working career, her life insurance policy paid out almost three quarters of a million dollars to her deceased son.

I head out for drinks after work with some of the other reporters from the newsroom. The four summer interns scurry along for the ride, hoping to do whatever it is you do when you're an intern trying to get into a big paper with little turnover and a dwindling editorial budget. I love acting jaded around them, grizzled fat fuck that I am. Crushing their dreams, telling them I hate my job, the pay sucked, the hours sucked, the recognition sucked. You can see the dimmer switch in their eyes starting to turn down ever so slowly as they watch me and the other journalists pound beers with ferocity as we exchange horror stories about living paycheque to paycheque and getting fucked over by advertising and our publisher at every turn. Every summer we have a bet, usually one intern will quit within a few weeks, one will cry in the newsroom after a serious chew-out for shitty copy, and one will actually do their job well. This summer is no different than any other of course, and they are dropping like flies.

About an hour into nachos and pitchers I can see the interns are getting a little woozy. Zack, the city reporter, is already drunk. He's a bit of a lightweight, but a good guy all in all. King's grad, some radio work with CBC, and presently in the same boat as I,

88

almost half a decade into the same job staring at the longest hallway to freedom imaginable. He's a much better reporter than I
am however, with a knack for compiling information and gaining
trust. Me, I get by on basic street smarts and university English
skills. Anyway, his black-rimmed glasses and cardigan are hanging
off him now that he's a bit tipsy, and he looks tired of talking
about how much we hate the industry, so I crank up a few stories
that should lighten the load.

"So you guys wanna hear a funny story?" I say to the three
interns sitting there at the end of the table. They all consent eager-
ly. Zack looks at me. He knows I'm going to tell the Spic 'N' Span
story, because I always do.

"Fuck your mother," he tells me.

I stare at him, hard, then forgive him for the comment as I'm
sure he has no idea about my mother's situation. "So this happened a few years ago," I continue. "Zack here's in the newsroom,
and it's the day after an election and everyone is really tired, hungover and pissed off that Harper got back in."

Zack doesn't look pleased. Every time I tell the story he gets
angrier that I keep telling the story.

"So we're on the desk, because most of the deskers are off
due to the election of the previous night. And we're laying out the
back section of Lifestyles or some random shit pages, just trying
to get the paper out so we can all go home and catch up on our
sleep. So Keith throws Zack here a page—it's just a little dogleg—
a brief and a standalone. But this is our last page and he really
wants to leave, so he doesn't process the photo. Just asks Keith
what it's of, then he'll send it to the photo editor and be done
with it. So Keith says it's a photo of a guy cleaning up in a restaurant. Sounds harmless enough, so he throws in the cutline, and
writes in the head—'Spic 'N' Span.'"

The interns look at me, trying to formulate the punch line.

"Anyway, so he throws the page through, goes home, gets
some much needed sleep. Then at about eight o'clock in the
morning the phone starts ringing off the hook at the desk. Zack
gets this irate call from the city editor, 'Get your fucking ass down
here right now and field these fucking calls!'"

Zack smiles a bit, takes a huge pull from his drink. The interns lean in intently.

"So Zack is up now, wondering what the hell is going on. Runs down to the front of his apartment complex to grab a copy of the paper, flips through it, and finds the lifestyle page, and right there, below his standalone photo headline of 'Spic 'N' Span' is a picture of a Mexican restaurant worker dressed in full Mexican regalia, little sombrero with those fuzzy balls and all, scrubbing away at a table, looking at the camera grinning this big fucking Mexican grin."

The interns start laughing. Zack starts laughing along with them, then stops suddenly and sips his beer. "I've heard that story so many times," he says, "and it never gets old."

"So what happened?" asks one of the interns.

"Oh man this is the best part," I tell her. "Council for Canadian Civil Rights phoned, Spanish Cultural Association phoned, they all phoned. Also, numerous middle-aged men phoned laughing their asses off saying that was the funniest shit they'd ever seen."

Zack, mouth open in a blatantly theatrical way, bangs his hand on the table repeatedly as everyone laughs. He's about done with the story.

"Hey I have one about our court reporter here too," he quips, ready to get me right back. I'm fine with it, it's all in good fun.

"So around the same time both of us were on the desk, I think this was about a few months before my Spic 'N' Span incident."

"Social justice," I put in before he continues.

"So our budding court reporter here is laying out a city page, and it's a story about the mayor, Sullivan at the time. So he throws the story in, everything is fine, and then goes to write the headline. However, for some reason our lovely court reporter here is totally neglectful of the letter L, especially in the word 'public' for some reason."

I smile a cheeky smile, tip my glass up and take a swig. The interns start to chuckle.

"So our amazing court reporter here has a serious story about the Vancouver Police and the Mayor with the headline 'Mayor wants full pubic inquiry into police force.'

All the interns laugh as I chuckle and bang my hand on the table mimicking Zack.

"And to top it all off, it ran with a picture of Sullivan, in his wheelchair, standing beside Van Der Meer, that butch. So imagine the headline with a photo of Sullivan literally looking like he's staring at Van Der Meer's big ol' vagina."

More laughter, I can't help but laugh too, it was pretty funny.

We have a few more beers and the interns leave, at which point Zack and I polish off two or three more pitchers before calling it a night. We live within a few blocks of one another, which makes for great stumble-home-drunk conversations. It's dark out, and we're both dragging our heels like little boys being pulled through shopping malls with their moms.

Zack stops, bends over by a car. "I think I'm going to puke," he says.

"Don't be a pussy."

I walk up to Zack and try to kick him around the groin area. He backs off and stumbles up onto the sidewalk. "No seriously don't fuck with me right now."

I hold my hands up in a sign of stalemate.

Zack lets out a full-on vomit. Half-digested pub nachos and beer spill all over the road. He gags a bit, then wipes his mouth and comes back up to stare off into the abyss of the downtown skyscrapers. "You know what?" he says.

I cut him off. "No, not tonight. Enough shit."

"I wasn't going to say that," he spits back, literally. "I was going to say I was thinking about getting into fashion."

I start to laugh, a little at first, then almost uncontrollably. Zack grows displeased and runs up and tries to kick me, but I dart out of the way just in time. We continue walking.

"Fashion," I say, still chuckling. "You stupid motherfucker."

After losing his house, wife and job, 49-year-old Derek Clement was pretty much ready to call it quits. He fell into a cycle of depression and *alcohol that landed him on the streets. Then one day a passerby gave him a few dollars and Clement went and bought a scratch-and-win ticket. He won $100,000.*

The local television station came to do a story about him, asking him to reenact his winning, so Derek went to the store and bought another scratch and win ticket to scratch off on camera for filler while the host outlined his story. He won another $100,000.

The city editor calls me into his office before I can even get some shitty coffee from the lunch room. Keith only calls me into the office for two things: one, to hear stories about Zack's and my drunken exploits, or two, to chew the fucking shit out of me.

But he is a good editor. He rarely gives you praise, and when he does, he means it. If he tells you you've done a good job on a story, you know it's true. Positive reinforcement you can take to the bank.

Keith is a lifetime journalist, having gotten his start back when they were still on typewriters and chain-smoking in the newsrooms. Going on thirty years experience, he's literally seen and covered everything. Russia and the Cold War, a few years meandering around South America for a travel magazine, and editing nearly every major Canadian newspaper.

Now he's a few years from retirement, with two marriages behind him, a nasty case of carpal tunnel from endless InDesign layouts, and about four thousand cigarettes from a heart attack. He's grizzled as all hell, and I love it because he still hits on the young sales reps and gets drunk at company functions. This guy hasn't been within a thousand yards of a sexual harassment seminar, and still swears like a sailor.

But today he's not happy with me. He sees my slanting ways with the manslaughter trial, and doesn't like it. Wants company council to okay my articles from now on, which is a bit of a slap in the face.

But he relents a little, to the point that he agrees with me siding with the defense. Fucking kid should be able to defend himself up to and including the level of the assailant's assault. Matt was in his own right to fight back, and Sean simply got seriously unlucky.

Keith knows I owe him a favour now so he slides a press release across his desk. I pick it up and read it. A fundraiser for cancer. A young boy has cancer and his friends are organizing a huge soccer game in Stanley Park to raise money for expensive treatment.

I shake my head, "No."

"No?" says Keith.

"No, I can't."

"You can't? Why not?"

"I just can't. Get Michelle to do it, she loves that shit. Or better yet, one of the interns."

"Michelle went home sick again. All of the interns are out for the day."

I continue to shake my head. "I just can't do cancer, okay? AIDS, Alzeimer's, Hungtington's Disease, scurvy, leprosy—anything, just not cancer."

Keith looks across at me. I really don't want to have to explain myself. He keeps looking. "Okay," he says finally, "but you still owe me a favour."

I nod, and get my ass out of there. Out the door, into the coffee room, and outside on my way to the courtroom, promptly.

I check the docket dailies for anything interesting seeing as Matt's trial starts tomorrow with the prosecution's star witness, Sean's girlfriend, Amy. The only thing that catches my attention is an Aggravated Assault trial that's scheduled for the entire day. I chat up one of the clerks outside, and she gives me the goods in exchange for harmless flirting. I should check out the Aggravated Assault, she says. Should be interesting.

It is, but not in a cool science experiment kind of way. Drew Macintyre is charged with Aggravated Assault. He lives and works in the downtown core, at Future Shop's car audio department, installing everything from speaker systems to satellite radios. Drew's been working this job for six years now, and loves it. He's one of those guys with a souped-up car—custom interior, state of the art CD player with thirteen-disc interchangeable something-or-other. Black-tinted windows, custom-painted racing stripes and matching faggy draft fin on the back.

Whatever, some guys like cars. And he hangs out with guys who like cars, they have parties and drive their cars to those parties, talk about cars, watch *Pimp My Ride* and Speed Television and quote the *Fast & The Furious* series. But Drew is also a fine upstanding citizen. Never been arrested—a few speeding tickets, but nothing to look at. No priors, as we call it.

So one day Drew is walking back to his car after his lunch break at Quizno's and spots the front driver's side door open. Some crackhead is lying face forward in the front seat trying to rip his expensive CD player out with a butter knife stolen from the local shelter. Drew also notices the front window is smashed.

So Drew walks up to the crackhead, yanks him out of the car by his ankles, and proceeds to give him a substantial beating. Broken nose, two chipped teeth, separated shoulder, broken arm and ankle, and various bruises and stitches.

Crackhead lies there in a pile of his own blood, and someone watching the entire incident phones the police.

The police show up, and pretty much take Drew's story for fact because, well, it's true, and he tells them exactly what happened. He found some fucking basehead ripping the shit out of his car, and he gave him a beating.

The cops call crackhead an ambulance, give Drew a stern talking to, take his information, and decide to call it a day. Drew's CD player isn't totally damaged so it's no use calling the insurance company because the deductible won't even cover it. He just takes his car back to work and spends the afternoon fixing it up and replacing the smashed windshield.

Then about three weeks later Drew is visited by the police at Future Shop. They need to take him down to the station to ask him a few questions. Drew is puzzled, as he thought everything was fine. But it isn't.

Turns out the crackhead's name is Alexander Dumall, son of Dumall Developments Inc. Alexander is a rich kid who's been living on the street for the past year because apparently being filthy rich isn't enough, he had to get addicted to crack and get kicked out of his parents' house. Evidently the silver spoon didn't fit properly up his ass.

Alexander's parents get called to the hospital, find their son beaten up pretty badly, and want vengeance. Pissed their son is a total waste of space, they need to take their aggression out on someone else, because they're bad parents and that's what bad parents do, neglect the obvious.

So they follow the ambulance report which leads them to the police report. Drew filed no claim with the insurance company so the damage technically never took place. He repaired it on his own dime because he didn't want the hassle of dealing with the insurance company. Fuck, nobody wants the hassle of dealing with the insurance company, so who would blame him?

Alexander's father would. And so he pressures the police to press charges, which they ultimately do, because Crown is friends with Alexander's father. Drew gets shit duty council, which translates as some new guy handling the most important case of your life while he's also handling about fifteen other seriously important cases. And before you know it, a full-blown Aggravated Assault trial is taking place.

Alexander is cleaned up. He's been in rehab for five weeks now, and appears to have gotten over his drug addiction. Truth is, he's not over it. He just shaved and borrowed a suit from Dad. And Dad can't stand to see his only son take a beating for being a crackhead and not see some type of redemption.

A civil suit is also in the works. And as I sit there in the courtroom, watching poor Drew think to himself this world is probably the worst place imaginable, I can't help but feel truly sorry for him.

I take notes all day, then head back to the office and file a twelve-inch story. But it gets spiked, and never runs because Dumall Developments Inc. is one of the newspaper's largest advertisers. Keith was told to can the story, and because he's not pension-ready to be fired, he cans it.

I throw a hissy fit in the office the next morning, throwing my keyboard across the newsroom—the keys bust off and scatter all over the carpet. An alphabet spilled across the landscape of wordsmiths.

I'm told to take the rest of the day off.

A lifelong sleepwalker, Randy Commenford was known to get up, walk around his house, and sometimes make a meal. One night, Commenford awoke in his bed with McDonald's French fries everywhere. Surveillance tapes showed the next day that Commenford drove his truck through the drive-thru, somehow ordered a Big Mac meal, and then drove his truck home, promptly parking it on his lawn.

Commenford states he has no recollection of the event. The story made the local news as a lighthearted piece, and everyone had a good laugh.

The following year Randy stabbed his wife to death with a kitchen knife while sleepwalking.

I phone Zack. He's totally down for drinks. Wants to hear all about the keyboard smashing incident at work as he was at council at the time.

We end up getting totally smashed at a corner pub just down the street from my house. I'm sitting there in the booth when I notice that Sophie has texted me. I show the text to Zack. 'Hey, it's me Sophie, what are you up to tonite?' it reads.

"No no no no no no no," says Zack, waving his hands in displeasure.

Now normally this would seem like a normal text between two normal people. Problem is, Sophie is my ex-girlfriend, as of about a month, and I haven't heard so much as a peep from her other than her constantly updated Facebook status. *Sophie Bishop is no longer in a relationship. Sophie Bishop is single.* And of course the requisite ensuing comments from her female friends asking her what is going on and if she wants to come over for drinks and talk about the fact that some men are assholes and she needs to only worry about herself right now.

I subsequently deleted her from my Facebook, then deleted my entire Facebook account, having since taken up more productive internet-based activites like masturbating incessantly to YouPorn.

Anyway, Sophie and I dated for about two years. We first met at a party on campus—she was in her second year of a Bachelor of Arts and I was just starting my job at the paper as a night-shift desker after finishing my English degree.

We hit it off, had sex the first night, and before I could get my bearings I found myself in a full-blown relationship. We did the usual trips together, kayaking, going for ice cream, taking weekend excursions to the island. Wholesome.

But after a while it wore on me. She was good looking, sure, fun and pleasant to be around, but after a while I couldn't take the constant fucking nagging about every little God-damned thing. Apparently I peed all over the floor when I went to the bathroom. I ate too quickly at dinner. I walked too fast when we went walking, or biked too fast when we went biking, or bladed too fast when we went rollerblading. I switched channels too much. I didn't enjoy watching the same movies she enjoyed watching. I never listened to her when she talked about her classes. I looked down on her because she wanted to be a high school teacher. I was a bit overweight, not fat, but she constantly nagged me to get a gym pass and return to my previous university sports form. My feet smelled, I drove too slowly on the highway, I always wanted to have sex before we went to bed and she never wanted to have sex in the morning. I wanted to have sex in the shower, she thought it was gross. I flirted with other girls too much at the bars, or they flirted with me too much—it really didn't matter. I had too much chest hair and my hair was always crusted with gel, so that she couldn't run her fingers through it. I snored. I rolled over on her in bed. I farted and burped too much in public and didn't always introduce her right away to people I knew and she didn't. And all I ever seemed to want to talk about was journalism, my job, and how much I hated it.

So I broke up with her. I just told her one day I wasn't happy with the relationship and wanted to end it before I developed brain cancer or went on a preschool shooting spree with an AK-47. I'd say it was me and not her, but it was definitely her and not me. I hated her guts. The only good parts about the relationship were the intermittent blowjobs, and the fact she actually liked it doggy style. Other than that, I could have cultivated more feelings for a reasonably comfortable bean bag chair.

So why she would text me a month after I dumped her is quite perplexing, considering she marked the occasion by fucking some guy I knew she always thought was cute. That and telling every mutual acquaintance we had that she dumped me because I was cheating on her.

I really didn't care. I already felt like an asshole for apparently having all these faults I never knew I had. I let it go and decided to move on, but now I have a text from her on my phone asking what I'm up to tonight.

I text her back, 'Nothing.'

Five minutes later: 'Oh cool ha ha so do you want to come over and watch a movie?'

I'm sitting there beside Zack, who for good reason refuses to partake in this exchange anymore. He just waves his hands like I should abort and pull the chute, go home and stab myself in the eye with a pencil, and call it a decent night.

'Um not sure what you mean by that,' I text back.

She answers almost immediately, 'Just come over.'

I show Zack this last text. He looks at me, eyes glazed from three pitchers of Sleeman's. "I dunno," he says, "the only good thing that'll happen if you go over is you might cum in a vagina tonight as opposed to your washcloth."

I stretch my neck around, and stare off at the bar. Zack looks down at his cell phone.

"I should go. I have to interview the mayor tomorrow."

He pays for half, and leaves me in the bar.

Bill Vanderzaam loved Emily Gainsbourough. Bill worked at Office Depot by the mall in a suburb of New Jersey. He was a simple man, he had a job, a car, and he looked after his sick mother. He also had a serious crush on Emily who worked at the one restaurant in the mall, a Red Robin.

Bill would go to Red Robin on his lunch breaks and sometimes for dinner, and sheepishly try to talk to Emily. Finally, after two years, he asked her out, and Emily said yes.

After two years of blissful dating (apparently Emily was waiting for him to say something because she had a crush on him too) Bill decided he was going to pop the question. So he took her out for a romantic picnic, with a plan of dropping the wedding ring in a glass of champagne, the oldest trick in the book.

Unfortunately Emily unknowingly swallowed the ring, and began to choke. Bill rushed her to the hospital, where luckily she was able to ingest the ring fully before falling unconscious. The day was ruined, Emily had permanently damaged her windpipe, and Bill felt like an idiot.

Then the doctors did a routine MRI and X-Ray to find the ring in Emily's stomach. They also found a previously unknown cancerous tumour attached to the outside of her stomach lining that had just started to spread to her internal organs.

Surgery was successful. Bill does not feel like an idiot anymore.

Sophie is poking my shoulder. I'm awake, lying on her bed. I roll over slowly, exposing my naked front side.

"Hey," she says with a sense of urgency. "You have to go, I have to work. I don't start at ten like you."

I roll back over. "Can't I just stay here until I have to go? I'll lock up."

"Uh, no."

I sit up in bed and scratch my head, not looking at Sophie. She's just standing there staring at me, dressed for a day of school and work.

"I have class, then I have to work. You need to go."

I look over at her. "What happened last night?"

Sophie looks disgruntled. She huffs dramatically. "Well let's see. First you show up at my house drunk as heck. You try to fondle me while we're watching a movie, then you go take your clothes off and pass out in my bed."

I smirk, blinking one eye closed trying to right my hangover vision. "Why didn't you just kick me out?"

"I tried. I kept telling you to go sleep on the couch, but you'd just roll over and try to grab my boobs and I'd tell you to fuck off and you'd go back to sleep and snore up a storm. Very charming."

"I thought you were asking me over for sex."

She puts her hands on her hips, visibly displeased. "I asked you over to *watch a movie*. Didn't you read my text?"

"Yeah it's just . . . I dunno, how am I supposed to read into that?"

"Look, just go okay? It was a mistake, I shouldn't have invited you over."

"Okay then," I say, standing up naked to roam around the bedroom in search of my jeans, which I eventually find and slowly put on.

Sophie looks at me.

"What?" I say.

She shakes her head. "Nothing, just go."

I get dressed and leave.

Gary McKinnen is a bad drunk. When he was a kid, his mother was murdered by a serial killer terrorizing the East Coast, praying on young women. He never got over it, his Dad disappeared, and the killer is now in maximum security prison serving a 150-year sentence without possibility of parole.

Gary's girlfriend has been threatening to leave him for months. Gary, usually unemployed, or working some mindless labour job, has a bad habit of drinking after work, usually until late in the evening, and then driving home. He's hit fire hydrants, dogs, driven onto lawns, plowed through white picket fences, and racked up two DUI's in the process. One more and his license is gone for life.

One night after getting into a fight with his girlfriend, Gary heads out to the bar and proceeds to drink like a frat boy fresh from finals. He gets wasted, gets kicked out of the bar for being belligerent, and heads for home.

While driving, he inadvertently runs a red light and smacks into a pedestrian. He gets out of his car, tends to the injured man, calls 911 and waits for the police. He is soon taken into custody and charged with a whole host of charges that will see him locked up for years to come.

Turns out the guy he hits is William Creek, a suspect police believe to be the Red River Killer, the one who's been preying on young woman, and luring them into hotel rooms, in order to rape and kill them. The murders subsequently stop.

Gary is now housed in the same maximum security prison as the serial killer who murdered his mother.

I head straight to the office in the same clothes from the previous day. I'm hungover, so I fill my stomach with Booster Juice and McDonald's. Keith calls me into his office, tells me I'm having a meeting with him and the publisher later today after I get back from courts. I hate the publisher—she's a woman—but I don't hate her because she's a woman. I•hate her because she's a careerist, one of those "company line" people who speaks in bullshit rhetoric. I'm also sufficiently convinced she's eaten her own young to get to the position she's currently abusing.

It's one of many problems with the industry. The internet is eating us alive, sucking profit from newspapers like leeches, and for good reason. Who wants to pay for content you can get instantly and for free? Of course we have a website for our paper too, which we're forced to fill with content like some stupid form of self-destruction. It won't be long before we're online only, with a reduced staff, working for reduced wages. Everyone is ready to get their walking papers at any moment.

The company is hemorrhaging too, racking up mountains of debt it never intends to pay back. We've been in the red the majority of the time I've worked here, and there's no light at the end of the tunnel. We are governed by monkeys sporting captain's hats, steering the ship towards a rock bed, telling everyone that everything is going to be just fine if we work hard and keep our noses to the grindstone. It is the most depressing sight a working stiff can fathom.

I head back to my desk to find a press release laid across the new company-paid-for keyboard that has magically replaced my old one. A mother and father have set up a charity event trying to raise money for a program that helps educate kids about the dangers of crystal meth. Their son Billy killed himself while coming down from a bad binge, and they want to use his tragedy to help shed light on the issue. Normally media outlets won't touch suicides with a ten-foot pole, for obvious reasons, and I was no different personally.

One day I was riding the Sky Train out to a story in the suburbs when one of the train cops chatted me up. He told me how, on average, some six people a year jump in front of a Sky Train to kill themselves. So you know how every once in a while the train sits at the station for a few extra minutes, and that soothing female voice comes on and tells you they're having mechanical difficulties with the tracks? Yeah, not so much. Anyway, it was the greatest story I never wrote, but that's beside the point.

I take the press release into Keith's office. He beats me to the punch. "Nope, you cover that before you head to the courthouse."

I make a face like an eight-year old boy who's just been told he can't wear his spacesuit to the dinner table. "Fuck, really? C'mon."

"Nope. You ducked the cancer one, not this one."

"What about—"

"The interns are busy and Michelle is off sick," he interrupts. "Fuck me."

Keith just sits at his desk holding his ground. I stare at him, but realize I'm in no mood or position to try to explain myself today. I hold the press release like a dirty tissue while Keith and I stare at each other for a few seconds.

"Look," he says, "it's going on right now, a few blocks from the courthouse. Give me ten inches—photo's already assigned— and we'll call it even."

I take in a breath of disgruntled air and leave the room in a manner befitting my displeasure, but also confirming my compliance. I throw my blazer on and head out.

I get to the fundraiser, a sidewalk musical-food-jamboree mess of a thing raising money for a program that sends ex-drug addicts to middle schools to talk about the dangers of becoming a drug addict. I approach the mother and father of Billy taking in a deep suck of air and holding my breath. I shut myself off, turn off all the lights, and clog any mental leaks that might come bursting out of my past.

I'm done in fifteen minutes, at which point I exhale and wipe the story from my mind as I jot it down while walking to the courthouse.

I grab a coffee in the courthouse, chat with a few of the sheriffs about the Canucks, and wait for Amy to take the stand.

The prosecution starts by padding her reputation—she's a hairdresser, or was, but she's thinking of starting her own shop. I feel like coughing "Bullshit!" under my breath, but manage to contain myself.

Amy tells the jury and everyone else how much in love she was with Sean, and how by no means were they fighting that night before the fight between Sean and Matt. They may have had their disagreements, but she loved him.

According to Amy, she went outside to call a friend when Matt and his friends started hitting on her. She tried to walk away, but Matt persisted. So she went back to her boyfriend and told him what happened, and he said he would go and try to talk to Matt. But when he did, Matt, who was clearly ready to fight, initiated the violence and Sean simply defended himself. Sean was defending himself. Yeah, right. Amy is literally lying in the face of the justice system.

Sean wanted to stop fighting, but Matt persisted, pushing him into a car, and then when Sean started to walk away, hit him, knocking him unconscious, and ultimately killing him.

The prosecution asks Amy if they think Matt intended to harm or injure Sean. Yes, he did, he was looking for a fight. Everyone in the courtroom aside from the jury and the judge look like they just ate some bad Chinese food. They are sickened by this display of blatant lying, myself included.

We break for lunch. I can see the defense lawyer for Matt seething, waiting for his chance to attack this female with all his schooling and experience.

I come back from a few slices of pizza with some Tums. The defense lawyer comes back to beat the hell out of Amy's character. He asks her to prove how long they were dating, and that they weren't fighting that night because defense witnesses will speak to the contrary. He asks her why she's been unemployed these last four months, and why she got fired from her job. Seems she got into a fight with a customer one day and her boss fired her.

He asks her about her medical history, and the endless conveyor belt of prescription medications she was on. He asks her if it was for bipolar disorder, she says it was for mild depression. He asks her about the night she spent in the psych ward, she says her father had just died and she was extremely emotional.

The questioning gets heated, the room tenses up. I want to walk up and pat the lawyer on the butt and tell him to keep going, but I just sit there scribbling away in shorthand like a schizophrenic stenographer.

Amy breaks down when he asks her about that night, and the judge gives her a moment. But the defense persists, asking her if they were fighting that night, why she left, was she actually the one who initiated the conversation with Matt? Was she out looking to have sex with someone other than her boyfriend? Amy barks back at him, the judge calls a recess.

I head into the bathroom for a piss. Matt is in there now that he's finally out on bail, washing his hands. I come out from the urinal and wash my hands alongside him. We make eye contact, nod at each other. He looks tired, wrapped in his suit. He washes his face with water, then steps by me to get some paper towel.

I want to say so much to him but don't speak a word.

The defense continues their dismantling of Amy, and by the end of it, her character has been shredded, ripped apart at every seam. If one only saw the cross-examination, Amy would seem like the worst human being on the face of the earth. Psychotic, unable to keep a job, a liar, a whore, someone whose opinion or statement of fact should not be taken into any type of reasonable consideration.

I head back to the office with a smile on my face and file fifteen inches on how much of a shitbag Amy is, leaving much of the prosecution's questioning out. I paint a disastrous picture of this woman and file the story, neglecting to send it to company council.

Then I have my meeting with the publisher and Keith. I don't talk for the first fifteen minutes—it's all bullshit rhetoric about respecting company property, proper workplace etiquette, and so on and so forth. I try to bring up Dumall Developments, but all I get is run-around answers and more bullshit rhetoric. Keith just looks at me with glazed eyes. He's tired of all this too.

We get up, shake hands, and I apologize for my behaviour. The publisher says she's not going to put me on probation, but that I do have to replace the keyboard from my own salary—it will be deducted automatically, just like the shitty medical benefits we get that barely pay for prescription medication let alone dental work or physiotherapy. I smile a most pretentious smile and walk out of the office ahead of Keith, too fast for him to try to speak to me about the meeting.

When I'm back at my desk, Keith finally makes his approach. I'm sitting down with my recorder and headphones out ready to transcribe an interview.

Keith thinks about saying something. I look up at him. He takes in a deep breath like he's going to say something important. I'm still staring at him. He's searching for words and I'm staring. He looks like he's about to spew something deep and meaningful, something that might wrap this whole stupid ordeal up with a nice fucking bow.

"Sometimes when I shit now, it just falls out of my butt and into the toilet, splashing up and hitting my arse—I hate it," he says, then walks away.

I can't help but smile.

Many people have favourite numbers. Gilbert Varelez is one of those people. The Spanish soccer star wore the number 13 his entire career, even refusing to play for a team he was traded to as someone else already had the number and refused to relinquish it.

Varelez was born on Oct. 13. His father wore 13 during his professional soccer career in England—being a foreigner, he was literally stuck with the unruly, superstitious number. Varelez signed his first big league contract when he was 13. He married his wife Dayana, on July 13th. His son, Juaz, believe it or not was born on May 13th. Varelez scored 13 goals for his country, and played for 13 seasons in his professional soccer career. He currently lives at 1313 Alma Drive in Madrid. Varelez's son has just started his young soccer career, the 13-year-old is already garnering big league attention at such a young age.

He wears number 14. Doesn't want to live in his father's shadow.

I head to the courts with a coffee in hand, cheap blazer and tie dangling off me.

It's Friday, thank God. I say hi to one of the sheriffs I know, we make small talk about the weather. I talk to one of the defense lawyers who usually represents drunk drivers, and usually gets them off. He asks me if I'm covering the manslaughter trial. Says he might stop by and check some of it out when it resumes next week.

I head in to catch the verdict of a police brutality charge. A young girl, sixteen at the time, was picked up by cops outside of a house party. She could barely stand up, and vomited all over the place when they arrived. But she was also being extremely belligerent, and tried to throw a few punches at the cops trying to call her a cab home.

So after more physical and verbal abuse from this 90-pound, make-up-wearing walking disaster, the cops decide a night in the drunk tank is in store. More kicking and punching, biting, and verbal abuse ensue.

They toss her in her own cell, but then she just goes nuts, and starts banging her head against the wall. So they tether her, which is actually what they are supposed to do when someone plays the self-harm card in custody.

I look around the courtroom. Rudy is there. It's about an hour into the verdict and I can see he's fast asleep.

Rudy is the court reporter for *The Globe*. He's pushing sixty, and started working as a newspaper reporter straight out of high school. He has upwards of forty-five years experience, and now he'd nodded off during a verdict, his eyes closed, head slouched slightly forward.

I quietly move back three rows to sit beside him. I poke him with my pen, his eyes open, he adjusts himself, moves around like a sleeping dog who's just been roused.

"Ah thanks," he whispers.

The four cops are found not guilty. The girl's father stands up after the verdict has been read and spews out a profanity-laced tirade against them. Three sheriffs take him into custody after he doesn't shut up and throws a massive fit.

"Now that's colour," says Rudy, scribbling away.

I head outside with Rudy for a smoke. He still puts back about a pack a day, his teeth resembling little rotted kernels of corn.

The two of us are workplace buddies. We always hang out, exchange contacts, double-check surname spelling for cases, swap info, and occasionally wake each other up when we fall asleep during trials.

Rudy loves to go off about everything—politics, courts, cops, you name it. He is fucking golden, straight from a John Grisham novel, the old grizzled reporter with his tattered blazer and wise-cracking, self-loathing ways.

Rudy and I head to a pub for lunch, put back three or four beers each, then head back to the courts smelling like liquor. Nothing's going on though. The best is a string of bank robberies, but it's only a trial confirmation hearing.

I head back to the newsroom, file the verdict, throw in some colour about the father throwing a tantrum. Zack comes over, sits down in an empty chair and wheels his way over to my desk with his feet.

"What are you doing tonight?" he asks.

"Dunno."

"You wanna go to press club?"

I cringe. Press club is actually PR club, where they talk your fucking ear off about whatever it is they're peddling. New theatre companies, Telus walkathons, cancer fundraisers, stupid human interest stories, blah blah blah. However, the beer is free, and so are the nachos. And hot journalism students usually make the rounds with teachers to talk to industry stiffs like myself about the trials and tribulations of the job. It's a nice little ego jerk-off session sometimes, young go-getters asking you how you got to where you are and what it's like to be "inside" the industry.

"Sure," I say.

Keith comes over and hands me a few business re-write briefs to write up. I pump them out, then go chat with the photo department about finding art of the young girl who was tethered by the cops. Of course the photogs are busy, so I spend the next half hour sifting through the multiple files in the photo archive sever. I find a mug, send it to process, and head back to my desk.

One of the over-eager production workers comes over to my desk. She's an overweight middleaged woman who drinks Diet Coke, one of many I see every day.

She asks me if I want to help out at the barbecue next Friday, they're raising money for juvenile diabetes. I ask her if she sees the irony in selling hot dogs and greasy burgers for diabetes. She doesn't.

She scolds me quietly and leaves in a huff.

Zack and I sit around and bullshit with the sports reporters until we get the okay to leave. We head straight to the press club bar, an upscale place downtown. It's packed with other reporters, and we sit with some of the younger ones from the bi-weeklies and weekly arts rags, and two radio hosts. We don't sit with the TV guys. TV guys are assholes. Most of them, that is. My favourite line from Keith one day was his remark about the buffoon who did lifestyle pieces and was a supreme dickwad off camera.

"He's not a journalist, he just plays one on TV."

The six of us push down five or six pitchers and two plates of nachos quickly. Dave, one of the local afternoon radio guys, convinces me to come in for a half an hour on the manslaughter trial. He's a good shit so I agree, and besides I figure I can plead my case for Matt across multiple mediums.

An old professor of mine brings around a group of second year J school students from the local university. They look so eager and willing. He shakes our hands and introduces us all to the group.

One of the students asks me how long I have to write my stories. I tell him usually it's about a solid hour before my editor places a loaded gun to the back of my head while I type. They ask Zack about the mayor, because Zack has interviewed him about a thousand times. Zack tells them the mayor has bad breath, and that he's probably cheating on his wife with his secretary and that he quite possibly has a codeine problem.

Another student asks the radio guys if it's stressful being on air all day, live usually. OxyContin solves that. We all chuckle. The professor has had enough. He takes the group to another table, and we resume our beer drinking with smirks on our faces.

One of the PR guys comes over and tries to get us to sign up for a prostate cancer bike ride through the city.

"Fuck me, can't I just have a drink in peace," says Dave.

"My prostate would probably get cancer if I biked around the city," adds Zack.

After about three hours of good solid drinking, the six of us decide to head to a club. We walk a few blocks back towards the strip. Dave knows one of the bouncers at the place—Plush or Hush or Smush—something like that. We head in and order a bunch of beers and shots.

For some reason the gender ratio is good tonight, and before we know it a bunch of girls have joined our table. They're all college students, mostly Arts, and they're quite taken with the fact we're all in the journalism industry.

Dave tells us about the fuck-up last week at the station. He has to yell over the music. "So we've got this local singer-song-writer on, she plays a couple of acoustic songs and then we do a bit of an interview. So she leaves just before the hour mark, and I mean she's pretty hot, so we've been flirting with her all show, on the air."

He points to Ricky, his producer. "So then doofus here leaves the input on while we're running the promos, and of course I'm like 'I'd totally hit that.' And Ricky is like 'I'd hit that.' And I'm like 'I'd hit that so hard whoever pulled me out would be the King of England.' And we both start laughing."

All of us have a good laugh, though the girls seem perplexed as to why the King of England has anything to do with this.

"It wasn't all bad," Dave continues. "It was playing over some promo spots and we didn't have our mouths up to the mics. So imagine like 'Coming up at five, police reports on the gang violence, sports from Don and weather and traffic in five minutes.' And in the background Beavis and Butthead are talking about hitting shit like monkeys with sticks."

We all laugh again. I spot Sophie out of the corner of my eye and duck behind Zack. "Fuck me."

Zack sees Sophie. "Oh shit." Then he starts waving, yelling, "Hey Sophie! Sophie, over here!"

I smack him in the groin with my hand, and he keels over in pain. I head to the bathroom to take a long piss and wash my hands. I never wash my hands.

I come back to find Zack chatting with Sophie and a few of her friends. They're all as drunk as we are and before I know it I'm out on the floor dancing to Black Eyed Peas with Sophie grinding all over my crotch. I follow the three rules of white men who are drunk enough to dance: hands never above head, no spins, and no biting lip like I have to pee.

The girls tell us they're heading off to another club, and Sophie says goodbye to me in a way I can't translate. She keeps asking me what my plans are tonight, and I tell her I don't know. Then she says goodbye again. I'm not sure she said goodbye come follow me, or goodbye goodbye.

Either way I decide to stay. Someone buys way too many shots, a whole tray of flavoured something. None of the girls seem into doing any of them, so Zack and I end up doing about four or five each. After that blinking both eyes in unison becomes tough.

Zack and I head out for pizza off the strip. We talk about Sophie—Zack tells me just to ignore her, she's rebounding and can't pull anything off the boards so she's retreating back to her comfort zone, which she had with me. Like falling back on old habits, bad ones. I nod, pretending to agree, but in reality I'm just trying not to throw up pizza.

Zack grabs a cab, and I have the great idea of heading to Sophie's house, thinking she might be home by now. She was always one to leave the club early.

I ring her apartment. No answer. Then some guy comes down to leave and I slip inside and head up to her place. I knock on the door, but no answer. I figure I'll just sit down for a few minutes and catch my breath before I head home, but of course before I know it I've passed out propped up against Sophie's door.

She kicks me with her heels, her keys dangling from her fingers. "What are you doing here?"

I look up at her, shake my head awake. "I dunno, I thought you might want to hang out."

"Wow you're drunk, I can smell you from here," she says, waving her hand in front of her nose.

I stand up to tower over her, but I might fall down. I hold the wall to steady myself. "I'm sorry, I'll go."

She looks at me. I can tell she's drunk too. I just stand there, all of my brain and most of my body being used to keep me upright, until she opens her door and drags me inside her apartment in a huff. I pull my shoes off and wobble into the living room and land on the couch. It's weird seeing her place now that we've broken up. I feel like an intruder, even though I've been here many times before.

She comes over and hands me some bottled water. I chug the entire thing in one gulp, and lie there on the couch.

She frowns, "You're a mess, you know that?"

"Yeah," I respond.

She heads into the bathroom, then into her room. I lay my head down and before I know it I'm out again.

It's dark in the apartment when Sophie wakes me up wearing hot pants and a bra. She grabs my hand and pulls me up off the couch. "Look, don't get any ideas, okay."

"Okay," I say, though once again she's speaking in tongues.

She starts to kiss me.

Down in Florida, a large wedding was hit by a sudden tornado. It ripped through the reception in a matter of minutes, destroying the local community centre in the process. Many were injured, however only two people perished: the bride's mother and the groom's father.

Sophie kicks me out of her house at 7AM sharp. She's going hiking today with friends. I'm downtown, severely hungover, looking like a bag of shit dressed up to pass as human. I grab some food and go home to sleep until dinner time.

In the tiny Chilean village of Rio Claro, a statue of the Virgin Mary started bleeding from its eyes. Locals and people from all over the country flooded into the village to witness the miracle. People lined up for days to see the blood trickle down from the white statue. They set up camp and prayed endlessly.

The village blossomed in population and tourism. Then a group of scientists and historians came to inspect the statue and found two small pin holes fed by a tube implanted in each of the statue's eye sockets. It was cow's blood.

Police have now started a massive investigation into finding the perpetrator, while the whole country watches, hoping the scammer will come forward so they can chastise and banish him.

The prosecution has called a doctor to the stand, so we get to find out why exactly Sean died. Apparently the knockout punch rendered him unconscious, which led him to fall on his neck. We get loads of terminology, and the prosecution nails home the point that the punch delivered was obviously done so with enough force to render someone unconscious, therefore enough harm was intended to conclude that Matt wanted to seriously injure or maim Sean. Then there's about fifteen minutes of explanation of the word "maim."

The defense asks the doctor if Sean wouldn't have hit his neck on a raised piece of concrete on the way down, would the blow have killed him by itself.

Probably not, we're told. No further questions. It's the *Law & Order* moment of the case.

I head out for some lunch, then catch the verdict on Future Shop Drew's case. Not guilty. Frontier justice in small doses still suffices, I think. Drew is now the happiest man on the planet however. He will go out tonight and get drunk to the point his liver shrivels up and weeps. And he will wake up tomorrow with the best hangover ever.

I write up about twelve inches on the doctor's testimony, using the *Law & Order* moment as my lede. Then I write about six inches on Drew's acquittal, which gets buried way back on A22, down in the corner. You'd miss it if you weren't looking for it, but it runs.

The doctor's testimony runs off the front of the city section—no art—but gets chopped instead of turning to another page. Apparently our editor-in-chief is one of those guys who read that stupid report that people don't like to read articles that turn. Even though *The New York Times* has been turning off its front forever, he's going to take this advertising-sponsored poll as gospel and cast down his wrath upon us.

No turn policy. Another death by a million cuts.

In the Russian city of Penza, Mayoral candidate Vladimir Kirilenko beat Lev Stalin by a single vote. They recounted eight times, bringing the UN in for one of them, and still the same result: one vote.

Putin, who backed Stalin, ordered a recount, which Stalin then won by a few thousand. The UN was promptly kicked out of the country.

I'm at the radio station, inside the studio, ready to go on the air to talk about Matt's trial. Dave tells me the usual: Cut for two breaks, half an hour show. Half an hour in the radio world feels like five minutes.

I put the headphones on, and pull the mic towards to my face. Dave does his intro, introducing me, daily news courts reporter, such and such. Talks a bit about the trial, the questions it's raised about fighting, and about self-defense. Then I'm on. Dave asks me a question.

"What is really the defining issue with this case?"

"Well there's usually one defining issue with every case, be it a drug offence, murder, or manslaughter. There's a point in every trial when the main crux or issue surfaces, and this trial is no different. The underlying question is how much force was Mr. O'Connor allowed to use to defend himself. And was he defending himself to a reasonable degree? We see this all the time—I was covering a case last year where a woman was being beaten by her husband for over four years, and one night while he was physically assaulting her she got a gun and shot him."

"What was the outcome of that trial?" he asks.

"Well the defense made a sound argument of battered woman's syndrome, and she was acquitted. But the thing that was interesting about the trial was that her husband never used a weapon at all, never intended to kill her. However, in my opin-

ion, and the judge's too in that case, she was well within her right
to defend herself with lethal force given the history, the prior
confrontations where I'm sure she feared for her life, just as she
very well could have at one point that night."

"Okay, tell us a bit about the specifics of this trial, and about
what happened that night," Dave says.

"Well basically what happened was two guys were at a party,
both of them were intoxicated, and an argument broke out
involving Mr. O'Connor and Mr. Smith's girlfriend. One thing
led to another, and they ended up fighting in the parking lot of a
house party. Now Mr. O'Connor is an amateur boxer—I'm sure
Mr. Smith didn't know this at the time—however both consent-
ed to the fight."

"So it was a mutual fight."

"Of course," I say. "And what is definitely playing in the
defense's favour is that Mr. O'Connor was out in the parking lot
when Mr. Smith sought him out. Mr. O'Connor did not go looking for Mr. Smith. Mr. Smith came looking for him."

"But do you think that warrants the force he used in the
fight?"

"That's not for me to decide. I think Mr. O'Connor is definitely allowed to defend himself, and there's no denying Mr.
Smith intended to harm him. Kill him? Probably not. Seriously
injure him? Probably so. And so to what degree is Mr. O'Connor
allowed to retaliate?"

"A lot of the testimony is coming from the people who were
at the party. What have we heard so far about the night in question?"

"Well right now we've only heard from Mr. Smith's girlfriend, who is a witness for the prosecution. I'm guessing Mr.
O'Connor's friend will take the stand, and tell us a slightly different version of the events."

Dave signals for a commercial break. We take our headphones
off. "That was good," he says as I lean back in my chair. "So what
do you think? They going to convict him?"

I mull the answer. "Honestly, I don't know. I can't see a jury
convicting him of manslaughter, but I can definitely see a judge
overruling the jury and convicting him."

He shakes his head, mystified. "Why do we even have juries anymore then."

"Dunno. They don't even sequester them in Canada. Jury members for this trial could be listening to this bit right now."

"Crazy."

And then we're back on. Headphones on, intro music, another introduction.

"Now I want to talk to you about the actual punch thrown. There's been a lot of discussion and testimony from a doctor about what actually killed Sean Smith."

"Well there's no denying what killed him. He fell down unconscious onto a small piece of raised concrete, and it punctured his spine, severing a few key nerves that connected to his brain. His death was instantaneous."

"How much did the punch come into play then?"

"Well what happened was, according to the police reports, Sean came back at Matt, and Matt threw the punch as Sean approached him ready to fight. This was *after* they had already fought and Matt had pinned Sean against the hood of a car. He was overpowering Sean because of his boxing training."

"So it was a haymaker?"

"No it was a jab, one that caught his chin at the exact spot that would dislodge it, sending shockwaves up his face, causing him to black out. It was basically two extremely unlikely incidents that happened within about two seconds of each other. The chances of something like that happening again are a million to one, at best."

"So the chances of a conviction in this case, how do you see it going down?"

I think for a moment. "I personally have to feel for the defendant in this case. I do not think he intended to injure or seriously harm the deceased. Manslaughter is a pretty serious charge, and Mr. O'Connor is looking at five to ten years in prison for defending himself at a party. Now if he'd gone looking for a fight I might think differently, and I think the jury might not have as much sympathy for him considering he's trained as a boxer and therefore should have taken into consideration the danger he possesses with his hands. But like I said before, this one could go either way. It's in the hands of the jury, and I wouldn't want to have to make such a decision."

We're done, headphones off. Dave leans back in his chair.

"Thanks, man. So what did you and Zack get up to for the rest of the night? You go meet up with your ex and rail her?"

I scratch my head. "Sort of. We went for pizza."

"But you ended up with her at the end of the night."

I cough, smile.

"Nice. Atta boy."

I push my chair out from the table. "Anyway, I've got to head back to the office."

I head out. Tomorrow Matt's best friend and Matt himself should take the stand.

While rushing his wife to the hospital, Burt Smith hit and killed a woman riding her bike. The woman was Melanie Sampson, and she was actually crossing the street illegally at the time, and did not see Smith who was deemed to be driving under the speed limit.

Smith's wife was complaining of horrible stomach pains. She needed a liver transplant, and Smith already knew she had a rare blood type, meaning a match would prove difficult.

Melanie Sampson turned out to be a perfect genetic fit.

Matt's best friend, Riley, is verbally assaulting Amy from the stand. Every chance he gets he rips into her, calling her a liar. The judge in turn has three or four statements disregarded, but the damage is done.

The prosecution keeps it short and sweet. They ask Riley what happened between Amy and Matt, and he tells the court she came over and started hitting on Matt. I glance at Amy across the courtroom, glaring, huffing like a little child sent for a time out. Riley says Matt brushed her off, and that's why she was angry. Says he would have done the exact same thing in Matt's situation. He's sorry for Sean's death, but doesn't think Matt should be punished so severely. The judge cuts him off again, asking the jury to disregard the last statement. Too late. More damage is done.

We break for lunch. I grab a couple slices of pizza and sit outside in the courtyard before heading back inside to get a good seat. I notice Amy outside having a smoke, but don't speak to her. I don't even want to look at her.

Matt takes the stand, swearing that the testimony he gives will be the truth. The prosecution asks him about his life, and he tells them he's to become a carded electrician in a few years, likes to box on the side, and has a great girlfriend.

The defense asks him about that night. Matt says he had a few drinks, maybe more than five or six, and a few shots. He was drunk, he's not hiding that. He went to the party with some friends and was hanging out in the parking lot. Some girl came up to him and started hitting on him, he politely declined, she persisted, and he declined again.

Then some guy, apparently her boyfriend, came out and tried to pick a fight with him. He tried to talk his way out of it, and Sean threw the first punch. Matt felt he had to defend himself, threw a bunch of punches, then stopped. Sean came at him again, Matt said he was going to defend himself again, and just happened to hit him with a lucky punch.

He pauses. And then something strange happens.

Matt starts to break down. He can't speak. It's tough to watch, because the guy has been through so much. He didn't want to kill Sean, didn't even want to hurt him. He just wanted to go to the bar and meet up with his girlfriend. He cries.

Matt apologizes to Sean's parents, then stops himself. He doesn't want to go back to prison for five to ten years. He just wants to live his life, be left alone. His lawyer lets him go, as there's something to be said for sincerity on the stand. Judges don't buy it most of the time, but juries tend to eat it up.

Matt says he's sorry, and that he should've controlled himself a bit better since he's trained as a boxer.

We break for recess. Matt's parents hug him and console him outside the courtroom. The kid is shattered.

The prosecution, however, has little sympathy for Matt's display. He is prodded, and his story is picked apart. Matt admits to fighting as well as defending himself—yes he wanted to inflict a bit of pain. Someone had spit on his face for no apparent reason. Some girl was calling him an asshole to his face. He'd done nothing wrong, felt blindsided, and didn't know what else to do.

The prosecution asks him why he didn't just walk away. Matt says he would've felt like a coward if he had. Would've looked like a coward in front of his friends, and all the people at the party. He admits he got caught up in the moment.

He admits that when he trains for boxing, he trains to hurt his opponent, as one of the goals is to knock one's opponent to the ground, knock him out, inflict damage. Matt says this is only to win the fight, not to hurt the other person.

They go back and forth a bit more on boxing, then the prosecution goes back to the fight. Why didn't Matt ask some of his friends to back him up, to keep himself and Sean separated? Matt says he was drunk, and therefore made a poor decision.

They talk about what happened after the fight. Matt stayed around, and there was a few minor scuffles before the police and ambulance arrived.

And then it's over. People leave the courtroom, Matt is consoled by his friends, family and girlfriend. He looks utterly destroyed, completely broken.

I head back and file another story, talking about how Matt felt remorse for his actions and didn't intend to kill Sean with the punch at all. I throw in some colour about his breaking down on the stand. It runs on the front page, with two mugshots, one of Matt and the other of Sean. They could be brothers in another life, they look so similar.

I head home and fall asleep on my couch, not quite able to make it to bed. I toss and turn all night, suffering through multiple dreams, but only one really sticks. I'm in a forest, visiting what looks like a park. There's a wooden fence, and scattered stones on the ground. I bend over at one—inscribed in its face is the word "creator." I try to pick it up, but it's buried deep in the earth. It's there to stay. When I awake, I'm not immediately certain if it's a dream or simply a buried memory.

Mark and Amy Bell had always been a blessed couple, but in odd ways. They lost their first son at an early age to a rare blood disorder, yet subsequently had twin boys three years later.

They had always been involved in local charities, mainly for cancer, and so when Amy was diagnosed with breast cancer, the town they lived in quickly raised all the necessary funds for her treatment, which was successful.

While flipping through some old photos one day, Mark and Amy noticed that when they were kids they had both gone to Disneyland with their parents around the same time. Mark grew up in Sacramento and Amy in Portland, so this was quite the coincidence. Then Amy happened to locate a photo of herself with her sisters and Goofy, and in the background was a young boy in a black striped shirt wearing Mickey Mouse ears and distinct knee socks.

When Mark noticed the young boy to be himself, he pulled out his old photo albums and confirmed that it was actually him in the picture. The two wouldn't officially meet for another fifteen years. Mark also located another photo of himself with his family in Disneyland in his precious knee socks, and in the background was a young girl in a green dress with a red bowtie.

It was Amy.

I don't go out on the weekend. I spend much of Saturday and Sunday helping Julie in her garden. I just dig and pull weeds all day, Julie asks me how things are going, and I tell her I'm okay, but getting tired of the job a bit.

Julie tells me things will get better if I keep going. If I keep pushing, sooner or later walls will fall down and I'll find myself in a happier place. It may seem foreign and scary, but after a while it will get better. I look over at her, shovel in hand, sweating everywhere, and thank her. Advice from this woman is solid even if it sounds a bit Disney and cliché. She knows because she's been through it all and still has a positive outlook.

It calms me as I work, I sleep like a baby both nights, my hands blistered and worn from shoveling all day.

Sophie doesn't phone me either. Well actually she can't because I have my phone off all weekend. I head into work on

Monday relaxed and well rested, knowing the verdict should be delivered Tuesday. I head to the courtroom and catch a few trials, a break-and-enter that led to an assault, a drunk driving causing death, a gang murder between the UN and the Independent Soldiers, Asians and East Indians killing each other and those in the crossfire all over Vancouver like it's a warzone. Lovely stuff.

The day of the verdict I'm all over the place again, wound right back up. It's not until noon but all I do in the office is surf the net and write up some meaningless briefs. They ask me to write a column about the trial after its conclusion, and I grudgingly accept.

Matt comes into the courtroom surrounded by friends and family. His girlfriend holds his hand. There's a tense feeling in the air, everyone just wanting to hear the verdict.

But the prosecution has a motion before the judge. He wants to bring to light articles written about the trial from a daily news court reporter. As soon as he starts to talk, I freeze up. He tells the judge they've compiled eight articles and one radio appearance, each one written with a slant and intent towards the defense.

I feel like I'm in a dream. The judge asks me to stand up, and to address the court. I admit to writing the articles. He suspends the verdict to review the articles and the radio appearance. I may be held in contempt of court for my writing. This might be a mistrial.

The judge calls a recess and I'm escorted into his chambers by the sheriff. Everyone is looking at me—Matt, Amy, the lawyers. Suddenly I feel like a criminal.

I sit down by the judge's desk at a complete loss for words.

"Son, are these your articles?" he says, holding them up together.

"Yes, your Honour."

"Do you agree with the prosecution? Are these unfair portraits of the trial?"

"I don't know if I can answer that question, your Honour. I felt I was being unbiased."

"You know that, without jury sequestering, there is a possibility that jury members can read and be influenced by your reporting because there was no publication ban on this trial."

"Yes I know full well, your Honour. I've been covering courts for three years now. I'm sorry, sir."

The judge looks over some of the articles. Then he calls in the clerk and they set a court date for me tomorrow.

I've never felt so blindsided in my life. I just tampered with the law, and now I'm going to pay dearly for it.

By the time I get back to the office the news has reached Keith and my publisher. I'm called in for an emergency meeting with company council. Then I'm sent home immediately.

I walk home in a daze. I don't turn my laptop on when I get home, but go straight to bed and lie down, staring up at the ceiling with a sense of sheer wonderment at the insanity of life. I've gone from bystander to major player in a single breath.

While walking to a local bookstore to conduct a small book signing for his non-fiction book The Dangers of Driving Distracted: Texting, Talking and How Technology Has Made The Road More Dangerous, *author Tim Bergeron was struck and killed by a car.*

The driver had been distracted by a parking ticket stuck to his windshield wiper.

I'm before the judge, at the witness stand. Everyone is there. I'm now part of the trial. A few more reporters are there, having smelled a good story. Rudy is in the back. I don't make eye contact with anyone.

The judge has reviewed the contempt of court submission from the prosecution. He has determined that my articles painted an unfair, biased portrait of the trial which may have influenced the jury's decision-making process.

He calls a mistrial, and a hush falls over the courtroom. Dazed, I head back to the office for another emergency meeting. This time there are six people in attendance, including myself, and there's a sense of resentment towards me. Keith valiantly defends his reporter the best he can, but it's hopeless. My days with the newspaper are over.

The publisher looks over some papers. "We have an offer for you," she says, pausing. "We have no choice but to let you go, however we feel that since you've been a valued employee with this organization for close to five years, we would like to extend you the chance to hand in your resignation."

I look over at Keith. He gives me a nod.

"Okay. . . ." I say.

"And upon receipt of this resignation you will be provided one year's severance," the publisher starts up again. "Of course you will sign a letter of confidentiality concerning the severance, and with anything concerning this issue."

I look at the publisher. "A year's severance? Like salary?" I say.

She confirms this. I accept. This is the only card I can play, and it was played for me.

The papers are drawn up quickly. I head to lunch with Keith while we wait, sitting in silence most of the time eating lousy Chinese food. Then Keith pipes in. "Look, kid, take the money. Go away for a bit, do something with the money, write a book or take a trip, don't try to head back into journalism just yet. You need to get away. The last thing you want to do is stick around. I've seen this before, and this is not a fight you want to take on. Lay down your sword and walk away."

We head back to the office where I sign the papers and clear out my desk, then I'm gone. Zack just stands at his desk, hands on his head, staring at me. I take a cab home with all of my stuff— my recorder, headphones, contact lists—my email having been wiped clean before I had a chance to look at it.

I flop down on my sofa, put the box on the coffee table, and sit there staring at the wall.

I sit there for over an hour, just staring at the wall, thinking to myself that my career as a journalist is done. I feel dislodged from a comfort zone, my future suddenly blank rather than a recurring flash of images.

Julie comes downstairs to knock on the laundry room door that separates us.

She heard on the radio what happened. Tells me I'm welcome to stay rent-free for a few months until I can get my feet under myself. A simple gesture of courtesy. I tell her I was given a year's severance, but her offer still stands.

She hugs me and tells me I'm welcome upstairs for dinner. I politely decline, telling her tomorrow night maybe. She says she'll make pizza, my favourite.

Zack comes over with some alcohol. I tell him, off the record, in confidence, about the year's severance. He tells me this is the best thing that could have happened to me, minus the contempt of court bullshit. At least I popped my cherry. He says I can get back into the journalism industry slowly—maybe work PR for a few years, then slide into a paper again a decade down the line. Quietly of course. No more courts. Maybe I should be an entertainment reporter, he says, and we chuckle a bit.

Zack heads out after the booze is gone. I stumble around the house, lie down on the bed. Sophie phones me.

"Hey," she says.

"Hey."

"So I heard. Are you okay?"

"Yeah I'm okay."

"You're sure. I mean . . ."

"I'm fine, Sophie."

"Listen, if you want to come over and talk, you're more than welcome to."

"No, I don't want to come over and talk. Or have sex, or do a crossword puzzle."

A brief silence.

"You don't have to be snippy about it," she says.

"Why would I come over and get advice from you?"

More silence.

"What is your problem?" she asks me.

"You."

"Me?"

"Yes, you. You keep popping up back into my life. We broke up, now leave me the fuck alone."

"Who do you think you are, saying things like that to me?"

I chuckle sarcastically. "Look, Sophie, don't call me, don't text me, don't carrier pigeon me. As far as you're concerned, I don't exist, okay?"

Silence.

"You know, you're a real asshole," she tells me.

"Tell me something I don't know," I say.

While attending a Kansas City Royals game, Eric Murphy was lucky enough to catch a flyball that drifted foul of third base. Unfortunately, in the process, Murphy spilled his beer all over his date, Alyssa Gordon.

Later in the game, Alyssa was struck and hit by a flying bat that had been lost by a batter during an errant swing. It was all over the Jumbotron. She required medical attention in the stadium's medical room. Eric and Alyssa never had a second date.

Finally, in the ninth inning, a home run left Kauffman Stadium in a record breaking hit, some 602 feet. The ball smashed the windshield of a 2005 Chrysler Cavalier, which happened to belong to Murphy. It was the longest home run to have ever been hit out of the stadium.

First baseman Billy Butler hit the pop up, inadvertently flung the bat at Alyssa, and smashed up Murphy's Cavalier with his record-breaking slam.

Upon reading about the amazing coincidence in the paper, diehard Detroit Tigers fan Josh Buarrez, who had retrieved the ball from Murphy's windshield while taking a well-timed, and very lucky, smoke break, contacted Murphy. Admitting he was actually a Giants fan, having grown up in the Bay Area, Murphy told Buarrez he was only attending the game on a date.

Buarrez gave the ball to Murphy on one condition, that he sign a legal contract stipulating he never sell the ball to anyone affiliated with the Kansas City Royals, a heated rival of the Tigers. Murphy accepted.

The fly ball, the bat, and the home run ball were then stolen from Murphy's house. They later resurfaced on craigslist and the thefts were tracked back to Alyssa Gordon's older brother Mike. The three items were returned to Murphy who subsequently sold the home run ball to Butler, who had since been traded to the Detroit Tigers much to the delight of Buarrez, who rescinded the contract upon hearing of Butler's trade.

Butler was then traded to the San Francisco Giants and subsequently sold the home run ball to the Kansas City Royals organization for half a million dollars. He gave half the money to Murphy, and also signed the fly ball and the bat for him.

Three days later, Buarrez, who had been suffering from bi-polar disorder, walked into Murphy's work and shot him in the back of the head before taking his own life.

Butler played a season for the Seattle Mariners and has since completely disappeared from public life.

There's a bit of a going away party for me at the pub by work. It has the feeling of a funeral. People tell me they feel for me, and ask me what I'm going to do now. I tell them I don't know. I put back a few pitchers of beer. Everyone leaves except Zack after a while, and we sit there and drink in a bit of a slump, a telling silence.

Zack says we should go out on the town. I'm not really interested, but he convinces me after sufficient prodding. We head to a restaurant for some food and then to a club. I walk around with a beer in my hand, watching all the drunks dancing away. I just want to go home to bed for a few months.

Zack and I sit at a table and have a few beers. Some girls come over and we chat them up, but I'm a piss-poor wingman and they leave shortly after. I head up to the bar to buy another round. Someone taps me on the shoulder.

I turn around. It's Matt. Riley and his girlfriend stand behind him. Matt hugs me. "Holy shit," he says. "What are the fucking chances I'd see you here?"

I just look at Matt, confused.

"I've got some fucking news for you." He grabs my shoulders tightly. "Amy went into the psych' ward yesterday."

"What?"

"Yeah, she flipped out. Got pulled over by the cops on a random traffic stop, threw a fit at the cops, and fucking lost her mind!"

"*What?*"

"The prosecution wants to cut a deal. My lawyer says they've lost confidence in her and don't think she can make another trial."

"What the fuck?"

"Reckless endangerment causing death. Two years probation. Anger management. Some community service."

Matt stands there, a broad smile on his face.

"No prison for me, man. No prison because of you and your fucking articles," he says, literally, and emotionally, shaking me.

"What?"

He hugs me again. I'm so shocked I'm having trouble breathing.

"Fuck, man, you bailed me out. I'm totally grateful. I heard you lost your job though?"

All I can muster is a "Yeah."

He looks at me, concerned. "So what are you gonna do?"

"I dunno."

"Fuck, man."

"Yeah."

Matt stands there, looking at his girlfriend and his best friend for guidance.

"Well can I at least buy you a drink or something?" he asks.

"Yeah," I nod. "Yeah, another drink would be good."

I stand there, staring at the three of them. Matt's girlfriend steps forward and shakes my hand.

"Thank you," she says, teary eyed. All I can do is nod. She comes in and hugs me.

Matt places a hand on my shoulder. "What are you drinkin', my friend?"

I shake my head, inhale. "Whatever you're buying, man. . . . Whatever you're buying."

DAY 2

Imagine a world of fantastical caricatures, abstract acrylic paint sprung to life, but then drain off half the colour. Take out the softer tones, and leave what remains. Now imagine a city within this harsh, half-lit world, abandoned seemingly for years. Then see it slowly besieged by the impoverished, the downtrodden, the homeless and the drug-addicted, the low-lifes who leech off others and scrape by on handouts and illegal activities. And this dirt and grime and red lipstick overcompensation, imagine as it rises up to rule this place, where the sun never fully comes out but the heat still bakes the concrete.

The power lines droop halfway down the city streets. The streetlights never work. The kids, like dogs, run around in packs where there are few cars, and nobody seems to be going anywhere. And beyond the city limits there is nothing but barren rock and grey sand. Nothingness in every direction.

I'm in a dirty white suit. Worn, slightly beige, with an open collar shirt. No shoes, no socks, the concrete feels like sandpaper on my soles. A group of kids hover around a stoop as I walk down the middle of the street. They're all plasticized, with caramelized faces and painted eyes. They frighten me as they stare at me like a murder of crows.

I continue to walk. Past corner neon signs that burst with blush colours. Each sign post holds a black prostitute, dressed like a curious circus clown or Christmas tree. Some of them have their breasts or vaginas exposed, as if they were constructed that way. They speak, not in a language, but in a tongue. I understand not a word.

A retro railcar rumbles across the squeaky steel tracks carrying no one, with no driver. I stop to watch as sweat drips down my chest, stains my clothes. I can almost hear the heat.

Most of the windows are boarded up. Water drips from others. The buildings are all fifteen storeys high, at least, and made of old brick, decaying slabs of cement and rustic bronze metal. Nothing but fluorescent black light between, and bulging clouds of smoky powder overhead. Smog so thick it coats the lungs.

A young black boy holds a silver Nambu pistol in his mouth like he's performing oral sex on it. He pulls the trigger over and over, the hammer clicking incessantly. Beside him a naked middleaged white man, overweight, masturbates while staring at the ground in shame.

I turn a corner onto a barren street down by the docks. But there's no water, just what looks like acres of black soot. A river of tar dividing the city where tugboats chug along past plasticine fisherman at work on the dock. Smoking long skinny cigars, they never turn to look at me.

I step onto a sidewalk covered in badly drawn chalk graffiti, misspelled swear words and racial slurs. Horrible symbols and cryptic lettering. Patches of blood and thousands of gum wads trampled into the slabs.

Finding two black doors, I push myself into a dirty jazz club, the air literally crawling with cigarette smoke. Nothing but faded red lighting and neon darkness. The music is horrible, like an old record left out in the sun to warp, and then played on a decaying phonograph. At each table sits a character, some familiar, some not, each a boxy modular unit of stiff foam rubber coated with urethane. Their faces made up of latex prosthetics that look like they've been worn for decades with little nourishment or upkeep.

In the corner sits a cluster of unrecognizable religious figures. Across the way a pack of black men in creamy dark-peaked lapel suits with elongated faces sit staring at center stage, each accessorized with a long red feather. At the bar stand a line of generals and war heroes, dressed in full uniform with cheap metallic medallions dangling from their necks.

The jazz instruments not only emit noise, but a dry autistic colour that feels as cancerous as the smoke. The musicians are all black, dark black, bamboozled black. They have no eyes.

I sit at a table, and the waitress literally hovers over. My mother. Dressed as the dirtiest, sleaziest of cocktail waitresses, runny mascara like black waterfalls down her face, she does not recognize her son. I can't seem to jar her memory. She just serves me a drink and labours off halfheartedly.

A red stir stick, a cherry, a lime green drink with thick ice cubes, it sweats onto the napkin. I look around, everyone seems to know I'm here but nobody seems to care. I'm part of the scenery as well as the ambience, but not welcome, not entirely.

The jazz drifts around the mumbled conversations like the smoke. Nobody moves faster than a snail, as though everything is being dragged down by the somber weight of this place.

I take a sip of my drink. Salt water, dried lemon, a hint of gasoline, I swallow it laboriously with a demanding gulp.

Everyone in the bar looks at me. The music stops. Their eyes upon me, I'm frightened, and I start to heave oxygen in and out of my chest.

I stand up, stagger to the door, and burst outside.

The Academic

Looking around a campus, one can see a mass discrepancy between the asbestos-ridden buildings that house arts students and the vast, shining multimillion dollar complexes in which the hard sciences are disseminated. In but a fifteen minute walk around any decently respectable university, one fact will become glaringly evident to the observer: arts students are the slaves of the academic world. Substitute cotton fields for classrooms, and there you have it. And so I toil, beholden to the academy, doing nigger work for nigger pay, with a nigger's hope of my lot in life improving when I'm done on this plantation of pedagogy and rhetoric. I should start a movement.

Ivory desks, ivory seats, ivory windows, ivory teeth, even little fucking ivory ballpoint pens you want to ram straight into your pupils. The sweet stink of entitlement, a pulpy smog you can physically choke on, strangling the larynx, imbuing the senses with a sour distaste for solving the world's problems by midterm. If only those skinny bloated African boys could see us work, they'd fix it all in one breath, one swipe of justice. Sure, we love to hear the sorrowful sounds of our own educated voices, just don't you dare put us out on the streets, we'd shrivel up and die—our tusks are all show.

Incomplete horizons, half-baked ideologies. Here I sit, between two worlds, one ruled by thought, the other by action. But the thought believed it fed the action, and the action never seemed to be affected much by the thought. Two parallel lines that never seemed to meet. For whatever reason, the action was on its own.

~

Outside on the foyer atop the Vancouver General Hospital—where nurses go to chain smoke, arms crossed, one hand up,

puffing away—there resides a large bonsai plant in the exact cen-
trifugal middle of the square. This bonsai plant is apparently over
one hundred years old. It was brought here during the hospital's
construction way back in 1906.

Since then it's seen literally everything. Heard countless stories, arguments, fights, reconciliations, confessions, apparitions,
epiphanies, and even a few jokes.

It's grown through two world wars, economic depressions,
nuclear bombs and world leaders bent on killing for clouded
righteous causes.

I'm sitting here, wrapped in my university rugby tracksuit,
staring at this bonsai plant, supremely envious. All this plant needs
to survive, to flourish, is two atoms of hydrogen and one of oxygen, and a little ultraviolet light. Both of which it gets for free,
from the sky, rays beaming down on it until about seven o'clock
when the sun dips below the western islands. It's heard all the
world's problems at the worst possible times, and it just sits there
and grows.

A nurse across the way asks me if I have a light. I don't smoke,
I tell her, I quit. She says she wants to quit. I tell her Xanax. She
responds with a telling nod. Her face looks fatigued, but she can't
be older than thirty. She probably went into nursing straight from
college. Now she's seen it all, had feces thrown at her, stuck ene-
mas up obese men's asses, and watched multiple people die slowly on her watch. I am not envious of her.

I head back inside to the disinfectant, the glossy floors, the sterilized hand rails. A collection of wheelchairs sit in a corner on the
eighth floor where I get off. They sit in a disjointed mess, as if they're
all talking to each other, exchanging stories on a coffee break.

The eighth floor houses cancer patients. They walk around
the ward like zombies, carrying IV stations. No hair, unkempt,
follicles falling out. Their eyes sunken, cheeks sagging, skin a
milky white with a tint of yellow and beige. It's tough to make
eye contact with these people as they pass. You want to look, but
you want to just let them labour in peace.

Cancer is the lottery of hell. It strikes through genetics,
through bad decisions such as smoking or working in poor

conditions. But mostly it simply strikes without discourse, without warning, without consent or ample time for preparation.

My mother has pancreatic cancer. It was found during a routine physical, in an advanced or "stage IV" condition. It is now metastatic, which means the original tumor is now replicating and sending brand new malignant microscopic cells into both her lymphatic system and blood stream. Those metastatic cells are travelling throughout her body, in the hundreds of thousands, and have been attaching at distant locations and setting up whole new colonies of cancer. This will repeat indefinitely, until my mother dies.

The new colonies are seeding, and reseeding, and will continue to until her body is absolutely filled with this terrible disease. Three doctors have stated she has literally zero chance of beating it—no chemotherapy was prescribed—it would only cause her to grow weaker, and allow the disease more open road to explore the secluded corners of her once healthy body. Over a year ago she was given six months to live, and the prognosis now is to simply allow her as much comfort as possible until she eventually succumbs. Her bed is a coffin, a casket waiting to be closed. She is on constant painkillers, enough to send her into daylong slumbers where she forgets how old I am, and that I'm in my fourth year of an English degree, and a member of the university rugby team. She sometimes even forgets my name, albeit briefly. She knows full well who I am, but cannot make the connection between her son and his official title.

It's around six o'clock in the evening, and my mother is sleeping. I have a permanent station here in the corner of her room. There is one other patient in the room with her right now, an elderly man with lung cancer and advanced stages of dementia. His family visits him, even though he no longer has any idea who anyone is. I'm sure he doesn't even know he's in a hospital.

I type away at my computer, writing a paper on contemporary poetry. A criticism of the modern movement. Twenty-thousand words of beautiful drivel. Sylvia Plath, Robert Frost, Adrienne Rich, T.S. Eliot. Whores of the written word. Captives of the artistic elite. Forever now stuck within a movement, unable to get out, to roam free. I spin a silky thread of prosody analysis, rhythm dissection, meter length and metrical patterns. I'm talking about a movement I've only experienced on pages. There is nothing real about what I'm penning.

After a few hours I need another break. I head to the control room and get my mother's dinner from the fridge. When I come back she's awake.

"Hello," she say in her hoarse voice. Oxygen tubes wrapped around her cheeks, disappearing into her nostrils.

When my mother was young, she was a looker. Tall, slender, a beautiful woman, her name, Eve, was so fitting—you can already picture her. My father fought off countless guys to win her heart, and then lost her through divorce went he couldn't fight the urge to stick his dick in someone else.

She's about twenty pounds underweight, her elbows jut out like sticks from a rubbery tube. Crow's feet, sagging neck, her whole body is tired of living, tired of losing a battle it cannot win, and thus resigned to doing the only thing it can, to take in oxygen.

"Mom, I have dinner for you. Pasta."

I have to spoonfeed her most of the time. She takes small bites, grows tired quickly, her stomach always gets upset. Tonight she finishes everything, even her red jello cup.

"How's rugby?" she asks.

"Good. Practice again tomorrow. And I'll need to stop by the house after."

She nods, offering her hand to mine. I touch it, cold, clammy, and weak, holding it until she falls asleep, dozing off quickly into a medically induced slumber. At least she looks peaceful when she sleeps, her only escape from this world of physical terror.

~

I entered university not quite straight out of high school, after a year of mindless employment and crazy nights of booze, women and cocaine, in no particular order. My grades were good enough to get into first year arts. A star in high school, I walked onto the rugby team, but spent the first two years on the bench, and the third as a winger. Then Donny, the senior scrum-half, went down with a knee injury midway through my fourth year, tearing a ligament apart. And so I was thrown into the starting position with a year and a half of eligibility left.

When one goes through serious mental strife, it hardens the exterior, creating a metaphysical cast. A layer of protection develops, a shield by which one hides emotions from others.

It also meant my pain threshold was extremely high. I'd throw my lean, weight-room frame into scrums with six-foot five, 230-pound props. I was fearless, nothing could damage me, my physical body yearned for punishment. I enjoyed it, my coach hated it, but corralled it, making sure I channeled it properly. Pain was the simplest recourse.

We run a standard offence. Our number 8, Derek, is All-Canadian, and hopes to play professionally in New Zealand after graduation. Most of the time my job is to simply give him the ball out of a scrum or ruck, and then get the hell out of his way. He's built like a compact rhinoceros—thick thighs, granite chin, arms like a toy action figure. He runs like he's blind, straight into confrontation. I admire his lack of restraint.

We practice on our home field, in a stadium near the back of campus on the edge of a forest. The stadium lights come on around six, spotlighting the field at the expense of everything else. It centers everything. When I am practicing or playing, everything else becomes secondary. The pain and the pleasure of the physicality of rugby is my one avenue of escape. I engage myself physically to avoid the mental side of life.

We run some standard drills, some set plays from the line-out, and I work with the backs on passing. I've yet to earn much respect from the starting fifteen—I know my style will be something of an acquired taste. Donny was much loved by the guys, a selfless player who wasn't much of an innovator, but more of a solid part of an effective unit. Me, I want to run blindside passes, drop-kick field goals, string plays straight out to the wingers. I want to create.

After practice, the coach, a big burly man who once played for team Canada, pats me on the back and tells me I'm coming along nicely. We started the season 6-1, and with me at the helm we are 3-2, still in a playoff position. I need a win this weekend to keep my starting job, as there's a freshman winger named Billy they've been grooming to replace me if and when required, a typical succession any team deals with in order to regenerate itself.

Donny labours over as well, on crutches, while the coach is still beside me. He looks like Tie Domi with blonde hair. His neck is the same width as his head.

"Remember," says the coach, "the playbook is there for a reason. It's something the entire team knows, so you stick to the plays and everyone will be on the same page. You call the plays like you believe in them."

I nod. Coach ambles off.

"You're doing good, kid. Stick to your guns," Donny pipes in once he's safely out of range. I smile to show my appreciation.

The team is getting some minor press, mostly by way of the campus paper and the local rag. Four years ago, when Donny was a rookie, the team won a national championship, and now anything but another banner raised in the campus gym would be met with severe disappointment. That championship banner looms over the heads of the team now, telling us greatness might already be in the rearview mirror. It instills in us a thirst to return to our winning ways.

After practice, I take the bus back to my mother's house. It's dark, quiet, like it always is. I feed her two cats, Cleo and Maggie—not getting a lot of attention these days, they follow me around the small apartment the entire time. I rarely turn on the lights. I don't look at any of the pictures on the walls. I haven't been in my mother's room in over a year.

It's tough to be here, for obvious reasons. I minimize my time around the place. The air suffocates me. The silence feels deafening. The sights almost blind me. The apartment tries to talk to me through its creaky hardwood floors. I don't listen. I don't respond. I'm a ghost here, hovering just above the floor. I don't touch anything. It's like a period house on display for the public. Everything in its rightful place.

I sink into the couch for a night of reading. Textbooks, novels, notes, seminar readings, papers, essays, handouts, summaries. The cats jump up on the couch and sit with me, rolling around and purring, happy to have human company. I fall asleep sometime after late night becomes early morning.

~

I head to my Political Science class on the third floor of the arts building. The Politics of Social Movements. White kids from three-storey homes articulating about the American Civil Rights Movement, about Martin Luther King, Jr., alternative social movements, redemptive social movements, reformative social movements, revolutionary social movements. Pretty much every student in this room comes from a solid upbringing—from safety, assurance, security and shelter, a somewhat artificial sanctuary set apart from the very real ills of the world. Racism and oppression are utterly foreign to them, but they speak as if they've lived such things themselves.

"You push any group of people into a corner and they'll fight back," says one, and I smile to myself. I doubt this kid's ever felt what it's like to be constantly judged because of the colour of his skin. Or be shot at or bombed because of his religion. Exiled by force, separated from his loved ones. Oppressed so much that victory or death becomes the only option. Squatting in shit-filled holes for days, living in trees with a loaded gun, walking for miles through treacherous terrain for the minute possibility of freedom.

I sit here watching this entitled white boy rail off on what it feels like to be oppressed. His verbal diatribe feels like diarrhea being shoved into my ears.

The teacher cuts him off, rolls back into the curriculum. I want to scream, but all I do is take notes.

I head to the hospital after practice on Thursday. *Dancing with the Stars* is on, my mother's favourite show. Other than her son, it's her one real connection to the outside world beyond the occasional family visit. Honestly I couldn't care less about it, but I chat with her about who's doing well, who's on the bubble. It calms her, distracts her. It's all we've got.

We sit there watching some former football star dance the salsa with a five-foot-four girl who probably weighs less than a racehorse jockey. My mother watches intently, almost as if she's a judge. She remarks on his footwork, and how the other judges will like that. He's lacking some creative juices though, probably because he's a football player—a running commentary throughout the episode. She agrees with the judges' comments about the dancers' costumes. She's immersed in it, it dilutes us both.

My mother worked for the provincial government for seventeen years before she was diagnosed with terminal cancer. She had life insurance, a pension, severance, medical coverage. Since my Dad left, and I am an only child, I am the sole benefactor. I will receive close to $120,000 when she passes away.

I also have upwards of $80,000 of debt in student loans and credit cards. Chances are, when I graduate, that figure will balloon to at least $100,000. I couldn't work last year because I was tending to her, and I'll be unable to work during these last two semesters either.

I look over at my mother, watching *Dancing With the Stars*, knowing her death will set me free financially. My mind can only skim the surface of what this is doing to my psyche. Waiting for her passing. Waiting to pay off massive amounts of debt. I want her to live, obviously, but her prognosis said otherwise.

I have no idea what to think. I have no idea how to handle this. Layers of insatiable questioning, reasoning, imprisoning my mind within a terrible Rubik's cube of despondent, brutal truth. Like a soldier forced to leave his wounded friend behind in order to save himself, it is a situation no one should ever be forced into.

Not long after we return to the room, Emily comes in to give my mother her supper. She's a nurse on the ward, from Australia, and she's been in Canada about four months now. She's got dusty blonde hair she always keeps pulled back, and her eyes are somewhere between green and hazel. She looks like a girl who spent her entire childhood on some sandy beach beside a beautiful ocean. A permanent tan dotted by a spray of freckles across her cheeks, with milky white teeth and even whiter scleras.

We talk whenever she comes by. I think she likes the company. Working all the time, she hasn't met many people in Canada yet. Plus she's a real fan of rugby.

"How are you doing today?" she says to my mother, half looking at me.

"I'm good," responds my mother.

I nod in confirmation.

"You ready to eat dinner?"

"Yes."

I sit there in my little chair, watching Emily feed my mother. My laptop sits idle so long it goes into sleep mode. I stare out the window, out high above the buildings, to the city lights at night. When it rains, like it is now, the white lights smear into tiny photon packets. They scatter across the window, igniting the rain as it slips south, dripping onto the windowsill like tears.

"How is rugby going?" asks Emily while carefully feeding my mother.

I look back at her. "It's good, stressful, you know."

"I read in the campus paper—my friend showed it to me when she recognized your last name—you're the starting scrum-half now?"

"Yeah," I say, rubbing my face in displeasure.

"Lots of pressure, I bet?"

"Yeah. Lots."

Emily senses I'm a bit tense about the subject. She holds some apple juice with a straw to my mother's mouth.

"So you enjoying Canada?" I ask, keeping the conversation going.

"It's nice" she says, nodding. "I'm not sure about all this rain. I'm looking forward to spending a summer here. Still getting used to the fact that December is a cold month."

"Oh yeah, that's right. You guys are all backwards down there."

Emily smiles. There's a silence as she takes away the empty apple juice.

"Would you like your jello now?" she asks my Mom.

"No, I don't think I'm in the mood for jello today."

"Okay," says Emily.

Emily is by far my favourite nurse. Somehow she's able to come off as happy and pleasant without any degree of pretentiousness. Most nurses are just putting on a brave face, especially here in the cancer ward, but Emily has a hard beam of sunlight encasing her body that only lately seems like it might be cracking.

"You have a break anytime soon?" I ask her.

Emily looks at me, cleans up the plate from dinner. "Umm, yeah actually. I was going to go on break after this."

"Okay, do you want to walk to Starbucks? I really need a coffee, I have a paper to write tonight before I head home."

She nods. "Sure, okay. Just let me get my coat."

We walk free of the white walls and sterilized steel of the hospital. Past the ambulances and the lung cancer patients smoking outside. We share her umbrella in the rain across the street to the neon green Starbucks sign. It's late, a weeknight, so it's not busy, and cars splash by on the streets. I keep my tracksuit zipped up tight.

After we get coffee we sit down at a corner table. Emily seems a bit disarmed, less professional, which must happen automatically when she leaves hospital grounds. I'm guessing that's how nurses stay sane.

"You know, it's funny," she says in her thin Australian accent.

"What's that?"

"It's just you've been coming to the hospital every day now for like a year, and you rarely talk to any of the nurses. I mean I totally understand, what with your mother's situation."

I nod, pondering my response. "I'm just not really a talkative guy."

"Well all the nurses think you're cute. I'm pretty sure two of them have crushes on you. They call you TDH."

"TDH?"

"Tall, dark and handsome."

"Oh, yeah," I say, trying not to smile too much.

"But they're all scared to approach you."

"Huh. . . . I'm sorry, I guess."

"No, it's nothing you have to apologize for, they just have all these theories about you. About who you are."

"Oh yeah? They think I'm Batman or something?"

Emily senses I'm not really into this trail of conversation.

"Anyways I'm sorry. Nurses talk a lot. It's what we do."

"I understand."

We sit there a bit. I pick away at the lip of my coffee cup, take a small sip.

"So how long are you in Canada for?" I ask eventually.

"I dunno. My work visa is for three years, so I guess three years."

"Do you miss Australia?"

"Yeah I do, a bit. I miss my parents and friends more than anything."

"Can't you get a job nursing back in Australia?"

"I could, but I really wanted to try and make it on my own, work in a foreign country. I mean nobody in my family travels much, and all the time I see these Canadians coming down to Australia to work and party, and I figure why can't I do that?"

"So you did."

"Yeah," she smiles. "I did."

"Have you been to many parties?" I ask her.

"A few. Mostly with the other nurses."

I sense an opening to invite her to one of the rugby parties. I sense she wants me to.

"Cool," is all I can muster.

We finish our coffee and walk back to the hospital. Emily heads off to do her rounds, and I head back to the room to find my Mum asleep.

I finish my Contemporary Poetry paper in the dark. It's like a prison cell with no bars.

~

Philosophy 414. Early Modern Philosophy. Hobbes and Locke and Rosseau and Kant. Chit-chat about the nature of existence. Passing conversations about the wonderment of humanity, brief discussions on the existence of the universe, water cooler talk on the state of nature, individual liberty and rights, the basis of political obligation and state authority, and the rule of law.

Blood, sweat and tears jam-packed into hour-long seminars where we give passing glances to movements far too complex for anyone to truly comprehend. We would have to have been there ourselves, and of course none of us were.

Our professor, with his patterned tie, worn dress pants and dusty grey beard, leads us through a discussion of the hypothetical condition of humanity. A natural condition. Without laws, without discourse, without government, without jails and prisons and schools and museums and art houses and soccer fields, who would we be? I can barely concentrate. Starting to fade in and out, I doodle along the edges of my notebook.

A young blonde with a push-up bra starts off on human nature. She could be speaking Icelandic for all I know. Her mouth moves but I can't understand her drivel. I lean back in my chair. She has nothing to tell me of any signifigance, I'm sure.

Then the professor is off again. Anarchy. Beautiful anarchy. Fighting and fucking and looking for food. Wolves running in packs with nothing to do but hunt. My mind runs with them, into a million different places. Life. Liberty. Love. Reality television. Cancer. Toilet paper. Breast implants and fourth-year philosophy students.

I rub my face, feeling as though I might be having a panic attack, and excuse myself from the seminar.

I walk down the corridor, third-floor, large glass windows off to the left exposing a green courtyard. I stop, look out. It's quiet, no pedestrians. I stand against the glass window, hands on the railing, my face resting against the cold hard surface. I take a few deep breaths, huffing in and out. I'm tired. Oh so very tired.

~

Practice. I'm dragging my ass and the coach is yelling at me.

"Get it out! Move the fucking ball! No no no—stop!" he shouts, stopping the play just as I'm about to whip the ball out to my blindside winger. He yells so loud he doesn't need a whistle at practice.

"Why? Why are you going out there when you have four backs the other way! Why are you pushing it left when everything is going right?"

Everyone stops to stare at me and the coach. I wipe sweat from my forehead.

"Break it, okay?" he barks.

"Okay."

"Okay!"

"Okay!" I shout back.

My coach looks at me. Waves his hand. "Run it again!" he barks.

We run it again. The ball comes out, I whip it out to my standoff in a diving throw, he chips it up and over the line where the winger grabs it and takes it home for a try.

Coach claps while walking towards me. I just stand there with my hands on my hips.

"See?"

"Yes, coach!" I say.

We break, and I head over to one of the trainers for water. I lean over. We're scrimmaging for fifteen minutes.

I keep my distance off the kick-off. I start to eye up Billy, the second unit scrum half. The ball moves over, rucks and mauls. He squirts blindside, I come at him, shoulder down, hands out ready to scoop him up like a plow. I blast into him, pick him up and slam him onto the sideline. The air leaves his chest as I fall on top of him.

Whistle. Line-out for us.

Donny yells from the sidelines. "That's my boy! Eat his heart!"

I pick up the rookie. He pushes off me a bit, offering a disgruntled look. I just stand there smiling at him goofily, daring him to make his move so that I can unleash all my pentup rage on him. He relents.

Practice is over. I'm in the shower with the boys. I get changed and leave early, hopping on the bus to the hospital before anyone can chat with me, even the coach.

I almost fall asleep on the bus. Wavering back and forth with the road, my mind drifts into those of the passengers around me. People of various ethnicities, all here on public transportation, all staring straight ahead as if at nothing. All working for less, working for those who make more. I just close my eyes and try not to worry about anything. I'm tired of caring.

Emily is on shift again. I catch her as I walk into the ward from the elevator. She waves and smiles, and I give a small wave back. The other nurses crowd around her quickly to chat, apparently about me. One laughs.

My mother is awake, listening to a book on CD. She pulls her headphones off as soon as she sees me. I sit down, put my bag under the bed, pull out my laptop and put it on my little table.

"Hi, how are you tonight?" she asks in a way only mothers can.

"I'm good, Mom. How are you?"

"I'm okay. This new medication the doctor has me on, it's different. It makes me sleepy, but I can't seem to fall asleep. I've been listening to books all night."

"I brought you some new ones."

I open up my bag and hand her a few more audio books from the campus library. She thumbs through them.

"I've read most of these. I thought you were going to get me that one from Oprah's Book Club?"

"I tried, Mom. I'm still on the waiting list."

"Oh, okay."

I've told her this about seven times, but she forgets. I'm thinking I'll just go buy a copy and tell her it's from the library. She won't know the difference.

"That nurse, Emily, the girl from England," says my mother.

"Australia."

"No she's from England."

"Okay."

"Anyways, she's really nice. We had a nice talk today. You should ask her out on a date."

I just nod. "Did you eat your dinner tonight?"

"I had a bit. But my stomach. This new medication the doctor has me on, it upsets my stomach."

"I'm going to work on a paper. You can listen to your books, okay?"

My mother nods, puts her headphones on, and turns her book on.

She's out within five minutes. I take her headphones off and turn the device off.

Emily comes in carrying a small cup of medication.

"Hey," she says.

"Hey, how are you?"

"Good." She puts the cup on my mother's table. "Are you going to be here a while?"

"Yeah, for a few hours."

"Okay, if you're still here when she wakes up, can you make sure she takes her medication?"

"Yeah for sure. Apparently it's upsetting her stomach though."

"I know."

Emily stands there looking at me. I just stare off.

She moves over to the dementia patient and tries to wake him. He doesn't move, but snores and lets out a few noises instead.

She comes back over. "So school is going good?" she asks.

"Yeah."

"You're in your fourth year, right?"

"Yeah, English."

"Cool. Yeah I was pretty tired of school. Almost five years."

"Yeah it can get tiring."

"So . . . you graduate this spring?"

"Yeah."

"You going to stick around for another year? I mean, you have five years of eligibility, right? For rugby? That's how it works here, correct?"

I type away at my computer, then stop. "Yeah," I say. "I don't think so."

Emily nods, stands over by my mother. "So what are you going to do then?"

I give a confused look. "I dunno really. I might go travel."

"Where to?"

"I dunno. Away."

"From here?"

"Yeah."

"Good idea. Like out of the country?"

"Definitely out of the country."

"Cool."

We move into silence, and it grows uncomfortable. I've got an empty tank for conversation—even with her it's tough. I'm trying, but failing.

"So I was thinking," she says.

I look up at her.

"You guys play the Hawks Saturday?"

"Yeah."

"So would it be okay if I came and watched the game? I mean I'd bring a friend, she's never seen a rugby game. I've only seen a few here, at the park."

I cough a bit, think about it. "Yeah, that would be okay."

"Okay," she says, developing a smile.

"I'll get you some pom-poms. You can sit with my booster club."

"What? Really?"

I smile.

"Oh," she says, smiling politely as my attempt at humour in a cancer ward dies.

"Okay then, I have to make my rounds."

Emily leaves. I watch her go out the door.

I start on my Early Modern Philosophy paper, pushing it along until it gradually gains traction and takes off under its own power. Footnotes galore, quotes, anecdotes, words I have to look up in the dictionary. Theories I barely understand even after multiple read-ings. None of it seems relevant to any aspect of my life at all.

~

The rain is everywhere. Muddy, sloshy, I can feel the water's weight in my pores. My jersey must weigh at least ten pounds. I can't feel the tips of my fingers or my toes.

The Hawks are a dirty, vile team. My left eye is swollen, slowly dripping blood. The trainer taped it up with waterproof surgical tape, but it's no use—the left side of my face has a river of red running down it onto my neck.

We're down 15-12, and the game is almost over. Emily is here, with her friend, wrapped together in a blanket under the bleachers, out of the rain. I haven't looked at her once, trying to stay focused, staying in the zone, as they say. I'm pretty sure I have onset pneumonia. I'm simultaneously cold and hot, my body pulsing with heat, only to have it snuffed once it reaches the surface of my skin.

Rugby, when played by professionals, or experienced players, is one of the most beautiful games in existence. The ultimate display of selfless teamwork, players wait until they get hit, then give the ball to their teammate in successions like falling dominoes. Cascading plays develop where players move forward and the ball moves backwards. Men who try to physically destroy each other for eighty minutes, raking cleats into each other while they lie on the ground, afterwards go for beers together. Compare scars they gave each other. Gentlemanly, but barbaric.

I've been giving the ball to Derek all night. And you can tell—poor guy is getting tired. But he's valiant, taking the ball every time and pounding it down the field for yards. Our backs are useless—the rain means knock-ons are happening almost every play, and no one can get any speed in the sludge. It's trench warfare. Dirty, nasty rugby where the hookers and props are doing the grunt work.

Their scrum-half is much smaller than I, but he's built for this type of rugby, low to the ground, able to pick up loose balls dropped in the mud. He's running the same game as I am, keeping the ball tight to the scrum, short yardage, easy plays.

We work it down into their end after a line-out with just over five minutes remaining. The hooker calls a long throw, so I call a play out to the backs for a change of pace.

I watch the ball move out through our backs right to the out-side centre. I keep pace behind, waiting for a ruck. Billy breaks a tackle, and literally slips through the line. The fullback chases him out to the line, but Billy's too fast and beats him to the corner flag to slide past the try line almost halfway to the dead ball line in the rain.

I throw my hands up in the air and start to yell, running towards him. I grab him in a huge bear hug, and he yells some-thing in my ear but I can't make it out. Sounds positive.

Donny hugs me in the dressing room before I can even get my jersey off. He almost crushes me he's hugging me so hard.

He pulls back and grabs my face. "That's my boy. Gettin' shit done."

We look each other in the eyes, and I see a glimmer of pain. His last year of eligibility is quietly slipping away. No one has said it publicly but there's no way he'll suit up this year, and he's played too many games to default the season. This will be the end of his university rugby career, on the sidelines, on crutches, watching some punk kid like me try to fill his massive shoes.

Emily congratulates me after the game outside the clubhouse where I meet her friend. But I have to head to the hospital for six stitches. Emily offers to give me a ride, but I politely decline and take the bus even though it's an extra half hour. The whole left side of my rib cage is swollen, and my hands are still numb almost two hours after the game. I ask the doctor for some painkillers for my rib, and he offers me codeine. What a guy.

I head home to my mother's house, some chicken noodle soup and a hot bath to keep a potential cold at bay.

Then I wrap myself in clothes and blankets and lie in bed, feeling a slight sense of peacefulness. My body has been beaten severely, my mind too tired to think, or care.

I haven't felt this good in weeks.

~

My father nudges me. I'm asleep in my chair at the hospital. I rub my eyes, my mother is asleep. He hands me a worn copy of

Where the Wild Things Are by Maurice Sendak. My mother used to read it to me all the time before bedtime. I'm sure she's read it to me over a thousand times.

I look at the book, puzzled.

"I found it rummaging through some old boxes, thought you might like to have it."

I flip through it. Max with his crown, in his wolf suit. I smile and put the book down on the table.

"How is she?" he asks.

"She's okay."

My father stands there, in his tattered work clothes, his healthy five o'clock shadow. "You need any cash?"

"Umm . . ."

"For the apartment, there's lots of food there?"

My father has picked up the mortgage payments since my mother went into the hospital. He wants to sell the place when she passes away, give the money to me.

"Um, yeah, some cash would be good."

He thumbs through his wallet, pulls out five or six hundred dollars. I take it and put it in my rugby bag.

He stands there, looks at my mother, looks at me. "So she's doing okay?"

"Yeah she's alright. Good days and bad."

He nods.

My father makes these appearances, usually bi-weekly. He's good at timing his visits, as typically my mother is asleep. It's like he can sense when she won't be awake and I'll be there. I can tell he doesn't want to talk to her. But he feels an obligation to be here even though they'd been divorced for six years when she was diagnosed.

I lean back in my chair, adjust myself. He points at the stitches above my left eyebrow. "Rugby?"

"Yeah."

"How's that going?"

"Good."

"Looks like it."

He comes and watches me sometimes. Sits there by himself, never clapping, never showing emotion. Always shakes my hand after and tells me I played a good game. The guy is busy though, so I think I understand. He's a night-shift worker, on a different schedule. He lost a lot in the divorce for his infidelity. And I'd always suspected something else happened between the two that further drove them apart, but I could never put my finger on it. It's so far in the past now that we don't pick at the scar. It's healed. Faded. Masters of small talk, we keep everything on the surface.

"How is school?"

"Good."

"Good. You still set to graduate this spring?"

"Yeah."

"Good."

More silence.

"Okay I should go," he says.

"Okay."

"I'll try to stop by this weekend during the day when she's awake."

"Okay."

My father comes over and pats me on the shoulder in a way only fathers can. He admires my dedication to my mother. He can't do it, doesn't feel he should do it, or doesn't want to be there every day like I am. We don't talk about it.

He leaves. I take in a few breaths and start again on my philosophy paper. But I don't get anywhere. I open up *Where the Wild Things Are* and read it to myself instead.

~

Early Modern Philosophy. The Rationalists. Innate ideas. The Empiricists. Knowledge beginning with sensory experience. I know what I've experienced. Loss. Not just my mother. A friend too. What does it mean to gain knowledge through experience? Thought only applicable to itself. Wavelengths of trials and tribulations. Gaining insight through life, learning life the hard way. All I know is what I've been through, why I am where I am today. These shoes I walk in are my own.

I head to class. The professor starts in on empiricism. Evidence. Sensory perception. Some rationalist kid from the nice part of town argues that there are absolute truths we know, that we do not need to experience in order to understand or feel. He believes we are born with right and wrong, and know full well the repercussions of our actions even though we've never ventured down that road before. We need only learn from others, and at times, ourselves, in order for others to learn from us.

After class the professor asks me if I can meet him in his office. I accept, not sure what's going on.

We walk down the halls, behind the main hall to the professors' offices. Newspaper clippings, editorial cartoons, anti-war posters. I look inside each office crammed full of books, expensive Mac computers, and windows overlooking courtyards.

We head in and I sit down. He closes the door behind us, then thumbs through a notebook at his desk, cluttered with papers. He apologizes and introduces himself, says we've never met formally. He has a slight sense of awkwardness most professors do. I think it comes with higher education. He must feel so many planes above me when it comes to knowledge. Not that I give a shit.

"Look, the reason I called you in here today is because, truth be told, I'm very disappointed in your class participation."

I just sit in his chair by the door, offering a nod that comes off more as a ploy not to answer.

"Obviously you're doing fine in the class, well over a B average. Middle of the pack, as they say. I just really want you to take some of the viewpoints in your papers and express them in class. I know you're on the rugby team, and that must take up a lot of your free time and energy."

I just sit there, nodding, issuing a half-assed "Okay."

"Is there something wrong? Are you not comfortable speaking in front of the class?"

I don't want to get into this. Instead I'm just going to play my ace and get out of here.

"My mother has terminal cancer."

His head tilts back, mouth opens slightly. "Oh my God, I'm so sorry. How is she?"

"She's going to die. I'm really the only person she's got left. Nobody wants to come visit her anymore—they did all the time for the first four or five months, then it just dropped off. They got tired of being around that much sadness. So now it's just me."

"And your father?"

"Divorced. He comes around from time to time."

"My God. . . . Well I had no idea."

"It's okay. But can I just get away with not talking in class? I mean I only have the one semester left. I know the material, I'm not in the dark, I just don't feel like I'm in the right headspace to start philosophizing about life and death in front of people I really don't know."

He nods, runs his hand through his beard. "All right, that's fair. I understand."

We sit there for a second, in silence. Finally I pipe in, "I have rugby practice."

"All right," he says, standing up, shaking my hand.

I find a place to rest and read a while, killing the two hours until rugby practice begins.

~

One of the trainers takes my stitches out, two days ahead of schedule. I'm just not into going to the hospital unless it's to see my Mom. He tapes it up with surgical tape, and I'll have to wear a rugby helmet during practice and probably the next game or two. I look like an asshole. The whole practice the guys keep asking me where my baseball is. I take it in stride.

We have two games left until the playoffs. Then three wins to make nationals. We're ranked second in the province—chances are we could make nationals. Chances are we would get blown out at nationals too, my inexperience likely getting exposed quickly and painfully for all to see. A slight discomfort has taken up residence inside my stomach. I'm in no condition to lead a team on the field. But here I am, lieutenant's badge across my heart.

~

I'm typing away at an English paper. Prose fiction. Novels. Short stories. Novellas. Poems. Fiction. Non-fiction. Horror. Literary technique. Hubert Selby Jr. and Hunter S. Thompson all in the same breath. Techniques of the greats. Massive figures who've changed the world. I feel small and insignificant by comparison.

The doctor comes in, and I stop transcribing notes from a lecture. He's a younger guy, glasses, short hair, always looking like he's just arrived from a weekend of skiing and drinking cocoa with his young family at his expensive chalet. He must have a dozen pairs of impeccable New Balance cross-trainers he rotates through. But at least he's always straightforward with me, willing to hang around and explain the finer points of what exactly is killing my mother.

"We tried switching her onto this new medication, as the side effects are supposed to be a bit less harsh. But from what I've seen, what you've told me and what your mother is exhibiting, I don't think it's working."

"So what is it exactly?"

"Well it's called Sutet, and it's basically a life-prolonging drug for terminal cancer patients. Stomach cancer and pancreatic cancer more specifically."

"Okay, I don't fully understand. Life-prolonging?"

"Yes, what the medication does, or attempts to do, is slow down the growth of new cancer throughout her body, while also impeding a lot of the pain that accompanies that."

"So, basically, what the drugs are doing is drawing out her life, but in a less painful manner?"

"Well I wouldn't really look at it that way."

"What way should I look at it then?"

"Well what the drugs do is prolong your mother's life in the best way possible."

"But you guys have been telling me for over a year now she has less than six months to live."

"I realize our initial prognosis may have been a bit overstated. The thing is your mother is responding quite well to most of the medication."

"The medication that is keeping her alive, but not fixing her."

I take in a deep breath as my eyes well up. The doctor comes closer and sits down with a calming hand on the bed beside me. My mother lies there, asleep, oblivious. I clench my fists slowly.

"This is an extremely tough time for you. I commend you, you've done a very honourable thing over the past year, being here beside your mother. My job is simply to allow her to live the best possible life. I know this might not look like much. But if I can give you an extra few weeks or months together, shouldn't I try to do that?"

I'm welling up, holding back tears. "I know, I'm sorry," I sputter. "I just don't want to see her suffer. I don't want her to spend the last year of her life in a hospital bed listening to books on her headphones while nobody visits her. That's no life for anyone."

The doctor nods slowly. He leans in, looking at me, my eyes watering, my throat closing in on itself. "Your mother is a fighter. She refuses to let the cancer just take her. You should be proud—her body, her mind, is strong, she's resisting death. This is something that is inside you too. You must put yourself in her shoes. What would you do if a terrible disease just swooped into your life and tried to take you away from your loved ones? Would you fight, or just give up?"

I stand up, a small epiphany settling across me. Every day I come here to the hospital, I do the right thing. I am with my mother. I give her strength by being here. I am prolonging both her death, and her fight, which she will ultimately lose. I'm giving her the strength to keep fighting a battle she will not win.

I walk out of the hospital room. The doctor says something to me as I leave, but I ignore it. I head to the elevator, out to the foyer—the bonsai plant just sits there, almost staring at me. I look around through the light drizzle. Homes and apartment complexes lit warmly for the night. The ocean off in the distance, a black expanse of slate. I run my hands through my hair. The horizon draws across my attention like a dying pulse line. Black mountaintops, dark clouds. No stars. Not a single star in the sky tonight.

~

My head falls forward. I awake in my chair, my mother asleep by my side. I have spent the night in the hospital again. It happens from time to time. The nurses take pity on me and let me sleep, sometimes even taking my laptop off my lap and covering me with a blanket.

Emily comes in with a coffee. "I figured you might need this," she says with a smile, handing me the cup. "I couldn't remember what you drink, so I just got you a coffee with cream, no sugar."

"That's okay, I'm sweet enough," I tell her.

Emily smiles as another poor attempt at humor dies here on the ward.

"Do you have class today?" she asks.

I dart my eyes to the clock, it's only eight. "I don't have class until noon. You work night shift?"

"Yeah it was quiet last night."

"Why didn't you wake me. We could've got coffee or something."

"You looked so peaceful, I didn't want to disturb you. You were drooling a bit."

I check my mouth, finding a little crusted at the corner.

"Damn," I say.

"It's okay. It was kind of cute."

I stand up and stretch out. Take a sip from the coffee. "Did the doctor come around?"

Emily looks at my mother's chart. "Yeah he talked about the new medication."

She looks over the chart once more.

"Okay, well I'm off."

She starts to leave, but looks like she's waiting for something. I'm standing there in the middle of the hospital room, still half asleep. I take another sip of coffee.

"Hey," I say.

She stops and turns around.

"I, umm, would you like to maybe go for a bite to eat or something?"

"Like right now? I can't, I'm off shift and have to go to bed. I have to work again tonight too."

"No, like I mean away from work. Like dinner one night when you're not working."

She looks at me, taken back a bit. "Like a date?"

"Well, I'm not very good at this," I say, scratching my head. "Maybe we could call it dinner, would that be okay?"

"Okay . . . Well I'm off this weekend. But don't you have a game?"

"Bye week."

"Oh."

She stands there looking at me. I stand there looking like an idiot.

"All right," she says, "well how about I give you my number and you call me tomorrow and we'll set something up?"

"Okay."

Emily steps closer as I tear a piece of paper out of my notebook and hand it to her. She scribbles her number down.

"I, uh, is this like against protocol? I don't want to get you in trouble or anything."

She hands me the piece of paper. We're standing close, awkwardly close, as usually there's at least five feet between us. It causes my heart to heat up like a furnace.

"It's fine," she says. "As long as we don't broadcast it over the intercom, I think we'll be okay."

Emily leaves with a smile. I just stand there with the piece of paper a few moments, unsure of what to do with it. It feels like a loaded gun.

~

It's funny. I'm sitting in my English class, Studies in Prose Fiction, the professor has stepped out, and everyone is talking about their reading break plans. One guy is apparently going to Europe. Another to Vancouver Island. Mexico. Banff. Me, what am I doing on my reading break? Get this, reading.

They chat about the best hotels, flights, where to drink, where to party. Best way to blow their parents' money as quickly and recklessly as possible. I imagine them sitting in hot tubs sipping expensive champagne discussing the famine crisis in Africa. Debating the merits of the civil warfare in Iraq. Arguing over socialism in Columbia. Waxing poetic about race relations in South Africa. Some of these kids still get nervous when they see a black man on the street.

I head to practice after class. We're off this weekend, then next weekend is reading break, and we're back on Saturday before classes resume. This means only two practices before our game against the Island team, the top-ranked squad in the province. Coach is on edge, and wants to run practice long. Me in my stupid helmet, sweating up a storm.

We run some drills. Derek is off on the sidelines getting his shoulder worked on. It's probably separated but he won't admit it. He will play next weekend regardless. The man could get shot in the chest on the way to the game and he'd still suit up. Plead with coach to put him in.

Donny plays with a few young tikes who always hover around practice like alley cats. Sons of the trainers and coaches. He's off crutches, has surgery in three days, two months being the best recovery time one can hope for. Nationals are in exactly two months.

Coach calls me to his office after practice. I sit down, tired and worn from the exertion, relaxed. I take my helmet off.

"I just want to let you know, there is a possibility that we could make nationals. This is obviously a goal of this team every year, and we can do it again this year."

I nod, check the scar above my eyebrow.

"And I know you've probably heard Donny might get the okay from the doc to play by then."

"Yeah I've heard a bit of that."

"I just want you to know, you're my guy. If we go to nationals with you at the scrum-half position, it's yours to win or lose. I'm not going to put Donny on the national stage fresh off a two month layoff. He'll be too rusty, it's too much rust for him to shake off, and at that stage it'd be suicide. I might get him in at wing or somewhere."

"Okay."

"You're my guy, kid. We're stuck with each other. This is your time, your chance, you earn your way and I'll make sure you get every reward coming to you."

I just nod again. "Thanks, coach."

He looks at me, shakes his head. "You frustrate me, boy. But you've got some fucking moxie, I'll give you that. I've never had a kid like you, 190 pounds soaking wet, grinding up dirt with the props. I love it, believe me, but just keep it in check. I know you've got stuff going on outside of rugby. But you use that, you channel that, and you can help this team sip champagne from the cup. And trust me, it will be the best fucking drink you'll ever have."

I nod again, feeling a bit of confidence. "Thanks."

"Good," he says. "Now get the fuck out of my office and we'll see you Thursday. Keep your cardio up."

He shakes my hand. I leave. The bus ride to the hospital breezes by as I ask myself, Why can't I be that guy? Why can't I be the best scrum-half in the country? What's stopping me? I'm starting, and there's no backup plan. This is my chance to shine. My time to step the fuck up, or wilt away.

I check in with my mother. She's listening to her books. I tell her I'm heading down to the physiotherapy room to ride the bike for a half hour. Usually they let me if there's no one else around. The guy who runs the front desk is a rugby fan.

Mom is still listening to her books when I get back. I tell her *Dancing With the Stars* in on in half an hour. She perks up. I head over to my chair and pull out the copy of *Where the Wild Things Are*. My mother lights up as soon as she sees it, holds her hand to her mouth and starts to cry.

"Oh my God, where did you find it?"

"Dad brought it in."

"He did? When was he here?"

"A few days ago."

My mom thumbs through the book.

"You know, sometimes I couldn't get you to go to bed until I read this to you. You would cry and whine. But then I'd read it to you and you'd be out like a light."

I smile.

"You remember when you went as Max for Halloween? You were seven or eight and your father made you a costume and a crown. You looked so adorable."

I smile again, choke up a bit. My mother's eyes are watering as she opens the book to the first page and starts to read. I pull my chair over beside her, lean my head over, and she holds my hand. Holding the book open so I can see the pictures.

" 'The night Max wore his wolf suit and made mischief of one kind . . .' "

She continues reading. The she stops, looks at me. "You remember when I used to read this to you and Brad all the time when you two would have sleepovers?"

I nod and smirk a bit. I remember building forts out of the couch cushions with Brad and covering them with sheets. Then my mother would come in with a flashlight and read to us.

"You two," she says, starting to choke up, "you two really were like brothers, you know that?"

She looks at me with an odd expression, one I can't quite distinguish, one I'm not sure I understand. Perhaps it's the medication. I smile.

My mother keeps reading.

~

I glance at the page before me. Environmentally friendly, post-consumer, recycled paper sits empty while stains of dark blue ink crowd the margins. The tip of the pen seems to move on its own, tracing patterns of miscellaneous shapes. He talks, I write, encapsulating the crux of just what the hell prose fiction really is. Then someone interjects, cutting him off.

We're discussing post 9/11 American poetry. Some lesbian advocating for feminist equality tries to reinvent the sonnet better than Wyatt and Petrarch. No one is really listening, but she talks like we should be. She forgets she's advocating to an audience that doesn't exist. This room, these thirty-two students, are creating a canon that will disappear after exam season.

Class has been over for two minutes by my watch, but no one else seems to notice—this woman is still sounding off. Bare hands extended towards the ceiling are scattered around the room. These are the hands of the dead, reaching out of graves, struggling and competing to breach the surface of the earth, as though she's being called to save them.

I get up and leave. She watches me go, as if I should stay and stomach this shit. I don't, I just pack my binder up and leave, her voice trailing off as I walk out of the classroom and into the courtyard.

I stop by a water fountain to have a drink and calm my nerves.

I head to the library and punch out the rest of my prose fiction essay on my laptop. It labours onto the page, slowly, like a lazy dog being kicked out of the house. I head home after the last class before break. Everyone is buzzing, but I'm just leaving, ready to spend my reading break reading, mostly English literature. Fifteen books for one course. I put them back like a drunk knocking back drinks, barely retaining any information from any of them. They're like passing acquaintances, forgotten as soon as they're out of view. Robert Frost. James Joyce. Thomas Hardy. Joseph Conrad. Charles Dickens. Alessandro Volta.

I do some laundry. Wash dishes. Remedial tasks to fill the days. I vacuum the whole apartment and scare the cats away for a few hours. I sleep on the couch, falling asleep with a book on my chest. The cats lie around my feet and purr. They meow for their food in the morning.

I head to the campus gym every day for cardio. I barely talk to anyone, unless they approach me. I walk right by a bunch of teammates one day, but they don't see me. I float, a transparent figure, headphones on to signal my intentions. I'm not into talking much these days.

~

When I get to the hospital, my mother's bed is empty. I freak out, run to the desk. Hands on the counter, I yell down at Emily filing some papers, "Where's my Mom!"

Emily glances up, puts her finger up to her mouth in a shushing manner.

"Where is she!"

"Relax, she's down on the third floor. She's getting an MRI."

I just stand there, frozen. Then I turn and run into the elevator. A nurse comes in with a food tray. I ask her how to get to the MRI area. Out left, down the hall, turn right at the end. I'll see the signs.

I walk briskly, my shoes squeaking on the linoleum floor, past a wall of plaques commemorating donations made to the hospital. Shirley & Mike Dunne. Gratton Law Offices. Anonymous. Boston Pizza.

I'm in a rush but I don't know why. My mother is fine, or as fine as can be expected. I try to slow down and walk at a normal pace, but I can't. I have to see her, the need insatiable.

The nurse at MRI reception tells me she's probably done anytime now. I can't go back to see her. I just stand there until the nurse looks at me with a puzzled expression. She points behind me. "You can have a seat over there in the waiting room if you'd like."

I shake my head. "No I'll stand."

She flashes another weird look as my mother appears down the hall in a wheelchair, a young nurse pushing her. I turn and head to her—she sees me, waves me over with a weak hand.

"Is this your son?" says the nurse.

"Yes, this is my son," my mother says as I reach her.

I take control of the wheelchair, not forcefully, but the nurse notices. "Okay, you can take her back up to her room," she says. "It's nice to meet you."

"Thanks. Okay."

We wheel away down the hallway. My mother looks back. "She's nice, you should talk to her."

"No, I'm not in the mood," I say as I wheel her back to the elevator. "How was the MRI?"

"It was good. The doctors, they want to see where the cancer has spread in the past few months."

"Okay," is all I can say.

My mother is making small talk about the disease that's killing her. It's what mothers do, they make small talk in the face of overwhelming circumstances and insurmountable obstacles. But this is tough to swallow.

"They want to know if it's still spreading at the same rate it was when I was first diagnosed. I don't like MRI's though, they make me claustrophobic. The lady there was nice. She told me MRI stands for 'Magnetic Resonance Imaging.' I didn't know that. Did you know that?"

"No, I didn't."

We step out of the elevator and onto her floor to wheel past the desk. I see Emily, apologize for yelling—she accepts my apology and asks my mother how the MRI went. They make small talk with me standing there behind them. I look down at my mother's feet, her legs, varicose veins almost like track marks across the skin. They push out of her legs like bloated blue worms, twisting over themselves to reach the surface. I realize I haven't seen my mother's legs in weeks. They've always been covered by bed sheets or gowns.

When my mother was young, she had legs to die for. Long, slender, smooth, no definition but sleek. Barbie doll legs, perfectly sculpted, my father used to say God must have spent weeks on her legs.

Now they look like skinny tree trunks, with the bark falling off. Blotchy skin, two-day-old stubble, my mother still insists on shaving them once every second day. She gets a nurse to take her into the bathroom. She won't let me do it, and I wouldn't want to.

Tonight I'm watching *Dancing with the Stars* with my mother, then Emily and I are going out for dinner and drinks once she's off at seven. I don't know what dinner and drinks means. Do we have drinks at the same place as dinner? Or do we go somewhere else? I'm also not sure what drinks implies, and how that makes it different than a regular dinner. I'm confident we'll both have drinks with dinner, but not certain. I haven't been on a date in well over a year.

Tonight the former football star gets voted off the show. My mother agrees with the decision, as the hip-hop number they tried fell flat. He's a running back, not a dancer. My mother makes some quip about how it's weird a black man couldn't pull off a hip-hop routine. Her mild racism is endearing.

We sit there together on the couch, my mother in her hospital gown. She sips from a cup of water, having to ask me to get it for her every time as she has trouble leaning forward when sitting down.

During a commercial break she tells me there's over thirty versions of *Dancing with the Stars* all over the world. They have *Dancing with the Stars* in Belgium. She's tickled by this. Then she puts her hand on my leg. "I signed a few forms for my life insurance policy today."

I look over at her. I don't know if I can talk about this right now. "It's okay, Mom. We don't have to talk about this right now."

"No, I want to."

"Okay."

"I allocated some funds for the funeral. My lawyer will handle all the finances."

All I can do is nod.

"I've also made a decision too."

"Okay."

"I've decided I don't want to be cremated. I was reading about that natural burial, where they let your body naturally decompose. Like nature intended. And they have a rock too, so you can come visit me and you'll know where I am."

"Are you sure about this?"

"Yes. I told the lawyer, and he'll set everything up. You don't have to worry about anything."

Dancing with the Stars comes back on.

I can't envision my mother dead when she's sitting right beside me. The idea of her lifeless body buried under the ground is unfathomable. My mind fogs, I can't wrap my head around the concept, can't entertain the notion of her not breathing, living. It strangles my stream of thought. Death is looming once again and I have no recourse. I have no weapon to fight. I'm disarmed and susceptible, totally unprepared. When my mother finally passes away, I will not be ready. I decide when she finally passes away, I'm gone. I will buy an around-the-world ticket and leave. If I'm not done school or rugby, so be it.

Another commercial break.

"Mom, I was thinking. Would it be okay if I used some of the money to travel?"

She looks over at me. "Oh yes, honey. If I have one regret it's that I didn't travel enough. I always wanted to go to Asia. China."

I nod.

"I always wanted to see the Great Wall of China," she says.

"Okay."

"You stay in school though, you hear me," she says with her finger pointed at me. "I don't want you doing all this hard work, then throwing it all away for nothing. Okay?"

"Okay."

"You promise me you'll finish your degree. Then you can travel to your heart's content."

She holds my hand—she's cold, her bones push against my skin.

"I promise."

Dancing with the Stars finishes. I wheel my mother back to her room and help her up onto the bed, pull the sheets up over her legs.

"So Emily and I are going on a bit of a date tonight."

My mother's eyes light up. "Oh my goodness, why didn't you tell me?"

"I'm sorry."

"Okay, you remember: the man always pays for the meal. And holds the door open for her. And don't talk about yourself too much, but bring her flowers."

I nod at each directive.

Emily comes in, and my mother stops. Then she starts talking to Emily about our date. My mother is talking to her in a different tone, as if she's pretending Emily is my girlfriend, or fiancée. I guess she can fantasize. I'm not about to stop her.

"So I'm off now," Emily says. "I'll meet you at the restaurant in an hour?"

I nod.

"Where are you going?" my mother pipes in.

"Um, I forget what it's called."

My mom pipes in again, "It's not Boston Pizza. You better not take this nice young lady to Boston Pizza."

She gently smacks my arm. Emily giggles.

"It's not Boston Pizza, Mom. It's called Viewpoint Bar & Grill."

"Oh I've been there, it's nice," she says, and looks over at Emily. "You take care of him, okay. Be gentle with his little heart. He doesn't get much attention from women who aren't his mother these days."

I blush. Emily smiles. "I promise," she says.

~

I put on a nice dress shirt and slacks, gel my short hair for the first time in months. Emily is there waiting for me when I arrive, though I'm on time. She looks so different out of uniform—a nice black dress, not low cut. I tell her she looks beautiful, and she smiles and thanks me. It's dark inside the restaurant overlooking the bay. Huge windows off to the right of the dining area, people strolling by on the sidewalk outside.

We order wine and make small talk. Emily is calming. She's not confrontational or snippy. She always thanks the waiter when he brings something or refills her glass. You can tell she's been raised with courtesy and class.

Invariably the conversation shifts to old relationships. Emily dated a guy through university. He's an accountant for a big firm in Sidney now. Has a fiancée. Emily is pretty sure he cheated on her at the end with the girl he's with now, the one he's going to marry. But he's never admitted to it.

You can tell she's over it, her tone being one of experience and lessons learned. She's okay with it now.

She asks me about mine.

"I, uh, well I've never really had a full-blown girlfriend."

She looks a bit stunned. "Really? Why, you're not some creepy axe murderer are you? You're not going to chop me up and put me in your basement?"

I smile. "No, not an axe murderer. Just kind of shy. And I mean for the past year it's been tough to think of anything other than my mother."

Emily nods in an understanding way. "But you're a handsome guy. I'm sure the girls were chasing you in high school."

"Yeah," I say, then pause. "High school was a weird time for me. Girls weren't really on my radar, let's just put it that way. High school wasn't really high school for me."

"Okay," she says, signaling she won't push the subject. "You're not one of those players I see at the club are you. Those guys who try to sleep with women all the time."

"No, I'm not. But I have had a few one night stands."

"I think we all have. So you didn't like date anyone, not even for a few weeks?"

I look at my drink. "Yeah there was this one girl after high school. I had such a huge crush on her."

"What happened?"

"She moved away for school."

"You guys don't keep in touch?"

"Naw. I mean, it was better this way."

"How long did you date for?"

"Well we never made it official, but we were together for a few months, I guess."

"Maybe you should look her up now. How long's it been?"

"Like four years. Naw, it's fine. I'm sure she's happy. Doesn't need me jutting back into her life, or vice versa."

Our food comes, curtailing the conversation a little. We eat slow. I think we both like the company. We're two sad sacks, lost in a foreign country, here together partly out of loneliness. I'm not sure where this is going. I don't even know if I'm supposed to try to kiss Emily at the end of the night. We seem to be balancing between acquaintances, friends and potential lovers. There's definitely something here, but the timing feels off, and I can sense she senses it too.

We head to a small bar off a walkway near the outskirts of the city. Have a few drinks under candlelight. Emily talks about Australia, I listen intently. It sounds like a beautiful place.

I take a cab with Emily to her place. We get outside, the cab still running. She lives in a nice part of town, in a fairly new apartment.

I give her a hug. She doesn't invite me up, but there's a sense that she wants to. I'm okay with this. I have no game whatsoever, and it would just get awkward.

~

We're over on the island playing the top ranked team. Donny has been yakking my ear off the entire ferry ride over, talking about his surgery, giving me countless tips about how to be a good scrum-half. "Watch their backs on the line-out, they'll tell you what's going on. Be careful of their fullback. Make sure you don't tire out Derek, and don't be afraid to punt more. Watch their blind-side attacks." It's a bit tiring after a while, but I remain attentive.

We head to the field—it's chilly, and I wear my dry-fit under my jersey. It's cold enough I can see my breath. The trainer rubs my legs to keep them warm while I put on my helmet to cover the scar from my stitches.

I spend most of the game just whipping the ball out to the backs. I've decided not to try to be a hero tonight, but play the role Donny had moulded for the team, keeping the ball moving so everyone stays warm.

We go into the second half down three points. Which eventually turns into seven, then eleven. The clock winds down, the whistle sounds, I throw my helmet off on the sidelines and curse under my breath.

The mood in the dressing room is somber. Coach tells us we played a good game—we did—we just got beat by a better team. I shower, and hop on the bus for the ride back to the ferry. I put my headphones on and listen to music the whole way, walking around outside on the deck, watching the city lights from Vancouver grow progressively larger. It's cold. Winter is on the doorstep.

~

There's a weird feeling between Emily and me the next few days at the hospital. I choose to ignore it, not explore it. My mother has a bit of a cold anyways, but the doctors don't think it's pneumonia. They just pump her full of medication. I write my papers in my chair beside her. She's like a cat, sleeping almost eighteen hours a day. I rarely catch her awake.

I start my fourth-year English paper, History of Criticism and Theory. Gender, theatre, origins of criticism. Sex in Literature. The role of sex in literature. The pre-eminence of gender in literature. I rub my face, take a deep breath in. Each topic smears into the next, a blender full of ideas whipped together. Theories of theories and criticism of criticism. Johnson. Shakespeare. Milton. Manley. I type as if I know these people intimately. None of them have faces though. They're just words, letters in succession. They have no real weight.

I decide to take a break. I go looking for Emily, thinking maybe she'd like to get a coffee. One of the other nurses says she called in sick. I ask if everything's okay, and the nurse says she doesn't know. Nurses take sick days, she says. It happens.

A few of my mother's friends and relatives come to visit. Most of the time she's sleeping—I tell them it's not good to wake her. I fill them in on all the jargon, and they commend me like a brave little soldier, standing watch over his fallen kin. I'm sick of talking about it to others. I find it draining. Repeating the same prognosis over and over, the words start to roll off the tongue with little or no meaning, weightless.

~

School is back in session. A few students have healthy tans, and they chit-chat about all the good times, the hangovers, the skiing, the food, their families. Some girl in my philosophy class politely inquires into what I did for reading break. I tell her I read, and she laughs. I don't.

I head to the hospital in the early afternoon after practice. It's toque weather now, the buses are freezing, and I have to wrap myself in a thick jacket and mittens most days. It's still raining a lot too. Snow seems to be on the horizon. People make small talk about the weather all the time. Comfort food for the brain.

My mother is awake today. She has some forms from her lawyer for me to sign. I scribble my initials and signatures across a dozen or so papers. There will be a small trust fund set up in my name that will earn interest. My mother says my lawyer wants to talk to me, says I should go to the bank and look at investing after I pay off my student loan. The inevitability of my mother's passing looms over every successive word.

Emily comes in on her rounds. She looks different as she talks to my mother about her medication. The lung cancer patient with dementia is gone now, I don't ask where he went.

Emily asks me if I want to get some coffee when she goes on her break in a few hours. I accept. I sense she has something to tell me. Not sure at all what it is.

We head across to Starbucks, unwrap ourselves from our coats and jackets. I take my mittens off and warm my hands around a cup of hot chocolate.

Emily seems to be dancing around something in her head. "I have to tell you something," she says finally, looking at me.

A million thoughts appear in my head, but I shoo them away.

"My father has been diagnosed with cancer," she says.

My eyes widen. Emily looks like she's starting to slowly deflate.

"Oh my God, I'm so sorry to hear that. Is he going to be okay?"

I get a quick sense of what it feels like to be on the other side of this conversation. It's unsettling, uncomfortable, alien.

"Well it's prostate cancer. They're going to operate next week, and then he's going to do a few rounds of chemo. They think he'll be fine though, they caught it early. It runs in the family so he gets tested regularly."

"So he should be okay?"

"Yeah, it's just I think I need to go home and be there with him. My mother has to keep working. . . ." she trails off, looking as though she's about to cry. "I'm sorry, I'm going to head home in two weeks. I put my notice in at work."

All I can do is nod.

~

Everything is black. Dark. I can barely see. A figure comes up behind me, gloves on, balaclava over his face. I'm instantly frightened. He wrestles me to the ground from behind. I can't seem to escape his grasp and plead for my life. He could slip a knife into my back at any moment.

I awake to find myself lying in bed taking in short quick breaths. A cold sweat covers my body. That and urine too. I sit up in the spare bedroom at my mother's place, sending the cats leaping off the bed. They scamper out of the room and down the hallway in a huff.

I head down to the bathroom. There's piss all over my joggers. I just sigh. At least I'm alone. I take my joggers off and throw them in the laundry, then hop in the shower and wash myself off. I head back to my room naked, put some fresh clothes on, dry my hair with a towel.

I lie back down in bed and try to fall asleep wondering what possible emotions I could be burying so deep they're manifesting in the form of bedwetting.

~

The new patient in the room with my mother is a high school teacher, a Mr. McKenzie. Teaches P.E. and English, and has testicular cancer. I'm introduced to his whole family—his loving wife, his three sons all under ten, all blonde and full of pip. He tells me they caught it extremely early, so hopefully he'll just be in the hospital a few weeks.

Mr. McKenzie loves to talk to me when no one else is around. He says I should come out and help coach the high school rugby team, but I politely decline. He asks me about school, about going to university, tells me to tell his sons to make sure they go to university, he wants them to have a good education.

He looks like your typical high school P.E. teacher. Tall, lean build, welcoming face. A master at corralling little bastards all day and keeping them from driving him insane.

The first four days are a madhouse. About thirty different groups of kids come in and give him flowers and gifts and cards, wishing him well. It's tough not to like Mr. McKenzie. I can certainly see why the kids do. He jokes about having nut cancer and ball-sack disease, and they eat it up.

But then one night he asks me about my mother. She has aggressive pancreatic cancer, I tell him, and the doctors gave her six months to live over a year ago.

He conveys his sympathies, asks where my father is. He's not around, I say, they divorced years ago. I tell him not a lot of people come visit her anymore, after a year it's tough for them to see her. The novelty has worn off, I suppose.

The next two days I don't visit my mother at all. I've done this before, but only a few times. I'm just not in the mood to deal with the parade of positivity surrounding Mr. McKenzie. Somehow that turns into the weekend and it's four days before I return to the hospital.

Emily is on her last shift. She comes in and says she's heading back to Australia soon, probably permanently. It doesn't seem to register with my mother. I think she thinks we're dating and will soon get married.

"It was so nice to meet you," she says to my mother, moving closer to hold her hand. "You have a lovely son."

"Well thank you, he is a good son."

We stand there, and I look over at Mr. McKenzie. He's reading a magazine, and I catch him watching us.

Emily and I walk over to Starbucks for one last coffee. She tells me she flies out in two days and has yet to pack. She's leaving a lot of stuff with her roommate as she doesn't have time to sell it. It will be weird heading back home, she says.

"I wish you all the best," she says. "I mean that from the bottom of my heart. You're a good guy. Guys like you don't come around very often."

"You're not so bad yourself," I say in a winking manner.

She hands me a small envelope with my name on it.

"You can't open this until I leave, okay?"

"Okay."

She smiles delicately. "So'd you decide what your plans are?"

"Yeah. My Mom always wanted to see the Great Wall of China, but I have to finish my degree first. I'm going to be here until spring at least."

"That's good, you should finish your degree. I know it sounds kind of silly, but when I finally got my nursing degree it felt like a great accomplishment. Sticking with something, seeing it through to the end."

"Yeah, I have to do this for my Mom."

We talk about rugby. She wishes she could see my game Saturday, but she has to fly out in the afternoon.

We walk back to the hospital. Emily says goodbye to all the nurses on shift. There's plenty of crying, hugs, flowers. Emily comes into the room, her eyes red. My mother takes her headphones off.

Emily comes up close to me. She's within that five foot radius again, and my heart picks up speed like a little locomotive. Emily leans in and kisses me softly, her lips soft, slightly wet.

She pulls back and hugs me, then pulls me in tight. I feel her breasts against my stomach, the first sexual contact I've had in over a year.

"You take care of yourself, okay? You promise me that?"

"I will. Tell your Dad I said hello."

"I will."

Emily turns and leaves. I can see she's crying. I feel like crying too, standing here as though I've just been mugged. I look over at Mr. McKenzie. He gives me a telling nod. My mother signals me to come hug her, and I do.

~

The next day passes in a trance. I walk as if I have nowhere to go, in and out of class, in and out of lectures. Writing papers in the library, studying for finals, I'm like a ghost.

I have to write a final paper for my fourth-year English literature class. We're to choose a personally representative novel on the theory of art being in the eye of the beholder, and rail off on it for 8,000 words. I choose *The Old Man and the Sea*, by Ernest Hemingway. We read it in second year.

I start by explaining the premise of the book. Cuban fisherman Santiago has gone eighty-four days without catching a fish. He feels the biggest catch of his life is right over the horizon. He's lost his apprentice, Manolin, to the better fisherman, however the boy still visits his shack at night in secrecy. They talk about American baseball and Joe DiMaggio.

Santiago sets sail the next day, eighty-five days into his drought. He heads far out into the gulf, alone. Soon a huge marlin catches his bait, and Santiago and the fish begin a war of attrition that lasts for days. Too stubborn, too filled with pride to let go, Santiago is willing to fight to the death.

On the third day the fish starts to circle, beginning to show signs of fatigue. Exhausted himself, Santiago uses his last ounce of strength to haul the fish up to the boat and stab it with his harpoon. All but dead himself, he heads home with the marlin tied to his skiff and a valiant pride filling his heart, ready to show his prize to all.

However, as Santiago heads into the bay, the trail of blood attracts sharks from far out in the gulf. He uses his harpoon to kill one, losing his weapon in the process. He makes another out of his knife. He kills many sharks, but the marlin has soon been eaten away, leaving only a skeleton.

Santiago finally returns home, and heads to his bed, falling into a deep sleep. A group of fishermen measure the massive skeleton the next day. Manolin finds Santiago asleep in his bed, and brings him a newspaper and coffee.

Manolin asks Santiago if they can fish together again. He agrees, then falls asleep again, dreaming of lions on an African beach.

In the early months of 1961, after being admitted to the Mayo Clinic with a host of medical problems, Ernest Hemingway tried to commit suicide but failed. He then returned home to

Ketchum, Idaho, and in the early morning of July 2, put a shot-gun to his head and pulled the trigger.

He did not fail a second time.

~

Bent over, sweat drips out of my helmet and down my face. We're at war with the Barbarians. It's cold, the field is hard as con-crete, and every time I fall my left shoulder shoots lightning bolts of pain down the tendons of my arm.

The game is tied at 14. I take the ball from the line-out, fake a pass to the backs, and head straight for the heart of the defense. Mass confusion ensues, limbs smack into me, and my body is taken up and thrown hard to the ground. A cleat rips open my rib cage, someone falls on my neck, their elbow pushing hard into my jugular. I grind my mouth guard so hard I can taste blood, but I keep the ball.

Derek comes in behind me, picks up the ball, and carries it back into the violent blur of the opposing team. He drives his feet forward like an ox pulling a cart, and I lie there on my hands and knees watching as he pushes four opposing players back with his own strength of will. Then he turns and falls, his legs still churn-ing the air.

I'm there in a flash. Down on one knee I grab the ball and whip it out to the backs, then fall flat on my face, grass squeezing into my teeth. Derek is already up and running after the play, hungry for more.

The ball makes it out to Billy. He breaks a few tackles, gets caught up by their prop, then Derek comes in and pushes him forward. Half the team is pushing him now, huffing and grunting, myself included. He moves forward slowly, driving his legs.

We push past the 22 metre line where Billy goes down, and I pick up the ball and drive forward. I slam into their backs, car-rying three with me for a few yards. I turn, Derek is right there, and I pop him the ball. He heads right, rams into more backs, pushes forward, slips a tackle.

We all join him again, pushing forward, our legs pumping like pistons, driving turf up with our cleats. I have nothing left in the tank, but keep going regardless until we pass the try line. Derek rips his upper body free and falls to the turf. I fall on top of him.

He stands up with the ball in his hand, his neck flexing, his nose bleeding, and I grab him around the hips and hoist him up. He holds the ball high above his head in victory, celebrating the score, and our voices join the guttural choir of teammates as we head to the dressing room after the final whistle. Coach gives me the game ball. I feel supercharged. Beaten and bloody but supremely happy.

On the bus ride home to my mother's house, I open the card from Emily. It's blank except for a small drawn heart over the words, "Maybe in another lifetime . . . Emily."

~

I don't visit my mother in the hospital for two days. Exams have started, and I study predominantly at home in the peace and solitude of her apartment. Like a squatter I use it, abusing its comforts.

My mother is sleeping when I finally show up. Mr. McKenzie is reading magazines, *Sports Illustrated* mostly, but puts them aside when I come in.

"Hey there, it's the rugby star," he says.

"Hey, Mr. McKenzie."

"Call me Dave. You're not one of my students."

"Okay."

"I saw the writeup in the paper. You guys really sneaked out a win there. The writer said you played like a man possessed."

"Yeah," I say, cracking a smile. "Something like that."

Dave leans over to his table. "Hey one of my friends brought me something." He holds up a small bottle of imported tequila. "Can I offer you a shot?" he says, holding up two small glasses.

I smile. "Yeah sure, why not."

"Don't tell any of my kids though. Our little secret, okay?"

Hand over heart, I zip an imaginary zipper across my mouth. "Scout's honour."

Dave pours two shots.

"You sure you should be drinking?" I ask.

He waves me off. "One shot can't hurt, eh?"

"I guess not."

"Hey my balls have cancer. I think I'm entitled to a shot of tequila."

I can't help but laugh as he hands me my glass.

"What should we toast to?" he asks.

I think about it for a bit. "To life."

He nods in full agreement. "To life."

We do the shot, albeit wincingly. Dave lets out a whispered "Wow" as I flop down in the chair beside his bed.

"How's your mother doing?" he says, tucking the tequila and glasses away.

"She's okay. I mean, considering."

"That's rough, man."

"Yeah."

He shuffles through his magazines. "I lost both parents that way," he says.

I nod.

"It's tough, man," he continues. "I'd tell you the secret for getting through it, but there really isn't one. You just have to hold on, grind it out."

"Yeah . . . I think I'll make it. My Mom, she's had a good life."

The doctor comes in. "We have the MRI results," he says.

I stand up and walk back over to my mother's side of the room. The doctor comes over, opens a folder, and points to images of what looks like a stomach.

"You see these, these are all new seeds. New cancer growing. It's spreading all the way up to her lungs, her neck, down to her uterus. It's not looking good at all."

"What does this mean?"

"It means if she has a bad day, catches another cold, or doesn't respond to medication, it could be tough for her."

I nod. "So a year ago you said six months. What are you saying now?"

"Well we checked her blood pressure yesterday, her breathing. She's getting weaker every day. I can't see her holding on more than a few weeks at this rate. This MRI is over a week old. These things are spreading fast."

I place the palm of my hand on my forehead and take in a deep breath. "Okay. Thanks, doc."

He leaves. I look over at Dave.

"Bad news?" he says.

I don't respond, not right away. "You want some coffee? I'm going to Starbucks," I say eventually.

"Naw, I'm good. Thanks for asking."

I throw on my coat and toque and head outside to find it snowing. Fat little flakes of crispy white descending like leaves. They stick to my face, tinting the air with a sense of wonderment, a sense of unfamiliarity. White specs clouding my vision.

I think about Emily, imagining what might have been between us. Imagine showing up in Australia, doing something stupid like proposing. It never works. It never plays out like it does in the movies. It hurts, but I take solace in the fact the feeling will fade, as it always does with time. It's not the first time I've let someone walk away from me. I try to drum up something some-one once told me, something eloquent about lost love, but noth-ing comes.

I sit there and drink coffee alone.

~

Last essay of the term. Last test. Last assessment of my ability to retain the utterly impractical. My brain is full of endless, seem-ingly useless information—philosophy, politics, politicians, whores—my hand sore from scribbling lengthy diatribes about everything insignificant under the sun dating back to before the Greeks. I've written the history of the world in the past two weeks. A short history of everything and nothing.

I finish up my English prose essay in the gymnasium. Four hundred students exhibiting their declining penmanship through countless words. The last time some of us will ever have to hear about reformative social movements and philosophical context, but not I. I still have one semester left.

I take my paper up to my professor and slam it down on the table before him. Everyone in the gym looks up at me, the professor shooting me a concerned glance.

"Fuck me, am I ever done," I tell him.

"Okay," he says, unsure, worried perhaps I might stab my number 2 pencil into his throat. But I won't because I am a) stupid, b) overeducated, c) insane or d) all of the above. Please print your full name, student number and appropriate class at the top of the page.

I walk out of the gym, grabbing my bag on the way. Dump my six binders in the closest trash bin, emptying them like academic compost.

One piece of paper falls on the ground. Guidelines for writing a philosophy paper. There's a doodle across the top of the page from a lengthy lecture gone awry, a drawing of a stick man underneath a giant anvil whipping down towards his head. He's smiling away, oblivious to what's about to smash his skull.

I crumple it up and drop it in with the others. My pack feels lighter already.

Time for practice. Last game of the season tomorrow.

~

The lowly northern provincial university rugby team. The kids whose grades or athletic abilities weren't good enough to take them too far from the tree line.

We pound away at them without hesitancy. Beating them as if by divine right. In an efficient, inevitable display of social status on the rugby field, the second half hasn't even started and we're up almost 40 points. I'm just flinging the ball all over the place, dropping field goals, side-arming standoffs, and taking it to their scrum-half. He's small, too small to play in the big leagues, but he gets a taste of it, a lick, and a variable licking from me. An older brother showing the younger one how far he still has to go before he escapes the black eyes and charlie horses.

Coach takes me out for most of the second half. He appreciates a good beating, but not blatant disrespect of an opposing team. Soon thereafter, Derek gets his fourth try and then literally straight-arms their fullback three feet into the turf. Unlike our coach, Derek has no regard for opposing players. They're just numbers, potential hospital patients, notches on his belt. He wipes his face and heads to the locker room.

Billy gets his chance to run the offence. He opens up his legs, drags their backs outside, an up and under, a grubber and chip, a high tackle the ref misses, a coat hanger, a few slings, and even a chicken wing tackle. He starts going for the shoestrings, cutting his teeth on these poor little northern boys.

I just sit on the bench and warm my legs in a blanket, watching this clinic from afar. I feel disconnected, remote. Eventually I pull my toque down over my eyes, seperating myself further from the atrocities being commited before me.

The whistle sounds with exactly 68 points inflicted, zero sustained. Happy and hollering, we line up to shake hands. Coach tells us to shut the fuck up and be gentlemen. We shut up.

We finish second. Which translates to a date with the Barbarians. Then the Island boys for the right to go to nationals, if we get that far.

Regardless, I'm just enjoying the damage.

~

Today my mother is sick. Too sick to be wheeled down to the TV room to watch *Dancing with the Stars*. I sit by her bed instead, and we talk about my childhood, about her life, about anything she wants to. Talking makes her tired. Her nose dribbles, her lips chap, she has her oxygen tube put back in. The nurse gives her some pills, and then some cough syrup. After all these months and all these battles, the common cold looks like it could deal the final blow.

Dave comes back from a round of chemotherapy looking haggard.

"How you doing, teach?" I ask.

He walks slowly with his IV, his feet dragging in his slippers.

"Wakeup call," is all he says as he heads to bed.

"How many they have you in for?"

"Three. Well two, now, thank God. I don't think my balls can take much more of this."

I smile, chuckle a bit. "You'll be fine. I heard teachers have pretty thick skin."

"We do. Yes we do."

I head out to the nurses' desk to call my father at work. He picks up after the seventh ring.

"Dad, it's me."

"Yes."

"Mom's not doing too good. You might want to come down sometime soon."

"I'm on shift tonight. The morning work?"

"Yeah, call everyone else. I'm going to stay here for the night."

One of the nurses comes over. "You know, we can wheel the television in if she really wants to watch *Dancing with the Stars*."

"You can do that?"

"Just go grab the television. There's a cable outlet behind her bed."

I jog down to the TV room, unplug all the cords, and wheel the television back to my mother's room past all the other rooms, occasionally glancing inside. The same old faces stare back.

"Surprise!" I say to my mother.

She smiles. "Oh wow. Are you allowed to do that?"

"It's *Dancing with the Stars*, Mom. Of course I'm allowed."

I plug the television in, twist in the cable, and turn to channel 12. Dave looks over as I sit down on the bed beside my mother and gives me a thumb's up.

Mom and I watch some washed up TV actor take a nasty spill while doing the Cha-cha-cha. My mother says he's most definitely done, and sure enough he is.

We watch the whole show, my mother delivering her running commentary throughout. I remember as a child, when she finished reading me *Where the Wild Things Are*, she would stroke my forehead until I fell asleep. And then when I awoke up in the morning, it would be the same thing—her long feminine hands, perfect nails, stroking my head. I felt so safe with her, with this delicate woman, the only person I've ever really loved.

Sometime during the night my mother passes away. When I awake she's not breathing, and since she's not set up to a monitor, I realize I've probably spent a few hours sleeping beside her lifeless body, slumped over in a chair.

The nurses move the television aside so that they can take my mother away. Dave's curtain is drawn, so I sit there alone, staring out the window until I find *Where The Wild Things Are* lying on the floor beside me. I pick it up and begin to read, jumping in randomly, until my father interrupts me. He has a look on his face I've never seen before, as though he's about to reveal something he's long been hiding. But he just stands there like he forgot his lines.

I wipe my eyes. At some point, I realize, I must have started crying. My father comes over, sits down beside me, and puts his hand on my shoulder.

The marrow in my bones ache. My heart struggles, labours, but under it all I feel a slight sense of peace. No more pain for her, no more medically induced slumbers, no more hazy days of bodily treachery.

My father and I sit there a while, in silence. Then we walk out of the hospital together.

~

I walk into the dressing room. My teammates freeze. Then as one they stand and start to clap. I'm welling up, trying not to cry in front of them, but it's hopeless. Tears stream down my face.

Donny comes over and embraces me. "You're a good kid, you know that."

I tell them my mother would slap me across the face if I missed a game because of her passing. Some of them chuckle softly at that.

"Tomorrow," I say, "tomorrow I have to go to a funeral. But tonight we bury a rugby team."

They all cheer, so loud in fact I'm sure the other team can hear. These Barbarians don't stand a chance, and we know it. The game begins with an offensive onslaught that never lets up. We score, then score again, relentlessly pounding away at them. I dispense the ball with flash and fury, the cut above my left eyebrow opening wider with every toss and tackle. This time I let it bleed, the taste of it in my mouth comforting me.

The game ends in victory, and we head to the dressing room in a jovial mood. Derek comes up to me with the game ball, telling everyone to shut up. He pulls out a felt marker and writes "For your Mom" across the ball, and hands it to me.

"That one was for her," he tells me.

Afterwards I head outside to find my father. He comes over and hugs me. "Good game," he says. "Well done."

"Thanks."

"You did good, you hear me."

I smile a little, and he puts his hand on my shoulder.

"You hear me?" he repeats. .

"Thanks, Dad," I tell him, and he looks off over my shoulder.

"Yes," he says. "You did good, son."

~

The funeral goes as expected. I make a short speech, telling everyone the earliest memory I have of my mother is her reading *Where the Wild Things Are* to me before bed. I still feel like Max in his wolf suit and crown. Then I tell them how my mother spent her last hours watching her favourite show, *Dancing With the Stars*. To their credit, most everyone manages a good chuckle at this.

I tell them how my mother was a good person who succumbed to a terrible disease. I tell them how she fought for over a year, and how she showed us the human spirit is tough to break. I tell them how I loved my mother more than anything, and how I have one more semester left before I take *Where the Wild Things Are* to the Great Wall of China.

Afterwards, my father and I head back to her house. We walk around a bit, have a beer together.

"So you gonna stay here until you finish school?" he asks at one point.

"Yeah, I think so. Then we should sell it."

My father nods. "It's your decision."

We stand there together in our suits, sipping our beers. My father looks like he wants to say something. Eventually he does.

"The biggest mistake I ever made in my life is screwing things up with your mother. There's just so much that happened that we haven't told you."

"Okay," I say, not sure where this is going.

He looks like he wants to say something more, but doesn't. He doesn't have to.

~

Surrounded by his wife and kids, Mr. McKenzie makes the trip to the rugby field to watch us play the Island team. His treatment is over and he's out of the hospital. He gives me the thumb's up as I head out onto the field.

I go down hard in the third quarter, my shoulder breaking my fall. It separates instantly, breaking my clavicle. I'm forced to head to the sidelines, then to the dressing room. The trainer takes off my jersey as I wince in pain. I can see the bone pressing against my skin.

I tell the trainer to get me a sling so that I can go watch the game. We're down by five when I return to the sidelines, and things get worse from there. Today is not to be our day. Sometimes stories don't end the way they should, but I'm okay with this.

The referee blows the final whistle. We shake hands with the opposing team, congratulating them on their hardfought win, and afterwards Coach tells me if I don't come back next year he'll understand. He'll be upset, he says, but he'll understand. I tell him I'll let him know as soon as I do.

He puts his hand on my good shoulder. "It's just a game, kid. There's so much in life so much more important."

After they reset my shoulder at the hospital, I head home to my mother's place to feed her cats. Inside her room are pictures I've long forgotten—of her, of me. They each have a different meaning now.

DAY 3

Miles below the ocean's surface. A universe of water. I breathe with no gills, walk as if I belong here on the sea floor, the beige sand lifting with each measured footstep. Off to my left and behind me I see a huge underwater mountain. Jagged cliffs blocking out what little sun makes it down this far.

The water is clear ocean blue, but still dark. Coral reef off in the distance, just barely in sight. Ripples of sand from lunar pull. Seaweed tumbleweed. I start to float with the currents in my shorts. There's a line of pillow lava with a bluish cast, dotted with pink tube sponges, cardinal fishes, stingrays and wrasses. A school of Caribbean reef squid, opaque and completely translucent, swim by my face.

I stop. I can feel the saltwater deep within my lungs, filling every orifice. I suck the liquid air in slowly—it relieves my joints from stress, bringing an ease of gravity. Off to my right a pack of jet black hammerhead sharks slide on by. I can tell they notice me, though I don't appear to them to be prey, but quite possibly a colleague.

Underwater you can't hear much noise, your eardrums are flooded. One feels vibrations more than sounds, thoughts more than words. A helix of the senses.

Off in the distance appears a sunken submarine. A good one hundred and fifty metres long, a beast of a mechanical whale sitting on the ocean floor like it's been shot down in combat. It's slightly rusted, worn, yet still retains its alloy, metallic feel. As I start to near, I watch an explosion erupt from behind the tail, a plush silken pulse of fire. Seemingly impossible underwater, it pushes me and the sea back about a foot, then sucks us back again. A second explosion draws me closer still.

I enter the hull through a huge blast hole near the rear trim tank to find the rear of the submarine missing. From a distance it appeared almost intact, but once I enter the hull I find bits of metallic guts scattered out across the seabed. Black cords dangle like dead snakes, metal siding sticks out of the sand like shark fins. Documents, engine parts, the stethoscope, all lay strewn across the floor.

Two figures appear, both male, both dressed in uniform, one slightly younger than the other. They float as though hanging from submerged nooses, and the younger one carries my dagger. As I close in with the current, I recognize them. One is Michael, the other is Brad, and they float like wax museum portraits before me, not quite lifelike, not quite dead. Their eyes never make direct contact, though they come eerily close.

Michael holds the long dagger in his grip, his eyes off center, cast down and to the left. He has a vindictive, viscous look about him, while Brad merely floats in what seems like a hallucinogenic dream.

Michael's eyes lift to look at me. He's angry with me, and while his mouth moves I hear nothing.

He slowly turns to Brad, eyes still on me. His hand comes up, dagger angled up, until he slices down across Brad's throat.

I scream. Bubbles of oxygen run up my face and blotch my vision. Brad's mouth opens, and blood blooms out like a flowering rose but I'm stuck, unable to move, as if tethered to this very spot in the ocean. I yell at Michael, a long bellow of effervescence shooting from my tongue, as Brad floats lifeless in the cloud of blood filling the water around us.

Michael brings the blade up to his own throat. I yell for him to stop, but undeterred, and with one consistent slice, he opens in himself a garish grin of flesh and veins. The dagger loosens in his grip, and I lunge for it before it falls to the ocean floor. Taking hold of the handle, I plunge it into my stomach without hesitation. Blood bursts forth into the water as I plunge it in deep once more.

I try to cry, but I cannot. It seems impossible to cry under-water.

The Addict

Throw yourself off a twelve-metre industrial bridge into a river at three in the morning and most people think it's suicide. Do a back flip while high on coke and nine or ten beers after jumping out of a moving boat going fifty kilometres an hour and they think you're crazy.

Not only do you somehow talk yourself into such things, but once you're up there, on the bridge for instance, you're no less content to turn around and go ass over teakettle trying to find your feet again before the water comes rushing up at you like the world's biggest reality check.

It's about a full three seconds in the air, long enough to hear your body ripping through the wind like one of those hockey team flags tied to some idiot's car. That sound of fabric vibrating through the air at high speed. You even have time for a few profound thoughts, such as "If I die, this is what I'll be thinking about, I'll be thinking about dying." For some reason your life doesn't flash before your eyes. No, your mind just freezes like a computer screen, crashing for all eternity. Maybe if you were more eloquent, you think to yourself, you might conjure up some stirring statement to utter, but no—just static, no signal, blank screen.

All you can see is orange lights off in the distance spinning in uneven circles as your body tumbles around as if it's been thrown in the dryer. All your organs shift due to the G-force, your lungs up into your throat, your intestines up into your chest, blood and other bodily fluids trying to escape out your head like an overflowing pop bottle. And for a few fleeting seconds you're kind of flying, almost at home in a world of air. Moving in conjunction with gravity, you feel as if your skeleton is hollow and there is no up or down—just air.

You don't feel your body make impact, you don't even realize you're underwater, the mind has so blissfully enjoyed the freefall that it takes a few moments for reality to set in. Meanwhile, some distance away, a lone man outside his car hears that distinct smacking sound, that of a heavy earthly object impacting water from an elevated height. He stops from opening up his car door, his keys jingling quietly in the night outside the city, and the first thing that comes to his mind is suicide.

You start to struggle right away, swimming for the surface. But from that height the body slices into the water on a curve, and instead of swimming upwards you actually swim on an angle. Plus you have no air in your lungs—it having been abruptly forced out upon impact—so there isn't enough oxygen inside you to naturally float to the surface. Therefore your sense of north and south is shot, and your wonderful world of air is now an inhospitable world of water.

Your left ankle has a minor stress fracture, your shoe having snapped it sideways. Your right foot actually hit square, meaning four toes, all except the middle one, are broken. The pulling motion of your left ankle going outwards tore your left hamstring on the inside, right up to your groin. And while all this was happening, your knees buckled and slammed into your chin, knocking one tooth clean out and severly chipping another.

Concussion. Bruised ribs. The latter meaning that every time you inhale and exhale, it feels as though someone is gently, but firmly, pushing three or four knives through your rib cage. And the hearing is gone in your left ear, waterlogged like when you get out of the pool, so that changes in depth and pressure don't register.

Through all of this you're swimming, luckily up towards the surface, and you only realize you're going to live when you finally get that first intake of oxygen.

Swimming to the shore is a frenetic eighteen seconds of gobbling water, bobbing up and down as the overhead lights of a warehouse flash in and out of sight, their pale amber glow guiding you in like so many sirens.

You see the moon above the mountains, just a dot in the sky, as you find yourself walking out of the water with twenty-five extra pounds of waterlogged clothing hanging from your limbs.

You keep going though, like a struggling amphibious evolution, until you hit the beach and you're back on your knees before collapsing face first onto the sand, lungs heaving up and down. You roll over to find the dark starlit sky, pinpoints of light everywhere, and you breathe in the sheer immense beauty of it.

And you smile.

~

I sit there in the waiting room with Brad's mother. She just sits there silently, like she has since her divorce, left to raise her one troubled son alone. Eventually she goes in to see him, and I wait on my own. My father is here—he goes in with Brad's mother for some reason—and my mother is on her way. I'm not yet sixteen, and I have no idea what's going on. The gravity of the situation will only hit home after years of pondering and life experience. So I wait.

It's not that my mind can't comprehend what has happened. It's that my mind won't even register the appropriate response of feeling. I'm simply an emotional blank.

Six hours ago Brad consumed an entire bottle of Tylenol. Nobody has uttered the word suicide. I don't really even know what the word means. But maybe some background is in order.

Brad and I were born three days apart. Our parents were next-door neighbours in the same lower-middleclass neighbourhood in a town just outside the city—labour workers and receptionist mothers making ends meet through loans and credit cards. Just enough to get by, but never enough to feel comfortable. Always an accident, tragedy or job loss away from a quick descent into chaos.

Brad and I played together well before we could walk, even before we could talk. We shared dump trucks and sandboxes, soothers and crying sessions. Close by default. I knew everything about him, from the birthmark on his ass that looked like an apple to the exact time and place he lost his virginity. How to calm him down and how to piss him off. His deepest secrets and most chilling fears. We were beyond friends, beyond brothers.

We spent our early childhoods sharing rides to soccer and rugby practices. Backyard barbecues and long weekend getaways. We rarely spent more than a few days apart. One time while visiting a lake in the middle of the province, I almost drowned while swimming back from a dock. Brad pulled me up, and we swam to shore together. We never told anyone about it.

We fit together perfectly, as if emotionally compatible siblings. I was more ambient, he was more brazen and outgoing. When both our parents' marriages started to crack, we were each other's keeper. One time while my mother and father were arguing in the living room, coming close to blows, Brad went into the bathroom, filled up the small garbage can with water, and came down the stairs to chuck it at both of them. They both stopped dead in their tracks, soaking wet and stunned. Then Brad screamed "Shut the fuck up!" and we scampered out of the house for the rest of the afternoon, avoiding repercussion.

In elementary school we'd always sit beside each other, and drive poor teachers absolutely mad. I'm sure we sent a few into early retirement, or at least to the teacher's break room with tears in their eyes. We got caught once throwing snowballs at cars after school, and I took the blame for both of us. Payback for the lake, always unspoken.

And then another time we were walking home whipping snowballs at cars and ducking into the graveyard for cover. I smacked an old Buick with a good iceball right off the driver's side window, throwing it sidearm and with full force. The Buick rammed straight into another parked car—the horn honked, the hood popped up, and our teacher, Mrs. Lantrondeau, scrambled out four months pregnant. Thoroughly rattled, she quit two weeks later. Rumours still abound that we caused her miscarriage.

I had a best friend in Brad, and we tackled everything together. Our first erections, puberty, girls, what sex might feel like. We stuck up for each other, and got into fights for each other. We had each other's backs through thick and thin.

He played the piano, his mother a teacher at nights after work to make ends meet. He used to play *Moonlight Sonata* by Beethoven while I sat reading comic books and listening. It was the only thing he was ever really good at, and he had dreams of playing in a band to sold-out concert halls. It was the only thing he had to separate himself from all his damning thoughts. He'd entered a trance-like state of late, where the whole world simply overwhelmed him. But alone and seperate from his thoughts for a moment, he was somehow briefly able to forget.

I was the rugby star, at a school where rugby was bigger than soccer and hockey. We were both popular enough that the in-crowd just left us alone, a consensual stalemate. We'd rather just spend our time together anyway. It just felt natural that way.

But Brad also had his problems. He struggled with ADHD, and could barely sit still in class for more than a few minutes without fidgeting or speaking out. It was like he had Parkinson's—always tapping his fingers and rubbing his face, he just couldn't overcome the urges of his body with his mind. It pained him—he knew he was committing errors—but he just couldn't help himself. He was just a kid, and he never asked for any of this.

His parents tried medication, psychiatrists, dieting, hypnosis, but it didn't work, and in turn cracked their marriage even more. My parents fell apart simply because of my father's infidelity. Together we felt like helpless spectators most of the time.

When both families finally split up, it was within a few days of one another. Neither of us knew how to handle it. We acted out, got kicked out of class, sent to the Principal's office. We started trying to one-up each other—our middle school Principal called us Tweedledum and Tweedledummer—and in response we toilet-papered his car, then poured water all over it, twice. Then we lit his lawn on fire and tried to hold his cat ransom. The cops put us in our place after we mailed Missy's collar to her owner with a threatening note.

Upon separation from his wife, Brad's father literally vanished to the East Coast, leaving his mother to take care of him. The six of us never set foot in a room together after that as far as I can remember. It was like the two families got divorced as well, but the kids got joint custody of themselves. We both suspected there was more to it, but we were much too young to investigate with any real muster. I overheard a few phone conversations that involved both Brad and myself for some reason, like we were part of both divorces. It was simply perplexing to us.

But everything felt like it would be okay as long as we had each other when needed. One half of one another, we could recognize when it was time to cheer the other up. We had plans to move to the city, get jobs, live in an apartment together but no girls—we'd just live together and work. Be buddies until we were decrepit and pissing in cadavers in senior homes, probably still toilet papering cars.

But now I'm sitting here in the hospital, waiting to go see my fallen friend who tried unsuccessfully to do himself in with a bottle of pills. He always talked about it, what death would be like, and he always said he wanted them to play *Moonlight Sonata* at his funeral. I never took it to heart, but I should have.

Brad's mother signals me in to see him. We're both just about to head into Grade 12, our final year before freedom. We have big plans after graduation, ready to take the world by storm.

I sit down in the chair beside his bed. "Hey man," I say.

"Hey."

"How you doing?"

"I dunno, I'm okay. My stomach doesn't feel very good, but other than that."

"What happened?"

"I dunno, I wasn't feeling very good. I mean I just wanted to scare my parents."

"So you took a whole bottle? What was it like?"

"Well I had to take like ten at a time, but I think I took about two hundred. I felt fine for the first few minutes, then my stomach started to hurt, and I got really dizzy. I just went and lied down on my bed. Apparently I puked all over my face."

We both chuckle quietly at that.

"They said you flat-lined for a few minutes."

"Yeah it was so weird."

"What was it like?"

Brad pulls himself up in the bed. "It was weird, you know? When I passed out, it was like the light was bending inwards."

"Weird."

Brad arcs his hands inward, mimicking the sight of impending death.

"Yeah, bending in until it went dark, like *Star Trek* when the ship goes into warp speed. It was cool though. My heart felt like it was stopping it was going so slow."

I look at Brad. He looks as if he's seen the other side, popped his head into a parallel universe for a second.

"You're okay though, right?"

"Yeah I'm fine. My Mom is worried sick about me."

"Well don't do it again. I don't want to go to school without you."

"Yeah I'll be fine. I don't want to go back to school though."

"Who does?"

"Yeah."

I stand up.

"When do you get out?"

"I dunno, they said something about tests. Some psychiatrists."

"Another one?"

"Yeah, I hate them. Always asking me about my feelings."

I snicker. "Yeah, feel my anus is more like it."

We both laugh just as the doctor comes in. He may have heard the comment, but it doesn't matter. Soon my parents come get me, and my father takes me home to his house. My mother stays over for dinner, and we eat in silence. Eventually my Dad chimes in, "So we'd like to talk to you about what happened to Brad."

I look up from my food, defensive and ready to argue dismissively. My parents have no authority over Brad in my books.

"What's there to talk about?"

"Do you have any questions?"

"No."

"Are you sure?"

"Yes."

"Okay, it's just we want you to know you can talk to us about it."

"Yeah, no."

I'm not okay though. I can't stop thinking about Brad. I don't want him to die. What the hell was he thinking taking those pills? And where did he learn to take them? Why didn't he talk to me? Was life really that bad?

And I know my parents think this is a serious situation. They haven't been in a room together since Brad and I got suspended in ninth grade for discharging the fire extinguisher in the girls' locker room. That and in court for their divorce proceedings of course.

A few weeks later, Brad and I head to school for the first day of class. He's lost a few pounds since the ordeal. His parent's have him on some new medication, some brand new antidepressants, but so far we've mostly just fed them to my mother's two cats, making them walk around the house in a stupor.

We only have one class together first semester, P.E. It's fine though, as we always meet up for lunch, head to the store or my mother's apartment to watch television. School is something that really just gets in the way anyway, except for music class when Brad wows his teacher with pitch-perfect piano sessions. They want him to attend a college for the performing arts after graduation, and he seems okay with that. He's been writing his own songs of late, beautifully ambient piano pieces, elegant but strong. He has a future blossoming right before our eyes.

And then there's me, after school with the rugby team, roaring around the field in my own menacing way. A punishing little guy who loves physical confrontation, always eager to run towards the guy bigger than myself, always biting off more than I can chew. Brad and I, we did have our outlets.

It's not even a week into school when I see Brad isn't doing so well. He's had enough of being a teenager with divorced parents and a no-show father. School just adds to his anguish. He gets kicked out of class all the time, and in turn comes looking for me, at which point I excuse myself to the bathroom and we head outside to smoke or play Game Boy.

One afternoon Brad and I head to his mother's house to play video games and watch movies. We should be studying, but we don't care. We're sitting in his room, drinking pop and playing Nintendo, when Brad looks over at me during a break in the game.

"I was reading somewhere that some people think you get reincarnated when you die?"

"Reincarnated?"

Brad always talks about death. He is fascinated by it, but it is trying on me. I'm in high school, and that's bad enough. Thinking about the nature of existence is simply beyond me.

"Yeah, like you die, and then you come back as a dog, or a tree, or another human."

"Really?"

"Yeah."

"Do you get to choose?"

"I don't think so."

"I'd come back as a cheetah," I say. "Just hunt all day and eat meat, then lie around all night. What would you come back as?"

Brad thinks about it a second, holding his hand to his chin.

"Mrs. Perry's pantyhose," he says at last, and we both keel over laughing. Eventually his mother comes by, poking her head in through the open door.

"Aren't you two supposed to be studying?"

"We are," Brad replies in a confrontational tone, but we both know that's the signal for me to go home. Eventually I do, and like any other night sleep soundly.

The next night, after fighting with his mother, Brad catches the bus to the Ironworker's Memorial Bridge, just east of Stanley Park and the Lion's Gate Bridge. Sometime between seven and eight o'clock, he climbs over the side railing and jumps to his death, falling some hundred feet into the frigid waters below.

They find his body the next day, pushed up against a flotilla of timber, face down. I can't help but picture him falling, tumbling downwards, limbs flailing around, the mere thought of it sending bolts of terror through my skeleton.

A few days later I find myself at Brad's funeral, in the church down the street from our high school. I sit in the front row, unable to move, dressed in a suit, numb from the inside out. My tie is a noose, yet to be yanked up. Over three hundred people show up. They do not play *Moonlight Sonata*.

My parents, and the police, have been quizzing me these last few days, but I don't know what to tell them. A sixteen year-old boy forced to become an adult in an instant, I feel primed to fail.

And then something even more bizarre transpires the following day. Two passenger planes fly into the World Trade Center in New York, another one hits the Pentagon, and one more plummets to the ground in the fields of Pennsylvania. And suddenly, in the span of one day, Brad has been forgotten.

~

This city sleeps. In fact it passes out around 3 AM, going from bustling with drunken idiots to a desolate ghost town. No more collared shirts and platinum necklaces. No more choppers lined up diagonally outside the nearest Starbucks. No more high heels clipping along in herds, moving as though they're heading somewhere important.

No cat calls, no police sirens, no horns honking or traffic jams. This city shuts down at this hour. Rambling around with their shopping carts and staggered steps, even the bums aren't enough to keep it awake. The odd car flees along the street, dimly lit, but anyone driving now is either on their way to work or drunk and trying to get home.

This is when you have at it with a set of potted plants outside city hall. You and a friend, fresh out of high school, pick them up and heave them at each other, and they shatter with that distinct sound of hardened clay, sending soil and flowers everywhere. Then you proceed to the cars, keying them, breaking windows with your elbow, the sound of breaking glass sending you scrambling every time.

You can put your head through the side window of a Honda Accord with ease. You just have to be drunk and stupid enough to do it. Only when you hear the sirens in the distance do you run to hide in an alley and catch your breath, finally deciding to call it a night.

I'm just about to kick in a storefront window when my buddy's cell phone rings. Some girl I was chatting up earlier at the club wants us to come hang out. They have a hot tub.

We hop in a cab, taking it the few blocks to the party. And as soon as the driver puts it in park we dart out in opposite directions. Gone in an instant, the driver doesn't know what hit him.

We ring the doorbell. Sheri, or Teri—I can't remember—answers the door, and we head up to the kitchen to find a few people mixing drinks. Lines of coke stencil the kitchen table. I do a rail, snorting it up violently with a rolled up five dollar bill. I ask for another and get it, and then head out to the hot tub in my underwear.

I hop in, my boxers still on, to chat up two little girls just old enough to fake their way into the clubs. Still untainted from assholes like me, wide-eyed and ready to make terrible decisions, they quickly reciprocate.

Sheri moves in to intervene, her bra hovering just above the waterline. She says I'm cute. I agree. She asks me why I'm missing a tooth. I tell her I did a back flip off a bridge. She laughs because she thinks I'm lying, but doesn't seem to care one way or another. Then she leans in to kiss me on the cheek, her hand passing over my tented boxers underwater.

Before I know it I'm in her bed, still soaking wet from the hot tub. I can't seem to cum, so I just keep going, pounding away at her pelvis until her moans start to sound like squeals.

Finally I cum, no condom, and flop down beside her on the bed. She tries to snuggle but it's not happening. I'm snoring within a minute.

My buddy comes and wakes me up in a few hours. Teri, or Sheri—I still don't know—is fast asleep. We escape through the kitchen, lifting two large bottles of hard liquor for our troubles, then walk down to the main road to hail another cab we plan on running on as soon as we hit 7-Eleven. After plundering the store, I walk home to my mother's place to crash in the spare room, which is really my bedroom. I'm just never there unless I'm nursing a hangover or coming down from a coke bender. I curl up in the bedsheets and try to get a few hours sleep in before work.

~

I'm called into the counsellor's office across from the science labs, during first period. A school counsellor, a psychologist, a psychiatrist, and the principal are in attendance. I sit down in the chair closest to the door. The counsellor has a beard. The psychologist has a beard. The psychiatrist has a beard. My principal is bald.

I sit there, hands on the armrests of my chair, looking at three beards and a bald head.

"We just want you to know that we're here for you," says the psychiatrist.

"Like where?"

"Here."

"As in this room? You guys came to this room for me?"

"Yes."

"Wow."

My principal pipes in. "Look, I know this is a very difficult time for you, so we wanted to offer you a network. The four of us are here for you, any time you want to talk. At school, at night, whenever, we'll give you our home phone numbers so you can get a hold of us."

"So what if I call you at three in the morning on a Wednesday?"

"Yes," says the grief counsellor, "any time."

"What if I call you from a payphone outside a dirty diner and tell you I just murdered a trucker with a tire iron?"

Silence. My principal clears his throat. I look up to find one of those motivational posters with a picture of a cute little penguin looking across the water to another iceberg and a bunch of other cute penguins, contemplating the long jump. It reads:

~ DETERMINATION ~

The will to succeed can overcome the greatest adversity.

"Can I have that poster?" I ask.

They look at me, then at each other. The counsellor frowns.

"I'd really like to have it," I add.

He nods acquiescently. "Okay."

"Good," I say, standing up to head over to the wall and remove the poster, then leave the room. I head outside to the courtyard, outside the window of the counsellor's office, and look back to find them staring at me before smashing the poster frame off a picnic table. The glass breaks, pieces flying everywhere. I keep smashing it until there is nothing left.

Then I stop, dust off my hands, and head back to class.

~

Ryan and I are in the kitchen of a house party. We just got off work from the warehouse we've been employed at for about two months. Moving crates of wood, and more crates of wood, for minimum wage, no benefits and brutal hours. Dream job.

Ryan is also my dealer. He hooks me up with my coke. But then he always ends up doing most of said coke with me, so it's a weird relationship. Whatever. He's a good shit. And one of those guys who never gets annoyed. He has a mop of dusty blonde hair that has a life of its own, with a different cowlick every time I see him. He also has this really cool story he tells people. He was conceived in a threesome in which both women got pregnant. And his half brother, also a drug dealer, lives in the city. I'm not sure if it's true, but if it is, it's one hell of a story. He's the type of guy who's always there for a party and a gram of good times. Everything between us is superficial, and I like it that way.

Anyway, we're hanging out with some other guys in the kitchen of a house party where we know virtually no one, when some little chunky mini-mall dressed girl comes up to me. I'm holding a Smirnoff Ice. She's holding a Smirnoff Ice. Apparently she feels this to be too strange to be mere coincidence.

"Where did you get that Smirnoff Ice?" she asks, pointing at my bottle.

"Where did *you* get *that* Smirnoff Ice?" I answer, pointing at hers.

"Don't play games with me. You can't just drink other peo-ple's Smirnoff Ice."

"Sorry."

Her eyes narrow in on me. I have no expression.

"You're a buffoon. A big fucking blockhead."

I flash her an excited, perplexed face. Ryan smiles at me, holding his hands up like he doesn't know what to say. Some other guys chuckle.

"Well at least I don't look like a plus-size model from a Sears catalogue," I tell her.

She whips her Smirnoff Ice at me. I duck out of the way, and it smashes off the fridge and all over the kitchen floor. The party is too loud for anybody to really notice though.

"Whoa, honey. Alcohol abuse."

She just walks away.

"What the fuck was her problem?" says Ryan as she heads out onto the deck.

"Who knows," I say.

After the party starts to die down, we head out to the one club in town. We're so well known here the bouncer doesn't check our IDs. He just makes some quip about us being there all the fucking time. It's fine, he gets us in when there's a line, when Ryan greases him with some coke or cash.

We order some beers and make the rounds. Meet up with a few guys we know. Ryan and I dip out into the foyer to smoke and do a quick key or two.

I start hitting on girls, any girls, anyone who will talk to me. I get shut down a couple of times, the brush off, a hand in the face. Then I hit a group who seem interested. Some girls from the town over, here just for fun.

Ryan and I chat them up, and soon they invite us onto the dance floor. I start eyeing up the cute blonde, though I can't remember her name for the life of me, and we dance. Eventually she starts to grind me, kissing me a few times, so we head to the back of the club to make out. I feel her up. She doesn't feel right doing this though, she says, she has a boyfriend. I shrug, head back to the bar, and order some more beers. Bug Ryan for some more coke.

The night ends, the girls head home, and Tara gives me her number. I crumple it up and toss it as soon as she exits the parking lot.

It's only Thursday, so Ryan and I decide to call it a night.

~

I've moved into my mother's apartment. One, because it's within walking distance of school, and two, because my father thinks the best way to deal with Brad's death is to not talk about it at all and avoid everyone like the plague. Hard as fuck, he is. My mother, however, pampers me. Cooks my meals, does my laundry, takes me clothes shopping. I feed off her motherly instincts.

She tries to talk to me about it, dancing around it, coming at it from various angles, but I never bite. There's no bait I'm interested in. But she stays positive in the face of such rebukes, umbilical cord evidently still attached. It's commendable, if slightly uncomfortable, kind of like school.

Here's what happens when your best friend kills himself. Let's say you get a bad mark on a test, or play a bad game on the rugby field, or are walking in the halls between classes and a teacher sees you. They stop you, and ask in their concerned voice how you're doing. No, really, how are you doing? You tell them you're just fucking peachy. They ask if there's anything you need. You say no, there's nothing you need. Sometimes they offer you a hug. Tell you their door is always open if you want to talk about anything, anything at all.

"Gay German fetish porn?"

"Ummmm . . ."

The counsellor and the psychiatrist visit you weekly. They ask you about your feelings, and how you feel about Brad. Are you angry at him? Yes. Do you resent what he did to you? Yes. Do you feel lonely. Yes. Okay then. And then they shake your hand, call you a brave little soldier, and send you back to class to sit in your desk and stare at the walls.

You bounce from person to person, keeping genuine human interaction at bay at all times, your only solace coming in the form of all the 9/11 coverage on television. Hearing people talk about some other tragedy. "People love this shit," you think to yourself. You throw tragedy in their face and they can't turn away, they want more, they want to know everything about it. Every fucking thing. They want to talk to you all the time about how you're dealing with all this.

You tell them you're getting by, but you're not. Sometimes at night you sneak out of your room barefoot and wander around the streets alone. You key cars, throw rocks through windows, wander up and down the beach by the river and set fires in garbage cans. You head downtown when the only discernible movement is the blinking eyes of stoplights: green to yellow to red. You smash storefront windows, rip apart signs advertising great deals on carpets and meals, and wreak general havoc the rest of the time. The rush, the adrenaline, it quiets everything else as you scamper from the cops, hiding in bushes, dashing through alleys. Their search is futile.

You think about Brad a lot, and where he might be. You don't feel his presence, except in those rare fleeting moments in which you *know* he's still alive. You see someone from behind that looks like him, or you drive by his mother's house, and you suddenly gain a full understanding of the term ghost. A supernatural entity there only to haunt you at your worst.

The psychiatrist at school says you should find an outlet. Then gives you a journal and tells you to write your feelings down. You don't touch the book for days, almost throwing it out at one point, then one night at your mother's place scribble something down you immediately wish you hadn't.

~

It twists your heart sideways, upping the beats to about a hundred and twenty per minute. Your right ventricle feels like someone is stepping on it with a heavy foot, quickly and repeatedly, like a succession of pumps on a gas pedal. Meanwhile someone is blowing air into the blood of your aorta, giving you the slight sensation of fainting. It juts and gyrates inside your thorax, a fat man forever stuck on a treadmill going too fast for his own good.

Your lungs are so clear, they're taking in way too much oxygen. Your nostrils start to drip, then bleed, blood jiving and juking back and forth in your sinuses, filling and emptying cavities. Your larynx is open, wide open, and white blood cells crawl up your tongue, past your teeth, and out your mouth like poison gas.

The taste comes down like a post-nasal drip, chalk-like, acidic, sea-salty, coating the mucous membranes on its way to the bloodstream where it hops a ride to the rest of your body. It starts with a sniffle up the external naris, like a constant tick, a drug-riddled flu, then passes the inferior nasal choncha, pooling across the bottom floor, draining like a river down to your taste buds where it sticks and stings and coats your throat with the taste of Aspirin taken without water. But this is nothing compared to what's going on in your head where dopamine, let free like a pack of ravenous dogs, pillages and plunders your brain. Do one line, it tickles the central nervous system. Now do ten within the span of a few hours on an empty hungover stomach, and the cocaine jerks you off, over and over, masturbating the senses until they can take no more. Neurons of dopamine create a traffic jam between receptors. A bottleneck of ecstasy, pushing its way into your brain.

You sweat profusely, your clammy pores opening up, dripping water from every follicle. You can't stop twitching, moving, rubbing, a spastic compliance to anarchy.

Ryan is trying to calm me down. I'm sitting against the edge of my mother's couch—she's away for the weekend, thank God. Ryan gives me a sip of water as I rock back and forth, a bombastic beat that sends my shoulders straight forward with my head.

"Just say the word, man," he says, holding the phone, ready to dial 911.

"I'm okay, I'm okay, I'm okay, I'm okay."

"Okay how about I dial nine-one, then if you pass out I'll dial the other one."

I look up at him. "That's the stupidest fucking idea I've ever heard."

I stand up, and blood rushes from my extremities, B-lining for my head. It pools in my neck, in my forehead, and I wobble slightly, then sit back down on the couch.

"Just lie down, man," he says.

Lying down makes it worse, cocaine running all over a flat slippery surface like racing cars. They lap my legs and arms, zoom up around my skull, and come back and do it all again in record time.

I sit up, stand up.

"What do you want me to do, man?" Ryan asks.

"I dunno, you're the expert. Am I going to OD or what?"

"I dunno, man. I've never seen anybody OD except in movies."

"Well that's reassuring."

I stand up again, and walk over to the kitchen, kicking one of the cats out of the way in the process.

"I heard maybe a cold shower might work."

I glance over at him. "Really?"

"Yeah it slows down your heart rate or something."

I stumble to the bathroom and open the door—the lights flash on and scathe my retinas. I take my clothes off, Ryan standing right there.

"Dude!" he says, turning away.

I turn the shower on cold, letting it run a few seconds before I get in and realize this was a very bad idea. A noise rumbles up from my small intestines and out my mouth, a roar, a yell, a gasping breath as the cold water hits my upper chest, my forehead, splashing down my body. It trickles down my back and into the crack of my ass.

About fifteen seconds is all I can take before I get out and wrap a towel around my waist.

"Did that work?"

"No, it didn't. No more ideas from you, okay."

"Sorry, man."

I rub my face, walk over to the kitchen, slug down some more water. I need more drugs. Valium, painkillers, downers.

"Eat some food," Ryan suggests.

"Yeah I'll just fry up some motherfucking omelettes you retard!"

"You want me to make you an omelette?"

"No!"

I put my hands on my head. My towel falls off, I lie down on the cold linoleum of the kitchen floor, and start writhing around in a wet, slippery mess. I feel like a fish drowning in the foreign air of a fisherman's boat.

"Okay hospital, man, hospital."

I don't respond. High blood pressure, rapid pulse, tachypnea on overdrive. Agitation, confusion, irritability, perspiration and what now feels like hypothermia. My coronary arteries spasm over and over.

Ryan suddenly stops dialing. "Shit, dude, I have some valium in my car. Diazepam, it's called. Same shit."

"Okay get it," I say, still naked on the kitchen floor. One of the cats looks at me from across the room, sitting there watching it all with a blank look on its face.

Ryan runs out of the apartment, and I hear him rumble down the stairs outside. I try to calm my mind. Count to ten. Suddenly the buzzer rings. Idiot didn't take the keys. I get up, naked, and stagger over to the phone to buzz him up.

Footsteps up the stairs. I open the door.

"Dude. Clothes, please."

"Valium, please."

He holds out a small prescription bottle. Opens it.

"How many should I take?"

"I never take more than two."

I take four.

Ryan comes over with my pants. "Clothes please."

My chest heaves in and out as I pull my jeans on. I feel a bit better already.

I sit down on the couch. Ryan sits in the loveseat. "What do you want me to do?"

"Just sit there, watch me."

"You wanna watch TV or something?"

I look at him again. "Yeah, whatever."

He turns the television on. Starts flicking through.

"Stop flicking!"

"Okay." He stops on the Home Sense channel. Some couple are getting their bathroom renovated, southwestern style. I take in a few deep breaths. It's working. I'm slowing. Maybe I'll still be able to go to that party tonight.

"Let's go to that party tonight."

"Really," says Ryan.

"Yeah, the walk will do me good."

I put my shirt on, head to the bathroom, gel my hair, put on some deodorant. Cognitive deficits. Impaired motor function. My heart starts to smooth out. I take a deep breath in.

Ryan and I leave the apartment and head down the street, past a convenience store. Inside we grab some lemonade to mix with our vodka, but I get transfixed with the colours of the chip bags. Blue and red, shiny, plastic. I touch them, run my hand across them slowly. Cheetos. Ruffles. All Dressed.

"Hey you!" yells the Asian clerk. "Stop fondling the chips!"

I stop fondling the chips. Fair enough, I say to myself, I don't need his stupid chink chips. The only things inside my body at present a solid gram of coke, four hits of valium and about six beers, give or take. I walk up to the register just as Ryan comes up with the lemonade. "No ticky, no laundry," I say, this time almost to myself.

The clerk just looks at me, taking Ryan's money. Then he reaches under the counter and pulls out a shiny silver handgun and sticks it in my face.

My eyes widen. I can see right down the barrel.

"Get. Out. Of my store," he tells me.

I put my hands up. "O-kay. . . ."

He motions towards the door with the handgun, and together Ryan and I back out of the store with our hands up.

Outside, Ryan just looks at me. I smile. "Wow that was fucking intense," I say.

"No shit, dude. You're a fucking idiot."

"No, man, that was almost spiritual. I felt so alive."

"Dude, you're wacked on coke and valium. The chip aisle made you feel alive."

"True. Let's go to the party."

"Yes, lets."

We head to the party. The house is packed. Rap music blasts from the living room stereo. I'm just walking. Walking is fucking awesome. I walk like I've never walked before, past people, down stairs, around and around in delicious circles, my feet against the carpet tickling all the way up my legs to my ass.

Some blonde is watching me rub my feet back and forth on the carpet. She doesn't get it. It feels like a million little kitty cats are rubbing my balls. I giggle. She giggles. "You're high," she says.

I stop, standing there like a cowboy, legs apart. Okay, maybe she does get it.

"Kites don't get this high," I tell her.

She giggles again. I lie down on the floor and start rubbing my whole body over the plush carpet. Now she can't stop laughing. I stop, sit up, extend my hand.

"Hey."

"Hey. Kendra," she says, shaking my hand firmly. I glance down her shirt. She just looks at me, smiling. "Okay, I have to go back to the party. You have fun now."

"Thanks, I will."

I take off my shirt and lie back down on the floor.

~

I don't go to the Halloween dance at school. Some guy goes as Osama Bin Laden though, and gets expelled. Too soon apparently.

It's tough to take the eyes. The eyes say it all. Groups of girls off in the corner, they watch me while I'm down the hall. And as I pass with my backpack slung over my shoulder, they quiet up and throw glances at me. I know they're talking about me, but what the hell.

Teenagers can be inconsiderate pricks, if you didn't know. There's already been a few slipups and whatnot, like during P.E. class when I strip the basketball from some ignorant football jock and he proceeds with a "Why don't you go play with your dead friend." You want to punch them out every time, and ninety per-cent of the time you do, but it's tough. You just want it to go away and besides, fighting it only makes it stronger.

I head into the counsellor's office for my weekly session with the psychiatrist. It's just him now though, the other three having all but given up. Most times I just fuck with him, giving him runaround answers and making up lies about how my father abused me and my mother was a drug-addicted prostitute. He has trouble keeping me on track, and starts showing signs of cracking when I meander off on some completely unrelated bullshit story.

"And that's when I started turning tricks in truck-stop bath-rooms for smack. It was a good life though. Truckers can be oddly affectionate when they have you bent over a urinal."

Today he tries to switch it up. Asks me if I've been writing in my journal. I pull it out of my backpack, and toss it over to him. He flips through it, focusing in one little haiku-like blurb.

"This is a poem."

"Is that so."

"No, I mean this is really exceptional. It's short, but it's excep-tional."

I look at him. "Okay. . . ."

"Have you ever thought about writing more?"

"Like what?"

"Poetry. Prose. Anything."

"Not really."

"Well you should."

"Okay."

"Try writing another poem. Write about the world around you, how you see it. Just let it come out. I don't have to read it."

That night I watch the news on my mother's couch while she bakes in the kitchen. Interviews with people crying, television reporters spinning soliloquies about terror and tragedy. Clips of planes smashing into buildings, over and over, from different angles. Endless destruction and death. Oil and gas and the Middle East and it's all going over my head.

My mother comes over, oven mitts still on. "Do you have to watch that all the time?"

"Sorry."

She frowns at me, then at the TV. One of the buildings falls, and the camera shakes around, losing focus. My mother sits down to watch it for a second.

"Your father wanted to know if you wanted to go paint-balling this afternoon."

"Paintballing."

"Yeah one of the other Dads from his work invited him, and you."

"Paintballing."

"Yes you should go. It will be fun."

"Shooting people with rock hard little pellets of paint? You really think that's a good idea for me right now?"

She huffs. "I don't know. It's better than you lounging around this house all weekend, watching television and sleeping all day."

I roll over on the couch, lie down, keep watching TV. I don't go paintballing. That night I have a noxious dream about cramped spaces, a long exhausting dream I can't seem to wake from. I can't see more than a few feet in front of me. Black, opaque, translucent images hover threateningly, but nothing ever takes form. The air like cigarette smoke, ash-tinted and falling from the sky like snowflakes. Dark, creamy rivers. A bridge off in the distance, hundreds of people jumping from it in the span of a few seconds— they fall with the ash, splashing into the water below. Their tiny charcoal figures dive downwards, out of sight. I try to turn away but I can't, my face is locked, and I'm forced to watch. Finally I head back through a thick forest under a somber, sooty, starless night, into murky swamps with creatures slithering just under the surface. Dogs bark violently in the distance. I feel a creature bearing down on me, but it never materializes.

Then everything goes white, like an atom bomb dropped on the horizon. I run but I'm much too slow. I fall to the ground and curl up in a ball as the blast overtakes me.

~

My mother comes home Sunday night. There's water all over the kitchen floor, along with a wet towel. All the lights are on, and the cats haven't been fed. The house is a mess. I'm asleep in the bathtub, naked, with empty beer cans floating around me and a few lines of coke on a small vanity mirror beside my head. A straw cut up into small bite-sized coke injectors completes the picture.

My mother wakes me up, poking me with her broom. I grumble, cough, look over completely dazed. She just stands there looking absolutely furious.

"This is your last chance, you hear me?" she says.

I look up at her with glassy, empty eyes. I'm so depleted, viciously hungover.

"You're a mess, you know that?"

I roll my head around. "I know."

"You know! You know!"

My mother is very angry.

"Look, I'm sorry, Mom. I'm like . . . I'm, uh—look, I just need some time to figure things out, okay?"

"Figure what out? That you're a drug addict? An alcoholic?"

"I still have a job."

"A job? Moving plywood for eight dollars an hour? You can't even make rent here. You're just living off me."

"I'm sorry."

I actually am sorry. I feel like a total fuck-up, sitting here naked in her cold bath, coke rails beside me, empty beer cans all around. My body is so pale.

"I'm just going through some shit is all."

"Like what? Don't you make this about Brad again. You're using that as an excuse now. It's been almost two years, it's time for you to pick yourself up."

I nod, rub my face, cough. I can feel blood crusted under my nostril and try to wipe it off.

"I'm telling you, this is your last chance. I come home to a mess like this again, you're gone. You go see how your father likes it. See if he'll put up with it."

All I can do is lie there.

"Okay, get up. Get out of my tub."

She whacks me hard over the head with the end of the broom.

"Ouch! Fuck, Mom!"

"Get out!"

She whacks me again. And again. And again. I'm being attacked by a broom-wielding maniac. Finally I splash around in the tub and get up, pushing her out to close the door.

I pull my jeans on, then slip my shirt over my head. I glance in the mirror quickly, just for a second, then look away. I don't want to see that face.

I quietly scoop up the coke and put it back in the bag.

~

I'm sitting in my English 12 class. We've been asked to write a column about a current event, and of course everyone has chosen 9/11. Huge surprise, even though it's already November. Everyone has to read their writing in front of the class. Twenty-two teenagers trying to sound eloquent and educated about their generation's Pearl Harbour. I can't take it. I've already sat through four and I'm done. I'll just tell the teacher later I was having a "moment." I can do that. Perks, I guess.

Outside, the grassy fields are empty save for the goalposts in their chipped and faded paint. It's cold, so I head back in to walk the hallways. Most of the doors are closed. I head to my locker, grab my bag, and head outside and up the hill. The school overlooks the highway into the city, eight lanes of cars, trucks and buses. I sit down on a ledge, pull my rugby hoodie out of my backpack, and quietly watch the traffic. My mother is off today, flex day, so I can't go home. And my father's house is too far away to walk. I figure I'll just head back to class, but for now I'll sit and have a smoke, one from the pack Brad and I nursed over the first week of school. I light it up, and the first inhale I cough.

The traffic streams across my vision, moving steadily left to right, a wide spectrum of mechanization pumping poisons into the atmosphere. Over and over, endless. I ponder how many cars

there must be in the world, and how this is but one highway outside one city. I feel small, out of control.

I reach into the bag, pull out the notebook. Start writing
again.

Petroleum Sun

From the twisted sands of the Venus rivers
To the urban myths of the South Side

She wallows and spells out a gasp
The chemical tread has seeped inside
And laid its cancer
Inside her corners
The slowest suffocation possible

She knows the answers to all of life's questions
But will never live to share them

A young priest stands alone in His home
The smell of wood stain and the feel of cold linoleum on soles
A solace so rich in tale but sweltering in fable
He's realized that he hasn't lost anything
But gave away everything

Two worlds in one, cold bracelets and dirty nails
Sidewalk boutiques and Styrofoam coffee cups

A world of placement and requisition, to a life of denial
Once one was the other: and the other was the one

"Do we live to die or die to live?"
Asked the mechanic.

The substance of space can become so concrete
That even if chipped away, it will always leave its residue

"Is grace too cold for comfort, has warmth become the stability?"

Asked the addict.

Join in this elaborate circus
Follow us through the blur
That connects the real and reality

Walk with me amongst the crumble
For this be a twilight for the idols.

~

I'm sitting in the break room at work. Ryan and I take lots of breaks, usually to do coke. Just a bit though, as we don't want to get fired, not just yet. Our job is so boring we have to do coke just to get through it. This is how we justify it, at any rate.

We sit here, lounging in our chairs. Henry is here on his break too, a pudgy, balding 35-year-old who's been working this job for over seven years. He lives in his parent's basement. Surprisingly he's a nice guy. Ryan and I can't figure out if he's mildly retarded, suffers from Asperger Syndrome or Fetal Alcohol Syndrome, or is just really fucking slow. Either way he's like a teddy bear, and he's always happy to see us, sitting around with our legs up on the coffee table. I don't pity Henry, I envy him. I envy any man who's genuinely happy where he is in life. I envy a man who doesn't need to constantly search the road ahead for better times. The only time I'm happy in the present is when I'm stoned, that's the reality of it. Henry, however, is happy because it's Wednesday, and on Wednesdays Marie from reception brings us doughnuts from Tim Horton's.

I wish I was Henry. Ridiculous, I know—I mean unlike Brad I'm fucking breathing for Christ's sake—but for some reason that never seems to be enough. I envy simplicity, but avoid it perpetually.

Ryan always talks about sex in front of Henry. It goes right over his head. We smoke and laugh and joke about the parties and the girls and the booze and the drugs, then the boss comes in and shoos us back to work. Us "fucking cock-a-roaches."

After shift I head home to find my mother has cooked me a full meal. Steak, potatoes, green beans and salad. Milk and bread. She apologizes for hitting me with the broom, and I tell her I'm the one who should be apologizing. I still feel like an idiot.

"I'm just worried about you is all," she says. "You're all I've got left. I don't want to lose you to some silly drug habit."

I just nod and pick at my food. She stretches her hand across the table, placing it over mine.

"I'm willing to look after you, but you need to start looking after yourself. Your grades were fine out of high school—you almost made honour roll—so why don't you look into taking some classes at the university?"

I shake my head. "Can't afford it. Way too expensive."

"There's always student loans. You can work during the summer to pay them off. I want to see you being productive."

I'm starting to get emotional. I'm like a six year-old again, barely able to feed and clothe myself, let alone pay rent and utilities.

"Okay, I'll look into it."

"Okay. And you'll maybe go to an AA meeting?"

"Yeah, I'll look into that too."

She looks at me again. "Promise me you will."

"I promise."

~

I'm back in the counsellor's office, with the psychiatrist. He's reading my poem *Petroleum Sun*. He finishes, looks at me. "Wow."

I just look at him, puzzled.

"This is amazing."

I shake my head dismissively. "Hardly."

"Can I make a copy of this?" he says.

I stare at him. "Seriously?"

"Absolutely."

He heads out of the room. Comes back in with a copy, and hands me back my journal, sits down.

"I know one of the English professors at the university. Is it okay if I take this to him?"

"Sure, be my guest."

He nods contentedly. "Your poem is excellent. This is something that should be shared. Published."

I just shrug as though I could care less.

"Whatever you say, boss."

~

Panic attack. Intense anxiety. Mounting physiological pain.

I'm lying in bed, rolling back and forth. My body is cycling from dependence all the way through withdrawal and back again. It wants coke, bad. Needs it. Hungers for it. And I lie here starving, dying slowly, unable to do anything about it.

I'm coming off the bender of all benders. Government rebate cheque and payday all rolled into one massive blow that lasted six days, day and night. Alcohol, cocaine, and whatever else I could get my hands on—it all had me flying high. And now I'm coming down hard.

I let out a moan, pull the pillow down over my head. A whitewash of terror blankets my mind. Cold sweats, flashes of heat, uncontrolled—I'm not at the wheel of this car anymore. I don't know where I'm at. Trembling, hyperventilating, choking on air, I'm experiencing all the symptoms of a heart attack. And a realization of life gone terribly wrong.

A wounded dog moans over and over in the distance. It will die soon, I think to myself, but for now it cries. Such a sad, horrible lament, I wish someone would put the sorry beast out of its misery. Makes me want to jam knives in my ears in an effort not to hear it.

Dry lips and bloodshot eyes. Teeth grinding themselves down past the enamel to the dentine. White knuckles and curled toes. I can't bear the sound of my own thoughts anymore. Will someone please shoot that dog?

Makes me think of Pavlov's dog. And how in 1992 psychiatric research doctors at the University of Phoenix experimented with cocaine dependency on rats. In the study the rats were given a lever that, when pushed, administered a small hit of cocaine. They were also given food and water. The rats would press the cocaine lever again and again, forgoing food and water until they eventually died. Most passed within a few days. Some lasted a week. None of the thirty-two rats made it past eleven days.

The dog moans again, but this time from somewhere much closer, in fact somewhere deep inside me. This is the worst moment of my life, hearing this.

The dog is me.

~

I'm standing outside the courtyard at the local university. Everyone who passes looks so much older than I do. They all look so confident and mature, chatting quietly as they stroll with their backpacks and attaché cases. I just stand here, looking and feeling completely out of place. Little high school kid in his rugby hoodie waiting for someone to stop and ask him if he's looking for his big brother.

The psychiatrist is meeting me here at 4PM. He wants me to meet the professor he gave the poem to. I'm sure he's told him all about this poor little bastard who lost his best friend and writes poetry in order to get through. Poor little trooper.

Well fuck them both.

I see the psychiatrist come strolling around the corner. He waves. I just nod.

"How are you?" he says. "You ready to go?"

I shrug my shoulders, still seething at the idea of someone's misplaced pity.

I follow the psychiatrist into one of the large buildings on campus, its glass walls and windows, steel and concrete construction, making me feel even smaller than I already do. We walk through what looks like a lounge area, past a coffee shop abutting a small food court where students intermingle, young and old, brown and white.

We head up some stairs, the psychiatrist leading the way, almost as if he's bringing me along by the hand. We pass a group of young women, and one of them flashes me a glance. Maybe she thinks I'm a student here, I think to myself, feeling a small sense of accomplishment.

We turn a corner and continue down a corridor of offices.

"You'll really like Dr. Atrivosky. Nice guy, loves poetry, teaches it here at the university. He's also the head of the English Department."

I just walk, thinking about what it would be like to be in a poetry class. What do people actually *do* in a poetry class? Write poetry? Study poetry? It seems so foreign, so cultured.

We step into an office, down near the end of the corridor. Someone I assume to be Dr. Atrivosky stands up behind a desk to greet us with a smile. A tall lanky guy in glasses, he's dressed in a grey suit minus the tie.

"It's nice to meet you, young man," he says to me, extending a distinguished hand. "Please have a seat."

We sit. He pulls out the photocopied poem.

"So I read your poem here."

"Okay."

"It's quite exceptional, especially for someone your age. Not to sound too patronizing."

"No, that's okay," I tell him.

He looks at me, frowns a little. "This is an excellent poem, you understand? There's beautiful rhythm, imagery, and it's quite topical, especially now."

I don't know what to say, so I say nothing.

"So would it be okay if we published it in our literary magazine? We have one here at the school, and currently we're publishing some themed poems, some about 9/11, and this is sort of along those lines. It has a very worldly feel to it, an apocalyptic feel."

He frowns at me again. I'm supposed to answer this evidently.

"Yeah that would be okay, I guess."

He shifts back in his chair. "Good, good. It's settled then. It'll be in the next issue, out in a few weeks. We'll add that you're a high school student—I think it might be good to show some of the aspiring wordsmiths here that young guns like yourself are nipping at their heels. Have you given much thought to the next phase of your education?"

I shake my head. "No, not really."

"Well Daniel here took the liberty of forwarding me a copy of your grades as well. You've easily got a high enough GPA to get into first-year English here. . . ."

"Okay."

"And I am the Chair of the Department," he adds.

I nod as though I understand the implication.

"Okay then," he says, tapping the desk with his palms. "Let's get this poem in our magazine. You come see me any time if you're interested in attending school here. I hear you play rugby too."

I nod, watching a whole new life spring up in front of me. I imagine myself reading little weathered chapbooks in coffee shops while wearing a scarf, and heading to improvisational jazz shows at night before retiring to my loft. Whatever the hell that is.

We shake hands, and the psychiatrist and I head out. He asks how I'm getting home and I tell him I'm taking the bus. He offers me a ride.

Out in the parking lot we find his brand new BMW. Soft classical music emanates from the speakers. He drives slowly, almost cautiously, and I experience the sudden urge to rip apart his leather upholstery. Instead I tell him where my mother lives.

"That's pretty cool, huh?" he says at length.

When he says "cool" he slows it down, as if to show me he's adept with my generation's stilted lingo. Employing local techniques and imagery to communicate with the resident tribesman.

"Yeah, pretty cool. But are you sure it's good enough to be in that magazine?"

"Mike wouldn't offer if it wasn't. He was extremely impressed. He said he's going to hand it out to one of his first-year classes. You'll be showing up some educated kids."

"Huh."

He tries to make small talk. Asks me about rugby, my living situation, sports, the weather. It grows tedious after a while. I don't know what to think about my poem being published. I can sense he's doing his job, trying to give me a positive outlet, in an effort to get my mind off Brad. But I still feel like an assignment. Like a patient, or a project the psychiatrist must complete. I don't feel any connection to him otherwise.

My mother takes me out to dinner that night to celebrate. Boston Pizza. The waitress comes by, a cute blonde, and my mother tells her she's taking her son out to celebrate because he's a published writer now. Wrote a poem that's going to be published, in a university magazine no less. The waitress appears only mildly impressed.

"Mom, please," I say, embarrassed.

She waves me off, tells me I should be proud. She is.

We talk, eat. Chat about my father and how much of a dick he is. She brings up Brad, but I brush the subject off. We're at fucking Boston Pizza for Christ's sake.

My mother only has a salad. She's been having problems with her stomach, she says. Doesn't think it's a big deal though, it'll pass. Part of getting old, she says.

~

Ryan and I are at a party. He's not too happy with me. He's got a gram of coke and I only want the one line—just a bump to get me up—plus I'm trying to drink less these days. Idiot went and bought a case. I paid my share of course, twenty dollars, but now he's got most of a case and a gram left, and he's out over a hundred bucks. His party buddy is shorting him, and he's pissed.

"Look, my Mom is all over my fucking case these days, okay? She's gonna kick me out, so I've got to cool it down," I say.

"Oh, okay. Thanks for telling me after I bought all the shit."

"Sorry, man. It's just I can't keep this lifestyle up. That near OD fucked me up."

He just stands there with his beer looking angry, the mass confusion of the party all but cocooning us.

"So, what, no more coke for you from now on?"

"Well I'm hoping so. I mean how much longer can we do this?"

"It's only been like five months since we started hanging out."

"I know, but how much coke do you do? How much do *we* do? I don't want to have a fucking heart attack, man. I'm not even old enough to drink in the States yet."

He takes a sip from his beer. I take a sip from mine too.

"Look, you make ends meet selling it. I don't. All I get is easy coke, and an easy habit. You're doing fine financially, while I'm a minimum wage monkey."

"What, you want to start selling it? Just say the word, man."

"No! No, I don't."

"Christ," he says, shaking his head. "I feel like we're breaking up or something."

"No, man, you're my buddy. You'll always be my buddy. I just need to curtail this shit before I end up on the streets or dead."

He nods. "Fair enough, I guess."

We sit there in silence, surrounded by a wall of noise. Some little brunette comes bounding up out of the periphery.

"You want to dance?" she says.

I look down at her. At her too tight shirt and her little bitch beer. "No."

"No?"

"Yes. No. I'm gay and this is my boyfriend," I say, pointing at Ryan. "So fuck off."

She looks up at me, stunned. Then leaves.

"Look," I say. "Seriously. How much longer are we going to keep doing this? You can't sell coke the rest of your life—the cops will pick you up sooner or later. And what, we're going to work at that fucking warehouse the rest of our lives?"

Ryan contemplates a moment before answering.

"I know, man, I feel you," he says at length. "I'm a bit tired of it too."

"Good."

"So what then?"

I inhale. "Me, I'm going home, man. Sorry."

Ryan just stands there, nodding acquiescently as I put my beer down on the table in a dramatic display of finality. Just then two girls come over, both blonde and pretty. One of them comes up to Ryan. The other one looks at me.

"We heard you guys are the coke dealers in town?" the first one says.

Ryan and I look at each other.

"We were wondering if we could do some with you guys in the basement," says the second. "We've never tried it before."

Ryan smiles, shaking his head. I sigh.

"Right this way, ladies,"•I say, leading the one away by the hand.

~

Just before Christmas break from school, I meet with the psychiatrist again. He brings four copies of the literary magazine with him, and my poem is in it. It says I'm a Grade 12 student. There's an accompanying picture too, featuring the four horsemen of the apocalypse riding up to a desolate city of addicts, criminals and police in riot gear trying to contain the madness. It's pure chaos, rendered in graffiti-like style, and it's gorgeous. I just stare at the page. I still can't wrap my head around it. It feels like there's another Grade 12 student with the same name who wrote it.

"Pretty nice, hey?"

"Yeah," I say, still staring at the page.

"So I have another surprise for you."

I look at him. "Okay."

"Another friend of mine, he's a city editor at the daily newspaper in town. I talked to him a few days ago, and told him I have a budding writer on my hands. I asked if maybe he might want to give you a tour of the newsroom, and maybe send you out on a story with someone. He said for me to give you his card and to call him—before five, that is, any day."

He hands me a small business card. I just stand there staring at it, turning it over slowly in my hands. "So, what, I like just call him up?"

"Yeah, give him a call."

I think about it a second. Another life flashes before my eyes. Newspaper reporter. I imagine myself with a little notebook, in a full suit, running around town chasing a story, shaking hands and getting the scoop, then coming back to a smoke-filled office and typing it out in a mad dash of inspiration as deadlines loom. Seeing my name in the paper, and people reading my columns in coffee shops.

"Give him a call," says the psychiatrist, reeling me back to reality. "Just go hang out with him, he's a great guy. See if it piques your interest. Lots of writers get their start in journalism. It's a great way to get into the business."

I head home after school, show the magazine to my mother. She cries, she's so proud of me. She's going to take it to work tomorrow and get it framed, she says, and put it up in her bedroom.

It's four o'clock, so I call the number on the card. Reception puts me through to a bustling newsroom. I•can hear people yelling in the background, shuffling around, a conversation going on right behind the phone.

"Mike Hadden," says a deep baritone voice, delivered like a statement of fact.

I tell him my name, and that I got his card from the psychiatrist.

"Oh yeah. Hey, kid. Good to hear from you. Dan is a good friend of mine. Helped me through some tough times."

"Cool," I say.

"So I hear you're a budding writer, eh? Got a poem published in that university rag."

I don't know what a "rag" is, so I don't say anything.

"Well why don't you come by the office tomorrow. It's Friday, so it won't be too busy. You have a beat you're interested in?"

"Beat?"

"You know, like a subject. Arts and Entertainment. Sports. Politics. Courts."

"Courts? What, like covering trials?"

"Yeah, Mickey is our court reporter. Mickey!" he yells out away from the phone. "You got a job shadow tomorrow. High school kid."

I don't hear Mickey's response, but it can't be good.

"Just do it or I'll fire you," Mike retorts.

I hear Mickey yell something. Mike laughs.

"Now you be good, okay? Take the kid to that drug rap maybe."

Mickey says something else. Mike laughs again.

"Okay, Mickey. Now shut up." He comes back to me. "When you get off school, kid?"

"Uh, tomorrow's a teacher's day. It's a day off."

"Well shit, show up at eleven. Mickey usually rolls his ass in here around then."

"Okay."

"Okay then, see you tomorrow."

The line goes dead, and he's gone. I feel as though I've just been mugged, but in a good way. Even over the phone the chaos excited me.

The next day my mother cooks me an omelette. Then dresses me in a blazer and tie, helps me gel my hair, and drives me to the newspaper. I'm so incredibly nervous my armpits are dripping sweat.

I make my way to reception, through shifting crowds of slightly agitated people. A huge sign behind a woman's head tells me I'm in the right place.

"Hi, I'm here to see Mike," I tell her.

"Which Mike, honey. We have five Mikes."

"Hadden."

Her eyes widen mockingly as she picks up the phone. "Yeah, hello, there's some kid here to see you," she says, hanging up seemingly without a response. "Just have a seat over there," she tells me, pointing to a couch by the front window. Pictures of the front page of the paper decorate the walls. I sit at the edge of the couch, too wired to lay back.

Mike comes around the corner. I can tell It's him right away—worn dress shirt, short grey hair, with a tint of black. I stand up to greet him.

"Hey there, kiddo," he says, shaking my hand. His grip crushes my knuckles. He's got to be at least six-four. "C'mon back," he adds, his free arm waving in the chaos.

He quickly introduces me to the staff. Entertainment writers. City reporters. Deskers. A lowly intern whose name he evidently gets wrong.

"This is Harold," he says, indicating another man about his age. "Harold's been here a while. Covers council. I just haven't gotten around to firing him yet."

"Go fuck yourself," Harold says to his computer screen, still typing.

I get introduced to the Editor-in-Chief, in his corner office. He's wearing a full suit, though he's seated behind a desk.

Mike puts his hand on my shoulder. "This little tyke here got a poem published in the *Review*."

The Editor-in-Chief comes out from behind his desk and shakes my hand. "Wow, not bad. Those ivory tower boys came down from their perch a bit."

They both chuckle. I just hope I don't have to take my blazer off, I'm sweating so much.

"That's good, eh? We should do a story on him maybe"

Mike nods. "Yeah I'll see if Jamie's interested."

We head back into the newsroom, over to Mickey's desk. He's a thirty-something guy wrapped in a brown blazer, with thin blonde hair and a slightly wrinkled face. An unlit smoke hangs from his mouth as he types.

He stands up to shake my hand. "Hey there, kid."

"So you wanna take him over to the courthouse?" Mike says.

"Sure, but I've got to get a coffee first. Bit of a hangover."

Mike nods knowingly. "Weekends start early at this desk."

Mickey and I leave the office a few minutes later, and make our way down the street on foot. He stops to get a coffee, and asks me if I want one. I say yes, even though I've never had a coffee in my life.

He lights up his smoke and sips his coffee as he walks. Notebook in the outside pocket of his blazer. I take a sip from my coffee—it tastes awful, and it's far too hot. I try to sip it causally, but still manage to burn the roof of my mouth right off just about.

Mickey talks about the drug bust he's covering. About the four guys going down for smuggling drugs, caught at a routine traffic stop. He talks, and I listen.

We head inside the courthouse where Mickey seemingly knows everyone. Lawyers, security guards, clerks, sheriffs, even some of the criminals—he talks to them all—and I'm introduced to each and every one of them. They each make quips about me job-shadowing him, and how I'm just asking for trouble. It all seems like an inside joke somehow.

We move into a courtroom where a trial is well underway. In a whisper he tells me to bow to the judge. I do, and then we sit down.

A whole world reveals itself in words. Four men. Drug charges. Eight pounds of coke discovered in the trunk of a car. One of the men is on the stand. The prosecution grills him. Mickey scribbles away in his notebook, then leans over to me and whispers, "You see that lawyer there?" He points to a young man in an expensive suit questioning the accused. "You don't want to fuck with him. He's hard as hell. Takes down drug dealers like you and I take down coffee."

I look down at my coffee, still pretty much untouched. Mickey indicates a huge black man in a tight black suit sitting off to the side. "That's his protection. Guy's had death threats. Doesn't phase him."

I watch the lawyer go after the drug dealer. He picks away at every statement, unraveling the accused like a yarn of thread until there's nothing left. He basically gets the man to confess on the stand. The defense attempts to interject, but it's of little use. Speed bumps for this guy.

There's a recess, and Mickey and I head back to the office for lunch. We bow again on our way out of the courtroom.

Back at the office, Mike introduces me to Jamie, the Entertainment Editor.

"So they want to do a story on you and your poem," he tells me.

Jamie shakes my hand. "Yeah that's a big deal. High school kid published in a university magazine."

Jamie asks if she can stop by my school next week at lunch. Tells me to bring a copy of my poem. We'll do an interview, she says.

"Okay," I say.

Mike shepherds me around some more, showing me the production side, the sales side, introducing me to literally everyone. He's a seasoned veteran and they all seem to love him, even though he tells half of them he wants to fire them.

At the end of the day my mother picks me up outside, bombarding me with questions. I have difficulty answering, as it's hard to put it all into words. I tell her I liked what I saw.

~

Ryan and I are at the bar, and I'm fucking loaded. High and wobbling around. I'm cursing myself for doing this. I thought I had it under control. I head out onto the dance floor, into the flickering lights, into the Top 40 blaring out of the speakers. I move up to a group of girls and start dancing like an idiot. They love it. Laugh and giggle. They're a bit older, and I'm just dancing my little heart out.

I lose my balance and fall into a table, taking everything down with me in a crashing confusion—drinks, bottles, some girl's purse. I knock over three chairs as well, sending a group of people scrambling for cover. A rum and coke splashes all over my face.

The bouncer picks me up by the scruff of the neck and walks me swiftly to the door. Then chucks me out. I stumble a few steps, turn around, brush myself off.

"What! So I'm banned? For how long?" I ask.

"Just get out of here, kid. Go sleep it off," is his answer.

"Sounds good. Where's your mom's house?"

He starts coming towards me. I take off running. After about a block I stop, panting away. There's no one behind me.

I stumble a few blocks until I hear cheesy 80's music pumping out of a pub on the corner. It's one of those Irish neighbourhood pubs, serving shitty pub food during the day and attracting the has-beens at night. Hairspray cougars and fat Italian men fresh off divorces. Lovely.

I head inside. It's about half full. I look to be the only guy under thirty.

Karaoke. Two cougars belting out Journey. I grab the song book, its pages laminated so people can spill beer on them when deciding between "Sweet Child o' Mine" and "Livin' on a Prayer," and make my decision. I return the book to the DJ, then head to a table and order a pitcher, drinking it straight from the jug while awaiting my song. I finish half the pitcher by the time the DJ calls me up.

On my way to the stage I notice a husky bartender behind the counter. Shrugging at him, I stagger up with pitcher in hand to jostle with the microphone, sending feedback screaming throughout the pub. It goes dead quiet. Eventually a cheesy piano track starts up, and the screen starts playing the video for "Making Love Out of Nothing at All" by Air Supply.

"This one goes out to my special gal right there." I point at an older woman sitting with what I assume is her third husband just behind the front row of tables. She fingers me.

"Aw baby, don't treat me like that."

I put my hand to my ear like a phone and mouth the words "Call me." The lyrics prompter comes up but I keep talking.

"Okay then, this one is for my homies in the back." I point to the back where two Native men sit hunched over their drinks. "Much love and respect."

I pound my fist into my chest, then start singing along in my blatantly racist Chinese accent, " . . . and I know jud how to scheme. I know jud when to face the tooth, and then I know jud when to deem."

I manage to get two full verses out before the TV is turned off and the microphone cuts out.

"Hey, I wasn't finished!"

"You're done," the bartender informs me.

"No, *you're* done!"

"That's enough, you're out. Get out!"

I hold the dead mic to my mouth. "Suuuuck . . . myyyy . . . ballsssss. . . ."

The bartender starts towards me. I hold my hands up, drop the mic, and walk backwards off the stage.

"Okay, but don't call me tomorrow all flustered because you can't get Air Supply out of your head and need my beautiful renderings to help you sleep."

I•back my way towards the front door, then wheel around to kick the doors open. Bursting out of the pub, I head further down the strip, putting a few blocks behind me before I stumble upon a house party just off the main street. I head right in, take a few beers from the fridge, and make my way downstairs to where the music is playing. It's too loud though, so I head outside in search of a smoke. Two people occupy the entire backyard. It looks like they're about to break up.

"Either of you two happen to have a smoke?" I ask.

"Sorry, man," answers the guy, still staring at the girl.

"Some coke then? You guys have some coke?"

"Dude, no. Leave us alone."

I just stand there. Finally the guy looks at me.

"Dude, seriously, what's your problem?"

I could take him. Even like this I could take him. You can always tell.

"Nothing, man," I say at length. "I just kind of don't like you. You're kind of a fag."

"What?" he says, turning to me. Meanwhile his girlfriend, or soon-to-be-ex-girlfriend, knowing he'll probably get shit-kicked, grabs him by the shoulder.

"Just fuck off okay," she tells me.

I just stand there smiling. He doesn't do anything.

I keep smiling, and he keeps looking. I've got at least four inches and twenty-five pounds on him, never mind the fact I'm railed on coke. Kid has no idea what he's getting into. Or maybe he does.

"I fight guys like you on the way to fights," I tell him.

"Okay you want to go then?" he says.

He backs up a bit, holding his hands up like a boxer.

"Where are we going? We gonna race up the streets? Paper-rock-scissors?"

"You're both assholes, you know that?" the girl interjects.

I wink at her, blowing her a kiss. That gets the guy right in my face, so close I can smell his breath.

"How about I just knock you the fuck out right now?" he says.

I just rub my face in displeasure. This guy is all talk. If he was really a fighter he would've hit me by now. I tell him this.

"Fuck I need some more coke," I say. "You guys have any more coke?"

I look at both of them. No answer. Shrugging, I turn and leave.

Bored of this so-called party, I decide to try to find Ryan. As I'm walking out the door however, I see two girls getting into a car.

"Ladies, where you off to tonight?"

"We're heading home for a slumber party. We have some E."

"I love slumber parties. And I love E. We have so much in common," I say, leaning against the fender.

The two girls look at each other, smile.

"What's your name?" asks the driver.

"Enrique."

"Enrique," she says. "What do you do, Enrique?"

"I rock worlds."

Both girls laugh. The driver looks at me.

"Why don't you come have a pillow fight with us then, Enrique," she tells me.

"Yes," I nod. "Yes I think I will."

The other girl opens the back door for me. I get in, and promptly black out, waking up some twelve hours later in bed, pubic bone bruised and head ringing incessantly.

I•have no recollection whatsoever of what happened last night.

~

Jamie, the Entertainment reporter from the paper, has come to my school. She's a younger middleaged woman with signs of experience, and signs of stress mapping her attractive but tired face. She's brought a photographer with her, a quiet man with glasses, and together they take me to an empty classroom at lunch. The photographer says don't mind him, he's just going to snap photos while we talk. Pretend he's a fly on the wall. I do, but flies on the wall pester everyone, I can't help but think while he goes about his business.

She asks me about the poem, about high school. Then the conversation turns, as I should have known it would.

"So I know this is a touchy subject," she says, "but I heard a good friend of yours passed away recently."

"Yeah," I say, staring down at my hands. There's a tape recorder on the table between us.

"If you don't want to talk about it, I'm okay with that."

"It's okay, there's not much to it. He was my best friend."

"Did he help inspire you to write the poem?"

"Well not really, I guess. I mean the psychiatrist who's been visiting me in the school gave me a journal, and I wrote the poem in that."

She nods. "Well it's an exceptional poem, especially for someone your age. I have a master's degree in English, and I was impressed too."

"Thanks," I say. "But I just don't want to feel like a charity case. Like they published the poem and you're doing this interview out of pity for me."

She shakes her head. "Your poem is good. I hear your mother is quite proud of you."

"Yeah," I say, scratching my neck, feeling a bit embarrassed.

"So do you have any plans after high school?"

"I dunno. I'm not really thinking that far ahead."

We talk a bit more, and she mentions a few books I might like, writing their titles down on the back of a business card.

She gets the correct spelling of my name and age, then tells me the interview is over.

"That wasn't that bad, hey?"

"Naw."

"I bet your mom will like the article. You can tell her it'll be out in a few days. I'll find a nice spot for it."

And sure enough there it is, a few days later, with a picture of me sitting at a desk, looking pensive. The headline reads, "Young writer tackles adversity through the written word." There's a subheading that tells everyone my poem was published in a university magazine.

For a few days I'm something of a celebrity at school. It's slightly refreshing, as for once I don't feel like a dark cloud roaming the hallways. At least now people have something else to talk to me about.

My mother gets the article laminated and framed, and puts it up in her room alongside the poem. She says she looks at them before she goes to bed every night. It helps her sleep.

Christmas break comes. My Dad surfaces, hovers around the house a few days, but never for too long at one time. There's always a reason to be heading out for something when the awkwardness starts to feel overwhelming. I don't think he feels very good about himself in the presence of my mother. There's this wound between the two of them that still somehow separates them, a metaphysical wedge stemming from their past. But they put on a brave face for me, and my Dad sleeps on the couch Christmas Eve. It's the first time we've slept under the same roof in years.

Mom and Dad get me a laptop for Christmas, a really expensive one. The accompanying card says, "For our young writer." I try not to blush too much when I read that one.

We have Christmas dinner together. You can cut the tension with the knife Dad uses to cut the turkey, but it's alright. There are no blowups, no yelling matches, no slammed doors. We play make-believe family for a few days, and it's oddly comforting despite the obvious production.

And then just like that my father is gone and I'm back at school. I feel like more of a regular kid though I guess the break reset a lot of people's memories. I still hover, still keep my distance, but I feel less intruded upon. I feel slightly normal.

Rugby season blurs everything right up to graduation. We make it to Provincials, and place third. I get team MVP, thanks in no small part to the pure physicality and mind-numbing brutality of it all. Violence, it seems, is a newfound specialty of mine.

I don't go to grad. Not sure I want to see all those video montages of Brad, if there are any. I just stay home instead. My Mom tries her best to get me to go—takes me out to pick out a suit, even going so far as to badger her coworkers into finding me a date from another school in the area—but I don't bite. It's not right. High school was not something to celebrate, but something to endure. I'm quite alright not taking part in the parties and the photos, let alone all that yearbook crap.

I do attend the graduation ceremony however. People clap when I get my high school diploma. Then they stand and applaud like some sort of encore. I want to load an AK-47 and turn it on them, especially when the Principal hands me a special diploma inscribed with Brad's name. Not in the mood for charity, I toss it out soon thereafter. Brad wouldn't have liked that sort of thing anyway.

~

The fucking shakes. So bad in fact I have to call in sick to work. My Mom has to call in sick too, in order to tend to me all day, which makes it even worse. The withdrawal from a weekend which included about twelve lines of cocaine, however many hits of E—I honestly can't remember—about four dozen beers, a pack and a half of cigarettes and about seven Red Bulls has finally caught up with me. I ran hard, but it caught me anyway. It was simple inevitability.

I toss and turn all over the bed, biting the pillows and drooling on the sheets. I can't call Ryan for valium—my Mom won't let me. No curing drugs with more drugs apparently. All she'll do is keep bringing me ice packs, water and morsels of food. I don't eat though, so the cheese and crackers just sit there on my bedside table going stale.

I have a nauseous headache. And an anxious heartbeat. I keep falling into fitful sleeps, which in turn pulverize me with terrifying nightmares. Guns shooting at me, people chasing me with knives, bombs exploding nearby, I run—all I can do is run—until eventually awaking in a sweating, trembling mess, only to immediately fall asleep again. Brad never surfaces in any of them. Everyone in my dreams is foreign, a product of my imagination, a vibrant villain whose sole purpose is to corral and frighten me into paralyzing stupefaction. Each time I awake exhausted, which only leads to more sleep, to more nightmares. It's a cyclical beast, one which strikes without warning, then hides just out of sight and awaits the next opportunity to terrorize me. In this way I'm soon worn out, exhausted from fear, and after a while stop running altogether. They catch me immediately, and I let them slip the blade in easily.

In the afternoon, my mother takes me to see her family doctor. She does not give me the option to say no. I'm still jumpy and skittish when I arrive dressed in my joggers and hoodie, my skin a milky beige and my eyes bloodshot. I have trouble gripping things like magazines and door handles—my hands feel slightly frozen. I walk like someone shoved a twelve-inch rod up my ass, labouring from one prone position to another.

Dr. Bill McKinley takes my pulse. He checks my heart. Checks my eyes, my ears, my throat. He asks me to list off the drugs I've taken over the past four days, and I tell him. My mother cries at each transgression as though I'm listing off criminal accomplishments.

He tells me I'm a binge drinker and a cocaine addict. And that it'll be six months, a year tops, before I wind up dead, in prison, or in the hospital from cardiac arrest. Six months if I'm lucky, he points out.

He gives me a pamphlet for NA, and AA, and sets me up with a drug and alcohol counsellor. But I don't feel as though I'm ready to quit. I'm already scheming of ways to get back out there this weekend, for one last kick at the can. Maybe, I think, I'll just get drunk.

At home later that night, my mother cooks me dinner. Homemade pizza. We eat in silence a while, but then she eventually comes at me. I can see the tears in her eyes.

"I don't want to lose my son," she says as if she's talking about someone else. "I want to see him grow old, find a wife, have kids, do whatever it is he wants to do. Travel, find a career, fall in love. I want to die before he does."

All I can do is nod.

"You promise me that."

"What?"

"That I die before you do," she says.

"How can I make that promise, Mom. I mean what if I get hit by a car tomorrow?"

It seems like such a ridiculous thing to make a promise about.

"You promise me," she insists. "This isn't a choice. I gave birth to you, I created you, so you promise me."

I take a deep breath in, but don't answer.

"Promise me."

"I promise, Mom."

"What do you promise me?"

"That I won't die before you."

"Okay."

We resume eating, and it suddenly occurs to me that it's been almost a year since I graduated from high school. My mom keeps bringing home pamphlets from the university, leaving them on the kitchen table for me to read, but I never do. I just lie and tell her I do.

~

High school is done. Just like that, it's over. I'm no longer a high school student, but an unemployed teenager. The psychiatrist is gone too. Part of the high school program, the district was paying for him to see me, and since my my mother can't afford his services, our visits end abruptly. And once again I'm alone.

I spend the first few weeks after graduation handing out resumes. I feel so stupid walking around town with my little shirt and tie, clutching my envelope of resumes. I ask to see the manager, and they tell me they'll put my resume on file. They're not hiring right now, they say. Come back in a few months and try again. You need your First Aid, Serving it Right, Class 5. All this shit I obviously don't have.

Finally I walk into a packing warehouse, catching the manager alone at the front desk. He notices I played rugby in high school, and asks if I can do physical labour, heavy lifting.

"Someone quit today. Can you start tomorrow at, say, eight o'clock?"

"Yeah."

And just like that I'm hired.

I show up for work the next day, follow the boss around. Wood comes in the back door, where myself and another guy, Ryan, pack it in. Then along with some older guy, Harold, we package it up and ship it out the front. It's mindless labour, tedious and dull, and after the first four hours I'm ready to quit. But I make it through the first day.

My mother cooks me a special dinner that night. Pasta. She says we're celebrating my employment. I don't feel much like celebrating though, I tell her, but she doesn't seem to hear. The woman is nothing if not an optimist, it turns out.

My second day of work I hang out in the break room with Ryan. He seems like a cool guy, always either full of energy or looking like he's going to pass out.

"Hey man, what are you doing tonight?" he asks me.

"I dunno."

"You wanna go to a party?"

"A party?"

"Yeah, a party. You know, with people."

"Where?"

"In town."

"Huh."

"Shit, man, it'll be fun. You look like you could use some fun."

"Do I?"

"Yeah, you do."

Ryan pulls out a little baggie of white powder. He sticks his car keys in the bag, checks if anyone is looking—I'm looking—then shrugs and sniffs up a small key of cocaine.

"You want some?"

I look at him. "I've never done coke before."

"Shit, really? You look like a guy who's been around the block."

"What the fuck is that supposed to mean?"

"Nothing, man. It's totally cool if you don't want any."

I look at him. "Lemme try a rail."

He looks at me and smiles. "A rail, huh? Well look at you. Not so square after all."

He stands up, heads over to the door and locks it, then sits down and pulls out his wallet. He's done this before, this little routine, tapping out a small little snowbank onto a credit card.

He rolls up a five dollar bill, and passes it over. "Just snort it up. Like in the movies," he adds.

I take hold of the bill gently, leaning in awkwardly over the card. Ryan looks around, then looks up. I sniff up a few times.

"How long does it take to work?" I ask.

"Ten minutes max. You'll feel it pretty quickly."

"Shit, man, thanks," I say, rubbing my nose.

"Anytime, man, anytime. So you down for that party?"

"Yeah, dude, sounds good."

He gets up and unlocks the door, and we head back to work with a slow wave of euphoria descending upon me, a riptide of happiness sweeping into the bay of my mind. Pleasure, I feel pleasure, as electric limbs take control and caramel blood flows into my arteries. My mind becomes childlike, and I feel like a kid at a backyard birthday party with a whole slew of toys and friends to entertain me. Life is awesome. Life is great. Life is a wonderful journey down a magical pristine river. I love life.

And about thirty minutes later I ask Ryan for more.

~

My mother watches me gel my hair. She just stands there, staring at me, while I gel my hair in the mirror. It's uncomfortable, and she knows it. Wants it that way. There's this thick, hard silence between us that's been in place for a good thirty seconds when I finally snap into her reflection in the mirror, "Well why don't you kick me out then."

"I don't want to kick you out. You're my son," she snaps back.

I finish gelling my hair, then wash my hands and put on some deodorant and cologne. With my shoes already on, I walk right by her on the way to the door, grabbing my jacket.

I stop. "Look, this thing is going to run its course," I tell her. "Let me let it run its course."

"That's your answer to this? *Let it run its course?* Let you wind up in the hospital more likely. Or the morgue! You heard the doctor."

I don't answer. I just put my jacket on and leave. She doesn't say anything as I head down the stairs to find Ryan waiting for me in his car. I get in, and we head off without saying a word to one another.

We're heading to a massive house party. A party I simply cannot miss. A party for which I'm willing to strain my relationship with my mother even more, and for reasons unexplained I feel utterly compelled to attend. Something is there for me, I'm sure of it. But I have no idea what.

We arrive at the address prescribed, a mansion up in the hills. Ryan and I carry our beer in, strolling through like we own the place. A small waterfall beckons us into a living room from which we see horses at play in the meadow out back. The place is packed. Everyone is here. Looking around, I'm very glad we've made it.

Eventually Ryan and I head down to the basement. We slip into a bedroom and stash our beer under the bed, sitting down to crack two. We sit there, quietly, unsure how to proceed. There's a sense Ryan knows what I'm going to say before I've even formulated the words in my head.

He pulls out a small bag. But he doesn't look at me. He just gets a binder from the table in the corner and pats out some powder, crumbling and smoothing it out with his credit card like he's done so many times before. He's been leaving coke residue all over ATM's and debit machines around town, I'm sure of it.

He cuts up two big lines, big thick snowplow lines, rolls up a twenty and proceeds with his work.

"You want one?"

I look over at the coke. He's holding the bill towards me.

"Naw, man, I think I'm just going to drink tonight. That cool?"

He looks at me, his blonde hair falling over his forehead like crashing waves. A moment passes, the telling end of a passing friendship.

"Yeah, man, sure. More for me."

He does a second line.

"Oh shit," he says, holding his nose. "Fuck me, I'm going to be high."

I sip my beer. He sips his beer, rubbing his nose.

"You alright?" I ask.

"Fuck me," he says, sniffing uncontrollably.

I stand up, chug my beer, drop the empty to the floor. Grab another, crack it, hoist it back. "I'm gonna take a piss. I'll meet you outside for a smoke, alright?"

Staring directly forward, Ryan nods. "God, I'm already fucking high. This is good stuff."

I smile, walk over to him, hold my beer out. He holds his up and we clink our cans.

I leave him in search of a bathroom. Finding a closed door, I try to open it but it's locked.

"Occupied," says a female voice from inside.

"Sorry," I say to the door, leaning back against the wall directly across.

I hear a flush. Then a rush of water from a sink. Finally the door unlocks, opens, revealing the most beautiful blue eyes.

"Hi," says the girl.

"Hi."

She looks at me, smirks a bit. "It's all yours," she says, starting to walk away.

I turn to watch her. "Hey, what's your name?"

She stops, turns around. Comes a few steps closer and eyes me up. "Why do you want to know my name?"

I scratch my head in a nervous manner. "I dunno. You just look like someone worth getting to know."

She focuses in on me, analyzing my motive. Then holds out her hand.

"Robin," she says.

"Robin," I repeat.

"And you are . . ?"

"Eli."

We shake hands.

"Eli, it's nice to meet you," she says.

Another tragic twist has occurred in the disappearance and death of 16-year-old North Vancouver resident Michael Vanbiesbrouck. The body of 29-year-old novelist Eli Anderson was found in the Burrard Inlet early Wednesday morning.

Anderson was the author of *Bending Light*, the bestselling novel in which Vanbiesbrouck penned his final suicide note. The note tipped off police to search for his body in the Burrard Inlet below the Lions' Gate Bridge after an unsuccessful province-wide manhunt. The similarities between Vanbiesbrouck and the novel's protagonist caused a media storm that landed the story in the pages of *Vanity Fair* and on *The National*.

Bending Light was largely believed to have been based on Anderson's childhood friend, Brad Schultz, who committed suicide at the age of 16. A promising young piano player, Schultz was dealing with his parents' divorce at the time of his death. Anderson won numerous international awards for *Bending Light*, and the novel topped the *Maclean's* Bestseller List for a record 16 months.

Anderson's father Jim admitted to police he spoke to his son on the phone moments before his disappearance, however was unaware he was suicidal. It was also revealed today in now declassified court documents that Jim was the father of both Eli and Schultz through separate mothers. Eli's mother Eve died over five years ago after a lengthy battle with cancer. Brad's mother Allie Munro could not be reached for comment.

Anderson was last seen visiting the parents of Vanbiesbrouck early Wednesday morning. His body was found submerged under the Lions' Gate Bridge three days later.

Bending Light has since been pulled from the shelves by its Vancouver-based publisher.